THE ANVIL

CHRISTOPHER COATES

Copyright (C) 2021 Christopher Coates

Layout design and Copyright (C) 2021 by Next Chapter

Published 2021 by Next Chapter

Edited by Tyler Colins

Cover art by CoverMint

This book is a work of fiction. Names, characters, places, and incidents are the product of the author's imagination or are used fictitiously. Any resemblance to actual events, locales, or persons, living or dead, is purely coincidental.

All rights reserved. No part of this book may be reproduced or transmitted in any form or by any means, electronic or mechanical, including photocopying, recording, or by any information storage and retrieval system, without the author's permission.

Prologue

IT FORMED EONS AGO. SHORTLY AFTER THE UNIVERSE SPARKED into existence. It spent generations orbiting a distant star before something changed. Something which knocked this simple comet out of its orbit and sent it streaking much further out into the galaxy than it ever had been before.

Over the centuries, its path was nudged one way or another by the gravitational fields of the stars it passed. During its travels, something happened. Maybe it collided with another celestial body and picked up some of its characteristics. Perhaps another civilization dumped deadly waste that this comet passed through. No one will ever know. But this simple but large interstellar comet went from being composed of only rock, ice, and water vapor to having another quality. A quality that no one will ever understand.

It now emitted massive amounts of powerful radiation. Something not typically seen in comets. Traveling at over 50,000 miles per hour, this deadly ball of ice would be making a very near pass on a small inhabited world.

The inhabitants of this world saw it coming, and a few even understood the peril they faced. But there was nothing they could do. Nothing other than to prepare for how to rebuild once the danger had passed.

When no one will survive, what do you do?

From "The Ark" by Christopher Coates

Chapter One

PRESIDENT DANIEL ANSON STOOD LOOKING OUT THE bulletproof windows of the Oval Office. The world was on the brink of destruction, and here he stood. Daniel was the most powerful political leader in the world, and he was helpless to do anything. Worse yet, to avoid panic, he had to keep this tragic news hidden from the people he swore to serve. He'd never felt more alone and ineffective.

He'd first learned about the impending disaster about a year ago when he was only a few weeks into his second term. He was thankful for that. Trying to manage this situation was bad enough, but trying to run his re-election campaign at the same time would've been unthinkable.

This morning, the President had asked to be left alone until his visitors were all assembled for the 9:00 AM meeting. That had given him almost ten full minutes of quiet time to contemplate the situation and the decisions he would make in the coming months.

The phone on his desk buzzed, and a voice said, "Mr. President. General Draper and his party are here."

"Thanks Liz. Send them in."

A secret service agent opened the door, glanced around

the room, and then allowed the trio to enter. The first into the room was General Draper. He was the acting Chairman of the Joint Chiefs. The sixty-three-year-old General stood six-foot-four and was relatively thin. His receding hairline left a large scar visible on his forehead.

Following the General was the National Security Advisor. Jeremiah Baker was a sixty-year-old African American man and a former senator from Virginia. He had extensive experience in areas of national defense and politics. He'd spent twenty years as an officer in the Marine Corps and later another eight years in the Senate, part of that time as the Chairman of the Senate Armed Services Committee.

The final person to arrive was Dennis Roberts. Dennis was the Deputy Director of Homeland Security. Dennis was also former military, having spent eight years in army intelligence before transferring to the Central Intelligence Agency. While at The Agency, he'd served for over a dozen years and distinguished himself on several occasions. He'd come to Homeland Security strictly to deal with the current crisis.

"Gentlemen. Please come in and take a seat. Where's General Fitch?" the President asked.

"General Fitch is busy, sir, and since this meeting is of limited scope, I instructed him to continue his work," General Draper explained.

The President nodded as the men came in and took seats across from the large desk. He too sat before continuing, "Dennis, good to see you again. I know when we first met a couple of months ago; we dropped a bombshell on you and gave you a difficult assignment. As you know, General Draper, Mr. Baker, and I meet weekly on this project. And they've been keeping me up to date on your progress. However, I wanted to have the four of us get together to hear where things stand with your branch of this effort and share any ideas that we may have."

"I understand, Mr. President. Now that I've had some time

The Anvil

to get a grasp on what's going on, I think it's safe to say that we'll have about 150 underground shelters available in time. We're working on two hundred locations but don't think we'll have time to get them all completed. The sites are mostly natural caverns or abandoned mines. All places where there's a year-round clean water supply. That's necessary for human consumption and reactor cooling."

"Dennis, if there's anything any of us can do to move your efforts along and make more shelters available, let us know. Each shelter means around a thousand lives saved and a better chance for the human race to rebuild.

"Now, what about the selection process? Who is going into the mines and caverns, and how are they being selected?"

Nodding, Roberts explained, "Sir, we're calling the selection process Project Anvil. I was amazed to see the detail of the records that Homeland has on US citizens. We started with tax records. That automatically will exclude anyone that doesn't pay taxes. Then we removed anyone with a criminal, drug, or psychiatric history. Since we're only going to save about one out of every 10,000 people, we need to select those that will function well and not cause problems while in an underground shelter for an extended time.

"There's also the problem with medications. While there will be medical services available in every shelter, including a pharmacy, we can't be storing the prescription medication needs of every shelter inhabitant for twenty years. Anyone going to a shelter must *not* be on any daily medications.

"We are then trying to locate people that reside relatively close to the shelters. When it's time to get to the shelters, there will be a massive logistical effort, and the closer, the better. Next, we're trying to make sure that those we're sheltering have valuable skills. We'll pick the electrician or trauma surgeon over the window-washer or birthday-party clown."

There was a brief chuckle at the last remark before he continued. "We also want families. It'll do us no good if most of the inhabitants are past their prime when the shelters open in twenty years. We're also trying to include a diverse range of ethnic backgrounds."

"Why 'Anvil'? Does it stand for something?" the President asked.

"Sir, as you know, an anvil was used by blacksmiths to take raw iron and pound and form it into something useful. We are using this project to take the people we gather and form them into a new society once the radiation is gone," Roberts explained.

"Okay, I like that. Now, how will it work when it is time to go to the shelters?"

"Everyone who signs on for this is thinking that nothing will ever happen. The idea is that in the event of a nuclear war, pandemic, or other devastating events, we'd bring them into the shelters. We won't inform them that we already know the nature of the disaster and the date this will all go down. They'll get the packing requirements and a limit of how much they can bring, and then go about their lives. Hopefully, they won't think much about being in Project Anvil, but they will know that it is real and urgent if they get the call.

"Forty-eight hours before the event, we'll collect them and transport them to the shelters. It's looking like there will be some people that we'll go out and gather from their homes. Others will get a text message, instructing them to meet at a specific location. We are still working out the logistics. We've already interviewed and signed on about forty percent of the shelter inhabitants."

Pointing at the other two men in the room, the President said, "If there's anything you need, contact them immediately. I don't want anything to slow your efforts."

The four men continued discussing details for several minutes before the meeting finally ended.

Chapter Two

2 YEARS LATER

Gasping for air, seventeen-year-old Lucy Wilson struggled to breathe as she ran. She could hear footsteps behind her, revealing that her pursuer was close, very close. Pushing herself even harder, she felt her speed increase slightly. The sweat was running down her face as she ran and it was stinging her eyes, but she couldn't wipe it away. She'd been running for almost two miles; her legs were burning, and she knew she was almost at her limit. Rounding the curve, Lucy saw her goal.

Seconds later, she crossed the line, followed immediately by her rival and friend McKenzie Reynolds. The 3200-meter run was the event they both enjoyed and only once had McKenzie won. It was usually close, but Lucy was always a little faster, even though she was a year younger.

The two of them had run against each other for three years. Their natural competitiveness made them work harder, and the two girls were better runners because of it. Even during today's practice run, they had both put in maximum effort, their drive to win not allowing them to hold back.

It was a hot, sunny May afternoon. The temperatures were in the mid-80s, and the heat added another challenge for the girls. They both collapsed on the freshly mowed grass and lay panting for several minutes.

After resting, the two friends went to the bleachers and retrieved small towels and water bottles from their bags. They drank most of their water and then turned to walk across the grass while waiting for their heart rates to return to normal.

"Our times were good. I think we'll do great next week," McKenzie stated.

Wiping the towel across her sweat-soaked face, Lucy replied, "Yeah, I think so too. We did really well, considering how hot it is." So far this year, Lucy was averaging a full minute faster than she had last year when she was a sophomore.

The girls discussed their upcoming track meet against the Upton Beagles. It would be the final meet of the season and their last race together since McKenzie would be graduating in a few weeks.

Their coach had told the girls that after this run, they'd be done for the day. After 10 minutes of cooling down and chatting, Lucy, while tired and sweat-soaked, walked away from the Armstrong Central High School track. She grabbed her bulging backpack from the base of the home bleachers and pulled out a second water bottle from a side pocket, sticking the first, now empty one, inside. Turning, the student athlete headed to the parking lot to find her car. Normally, she'd have taken the time to shower at the school before heading home, but things were different this week.

Early this morning, her parents had flown to Miami for a seven-day cruise to the Caribbean, leaving Lucy in charge of her twelve-year-old brother, Sam. Neither of the kids could understand why their parents had picked this time of year to head south when it was already so hot here.

This was the first time her parents had left them alone for this long, and Lucy was determined to make sure they didn't regret their decision. While she and Sam got along most of

The Anvil

the time, being responsible for him was a challenge. They both had busy schedules, and Lucy had to figure out how to make it all work.

Since Sam was only in the sixth grade, he was in a different school building located several miles away. Today, he had a baseball game after school and he'd asked Lucy to try to get there for some of it. She wasn't too concerned if she got to see any of the game, but she didn't want him stuck, waiting for her to pick him up.

Several years before, Sam was critically injured when he'd run into the street and was struck by a car. Lucy had tried to stop him but had been unable. For almost a week, it was uncertain if the boy would survive. During that time, Lucy had refused to leave his bedside. Terrified something would happen to her brother. Three weeks later, when he finally came home, she watched over him constantly. She even took responsibility for helping him several times a day with the exercises he had to do as part of his rehabilitation. Through that horrible experience, Lucy had become very protective of Sam, and the two had grown extremely close.

As she crossed the mostly empty parking lot, she started to smile. Standing by her car was Marcus Ditmore. Unconsciously, her pace quickened. Marcus stood just under six feet tall and had jet-black hair. He had a positive attitude about almost everything and people were naturally drawn to him.

Lucy and Marcus had been best friends since the first grade. Since children, they had held a deep trust in each other and had always confided their secrets. Their connection was deeply rooted and seemed unbreakable. It had taken until this school year for that relationship to transform and for them to start dating. This relationship didn't surprise anyone. Most everyone had already thought they were a couple, and the rest wondered what had taken so long.

Three weeks earlier had been their prom and, since that

night, they'd been making plans to look for colleges they could attend together.

Every time she saw Marcus, her hand instinctively touched the bracelet on her wrist. It was a sturdy gold chain with a flat surface that had Marcus' name engraved on it. He wore an identical but larger version of the bracelet with Lucy's name. Neither of them ever took them off.

"Hey, Lucy," he said as he went to give her a hug.

"Don't. I'm all sweaty and gross. I'm late to get to Sam's game and didn't have time to shower," she explained.

They kissed briefly, then he said, "My baseball practice just ended and I need to get to work, but I saw your car and wanted to say hi."

Lucy nodded. "Can you call me tonight?"

"Probably not. We won't be getting done until quite late, but I'll see you in class tomorrow."

"Okay. My parents are gone all week, but I should be available most days after practice."

"We'll figure something out," he promised. He kissed her again and headed for his car.

Getting in her four-year-old Chevy, she started the engine, cranked the air conditioner to maximum as she pulled out of the lot, and headed south toward Armstrong Middle School.

Navigating to the rear of the school, she looked for a spot close to the ballfield and found one easily. The attendance to watch the game was dismal for both teams. As she walked toward the home bleachers, she heard the crack of a bat making solid contact with the ball and saw the centerfielder for Armstrong take two steps back before reaching up with his glove and catching the flyball.

There was an eruption of cheers from the home team and its fans as the game ended. Lucy moved closer to the fence, hoping that Sam would see that she was there before the game ended. She glanced at the scoreboard and saw that the final score was 8-4.

As he was coming in from his position as the shortstop, Sam glanced up and saw his sister. His face, which was already excited from the victory, brightened a little more.

She waited a few minutes while the teams congratulated each other and then met with their coaches for a post-game discussion. When his coach dismissed Sam, he ran to his sister. Before he could speak, Lucy said, "Congratulations. You guys did a great job." She hoped he wouldn't ask how much of the game she'd seen.

"Thanks. We were expecting it to be tough, but it went real good."

"I remember you saying that this morning. Your team is doing great so far."

As they spoke, they headed back to the parking lot.

"I'm hungry. Can we stop and get pizza?" the young ballplayer asked.

"Sorry, not today. Mom left some chicken defrosting in the fridge, and she wants me to use it tonight."

Noticing the disappointed look on her brother's face, Lucy added, "We'll get pizza one day this week. I promise."

When Lucy made that promise, she never imagined that it would be impossible to keep it.

Chapter Three

THE YELLOW TAXI CAB MOVED SLOWLY THROUGH THE MID-DAY traffic as it approached the Port of Miami. Still over a mile away, the tops of the majestic cruise ships were already visible. There were four cruise ships in port today, each turning over their complement of passengers.

In the back of the cab sat Marie and Alex Wilson. The couple was eager to board their ship and enjoy a week at sea. They'd cruised nineteen years earlier for their honeymoon and had a fantastic time. Now that their kids were old enough to be left alone, they were excited to go again.

As the cab entered the busy port area, they passed a dozen motor coaches heading in the opposite direction. The buses were ferrying those disembarking back to the airport so that they could head back home, their wonderful vacations already only memories.

When they got closer to the mammoth ships, they could see the many semi-trucks parked close by. They were waiting to unload all the provisions that would be needed to keep the thousands of passengers well fed and entertained for a week.

Their ship could hold close to 6000 passengers and had over 1500 crew members. It was one of the largest in the fleet and indeed was the largest in port today. Alex enjoyed thinking how all the passengers, arriving to cruise on smaller ships, would look at theirs and wonder what their ships lacked that the giant monster had room for.

Marie took her husband's hand in hers, physically sharing the excitement of their arrival with him. He smiled at her, knowing the thrill she felt because he was experiencing it too.

"The ship is beautiful," she exclaimed.

"It's huge," Alex responded.

"This is going to be a great week,"

Nodding, Alex added, "Sun, sea, and no kids."

Marie laughed at his comment. They'd considered waiting a few weeks until school let out and bringing the kids, but decided that they needed time to themselves as a couple.

Thinking of the kids, Marie said, "I hope they'll be okay. We're putting a lot of responsibility on Lucy."

"Yes, but she's proven time and time again that she can handle it."

"I know," Marie agreed with a rueful smile. "I'm afraid that when we get home, if everything went smoothly, I'll realize that she doesn't need us as much anymore."

"She doesn't. She's growing up, and we did our part right. This trip is a chance for her to prove it and for us to learn to accept it."

Porters met them as they arrived at the embarkation area, ready to take their luggage. After paying the cab driver, Alex got out and showed their documents to the porter, who verified that they were at the correct ship and on the right day.

Slipping the porter twenty dollars, Marie watched as he took off with their six bags. If all went well, the luggage would arrive at their stateroom by dinnertime. Hefting their one carry-on bag, Alex led them into the cruise terminal building. From here, they moved from station to station, presenting their passports and making sure all their documentation was in order.

Since boarding had begun an hour before, the crowds in the embarkation area had largely cleared out, and the lines had shrunk, so they were able to move through the stations quickly.

After clearing the final station, they followed a few other passengers heading to the gangway that led to the ship. They made one last stop, where a photographer from the ship took every group's photo before they boarded.

Alex tried to bypass the photographer, but Marie grabbed his arm to stop him, saying, "Come on, let's get the picture."

"I'm not sure if you remember, but they'll be taking these pictures the whole week," Alex responded.

"I know," Marie said with a smile. "And this will be the first one."

Minutes later, they crossed the gangway and were officially on the ship. They paused to take in the amazing scenery. The spacious lobby was elegantly decorated, and there were three glass elevators whisking passengers to different levels. It was an excellent first impression.

Almost immediately, a member of the ship's crew approached them. She was a perky young woman with an Australian accent, and she held out a small folding piece of colored card stock. "Welcome aboard. Here is a map of the ship."

"Thank you. The ship is beautiful," Marie replied.

"I'm glad you think so. We're very proud of it. May I see your boarding documents?"

Alex held them out and she looked at them briefly. "Your stateroom in on deck six, midship. It's still being cleaned and should be available in about a half-hour. Until then, feel free to explore. There's a buffet open up on the main deck and also one on deck nine at the back of the ship."

"Thank you," Alex replied with a quick smile. He opened up the map and tried to orient himself.

The Anvil

Marie shook her head and said, "Just follow me. We want to go this way." And she took off across the lobby.

"How do you know which way? I have the map," Alex asked with a smirk.

"We don't need a map. I memorized the ship's layout a month ago."

They headed to the glass elevators just as a car was arriving. The elevator rose smoothly but stopped twice for other passengers to enter as it made its way to the top. Stepping out, the Wilsons approached a door that automatically opened, allowing them access to the top deck. The first two things they noticed were the blast of hot air as they left the ship's comfortable air conditioning and the calypso music playing from a live band on the deck. They made their way to the rail and looked down on the pier. There were still passengers arriving, and different semi-trucks were unloading their cargo. The ship would be departing in two hours, and everyone was finishing up preparations.

They enjoyed the view for a few minutes and then headed toward the rear of the ship, hand in hand, to look at the other ships that were also in port and loading passengers. As they walked, Marie asked, "How do you think the kids are doing?"

"They're fine. They're both trustworthy and are probably enjoying taking care of themselves."

"I know, but I worry about them."

"This is good for them. They get to taste a little extra responsibility, and we'll be back in just a week."

They approached the rear of the ship and looked at three other cruise ships. There were many others also enjoying the view and taking pictures. Many of the other passengers already had drinks in their hands.

"Interesting, how different they all look," Marie commented.

"They may be a bit smaller than us, but they're all impressive to look at," Alex added.

They waited for several minutes for those standing in front of them to clear out enough that Marie could get to the rail and take a few photos with her phone.

Seeing his wife finish, Alex asked, "How about we head over and get something to eat? I'm hungry."

"Okay. Do you think you can find your way without the map?" Marie teased.

"Yes, I can. It is on this deck. I saw the lines as we were walking here."

"Good, I was just checking," she said with a grin.

"I'm not *that* directionally challenged," Alex replied defensively.

Taking the lead, he guided them to the buffet line, where they waited several minutes. They could smell meats grilling and see passengers walking past with heaping plates; their hunger grew. Eventually, the line split, with half the people going toward the grill and the others toward previously prepared salads and entrees on the buffet table.

Marie had a grilled chicken sandwich and fries, and Alex went with a cheeseburger. They got beverages and took seats near the pool, which was closed since they were in port.

"We still have a little while before we can get into our room. What do you want to do?" Alex asked between big bites.

"Let's go down to deck eight and check out some of the lounges and the casino."

"Okay, that works for me."

As they were talking, there were two loud blasts heard from a ship's horn.

"Sounds like one of the other ships is leaving ahead of us. Let's go watch as it departs," Alex suggested.

Chapter Four

A FEW HOURS LATER, THEIR SHIP HAD DEPARTED BUT WAS STILL in sight of land as it was moving slowly. All the passengers were completing the mandatory lifeboat drill, and most were heading back to their staterooms to return their lifejackets to their proper storage compartment. The US Coast Guard required all passengers to show up to their lifeboats with their lifejackets physically in hand. Everyone needed to know what to do in case of an emergency.

Marie and Alex took seats on the top deck, not wanting to get caught up in the hordes of people heading back to their rooms. There was a great view of the shoreline, and they relaxed, planning to wait until the crowds cleared out. They sat, enjoying the motion of the ship as it moved through the ocean, and thought about how nice it was to be away. Their peaceful thoughts, however, were interrupted by simultaneous sounds from their smartphones as text messages came through.

"See, babe. Even out on the ocean, the kids manage to disturb our peace and quiet," Alex chuckled.

"I thought we'd have heard from them a little sooner,"

Marie replied as she stood and fished her phone from her pocket.

At first, Marie was confused. The text wasn't what she was expecting. Then slowly, clarity returned, "No. No ... *no!*"

As she struggled to make sense of the two words on the screen, Alex was also holding his phone and processing the meaning and implication of 'CODE ANVIL'. "This can't be real. It has to be a test."

"No, they made it very clear. It would never be a test. If we got the message, it was real," Marie reminded him. "What do we do?"

"There's supposed to be a second message. Meeting instructions and times."

"We don't dock in St. Maarten for a day and a half. How do we get off this ship? We need to get home now!"

"We can't get off the ship. Even if we could, we'd never make it to the meeting point in time. We were told it would all move very fast," Alex declared.

"What about the kids? We need to call them."

"Do you mean to send them without us? We might never see them again," Alex exclaimed, his voice growing unintentionally louder with each word.

"We don't have a choice. It's better than us all dying!" Marie yelled back.

A woman with her own cell phone in hand came around a corner. She was a medium height Caucasian woman in her thirties with short brown hair. There was a tattoo of a seahorse on her calf. She was hysterical and speaking louder than she probably intended. "What do you expect me to do? I can't get off the ship. We're in the middle of the ocean."

There was a pause and she spoke again, "How am I supposed to do that? I can't just swim to shore." She noticed that she'd wandered close to the Wilsons, and her conversation was clearly audible. "I need to go. Figure out your plan, and

I'll call back in a few minutes." She disconnected, lowered her phone, and turned to leave the area.

As soon as she turned, Marie said, "Miss, please wait a minute."

The woman stopped and looked at Marie. She seemed uncertain as to whether she wanted to stay as asked. With a trembling voice, she asked, "What do you want?"

Marie walked to her with Alex and said, "We weren't trying to listen to your call. But it was impossible not to hear what you said. Did you get a text message just before your call?"

Nervously, she replied, "Maybe, but I can't talk about it."

Alex proceeded cautiously, remembering how it had been drilled into them that they were never to discuss Anvil with anyone. He stepped forward, holding out his phone so she could see the screen. "Did it look like this?"

The woman burst into tears and Marie took her into her arms and held her while she too wept.

"What do we do? We can't meet up as we're supposed to," the woman declared.

"I know. That's what we were trying to figure out when you came up. Come over here," Marie said as she gently guided the woman to where they'd been seated.

Alex nodded. "I'm Alex Wilson, and this is my wife, Marie. Our two kids are at home in central Indiana. We were just trying to decide what to do. Do we try to get home to them or have them proceed to a shelter without us?"

Nodding, the woman responded, "I'm Debbie Maxfield. I'm here with my sister. Her husband died a couple of months ago, and I talked her into taking this trip to try to help her have some fun. She's not part of Anvil, and I'm not allowed to tell her about it. My boyfriend is at home with my kids and his. We need to decide if he leaves or waits. He's in a panic. I guess I am too."

Alex addressed both women. "I think we need to save our

families. Help them do what is needed to get to their shelters. Once we reach St. Maarten, we get tickets on the first flights back to the US. From there, we try to meet up with them. That's all we can do."

"I agree. I don't see any other choice," Marie said, fighting to control her emotions.

Shaking her head, Debbie said, "We don't even know what the threat is. Maybe it's not that serious. Maybe they sent the message by accident."

"You got the same information we did. They wouldn't activate Anvil unless it were something severe. If we get the second message, we'll know it isn't a mistake," Marie told her.

"I was listening to the news on the radio while on the way to the ship. There was nothing that sounded at all concerning," Debbie stated.

"I know," Alex nodded. "But there has to be *something* happening."

"I can't just leave the ship in St. Maarten. My sister is on board. She's my best friend. I can't abandon her and fly home. Even if we both got off to the ship and made it to my shelter, there wouldn't be a place for her."

As she was saying this, she was interrupted by another text message. She glanced at her phone and then at her new friends. "I guess it wasn't a mistake. It's the instructions. We live in Colorado. We're supposed to drive to a National Guard base to meet. The base is about thirty minutes from our house. They have to be there in two hours. I'm really glad we got to talk, but I need to call my family."

Hugging Debbie, Marie said, "We are going to call our kids too … but I'm not sure what we are going to say."

Nodding glumly, Debbie walked toward the bow of the ship while placing a call.

Alex was the first to speak after Debbie left. "Do you agree that we need to tell the kids to go?"

Marie was quiet for several seconds. "Yes. I guess we do.

But we get off the ship as soon as possible and try to get to them."

Alex and Marie would spend the next day and a half roaming the ship, observing other passengers. They didn't see anyone else who looked anxious to get home.

Chapter Five

AFTER BREADING THE CHICKEN, LUCY ARRANGED IT IN A GLASS baking dish. It needed to go into the oven for forty minutes. She planned to get dinner cooking and then take a quick shower. Still in her running gear, she wanted to get the meat in the oven so that it could be cooking while she was showering. When she got back down from her shower, she'd start the water boiling for the box of macaroni and cheese that they would have with the baked chicken.

As soon as they'd arrived home, she'd sent Sam up to shower and change. She'd heard the water shut off as she slid the dish into the oven and set the timer. As she started to head upstairs, her cell phone rang. She looked at the screen and smiled when she saw that it. "Dad."

"Hi Dad. You miss me so much that you had to call already?" Lucy asked.

"Hey kid. I need you to get your brother and put us on speaker. I need to talk to you both. This is serious."

From the sound of his voice, she knew that something was wrong. "What happened? Is Mom hurt?"

"No, Mom is here with me now. Just get Sam on the line. I'll explain then."

The Anvil

"Sam! Get down here now. Dad is on the phone. There's a problem," Lucy yelled

Seconds later, the twelve-year-old came running down the carpeted stairs. He was fresh out of the shower and was wearing shorts and carrying a tee shirt. "What's wrong?"

"Dad needs to talk to us both. Something's wrong," Lucy said as she pressed the button, activating the speaker on her phone.

"We're both here now."

"Hey, Sam. Can you hear me?"

"Sure, Dad. What's going on?"

Taking a deep breath, Alex Wilson said, "You guys remember how we talked about Code Anvil, and we kinda joked about the world coming to an end?"

"Yeah, I remember," Sam answered.

"Sure, I remember that," Lucy acknowledged and felt a knot forming in her stomach.

"Mom and I just got the Code Anvil text. It's real. Something awful is about to happen. We need you both to get the checklists from your bags and get packed. Also, take your backpacks with stuff for the trip. We don't know how long it'll take to get to where you're going. You'll then need to go to the Sherman Center Mall. There will be buses there. And remember, this is *super* secretive. You can't tell anyone what's going on."

Sam responded first. "Is that where you'll meet us?"

Lucy, who had turned ghostly pale, unconsciously shook her head.

"Guys, you need to be there by eight tonight. No later. We can't get off the cruise ship for a good twenty-four hours. You need to go without us."

Sam, still not grasping the meaning of his father's words, asked, "Then how will you find us?"

When their dad paused, Lucy answered her brother's question. "They won't." She felt tears running down her face.

23

"No. We're going to wait here. When you get here, we'll try to find where we should go," Sam said emphatically.

Marie's voice came on the line. "Sammy, we aren't going to get there in time. More than anything, we want you to live. That's even more important than us being together. You must do this. You must listen to Lucy and go without us. We'll try to find you when we get back, but that won't be for about two days."

Everyone got quiet for several seconds, and then 17 year-old Lucy Wilson felt something change. It was as if her mind shifted into a gear she'd never used. She picked up the phone from the counter and turned off the speaker, and held it to her ear. "I understand what I need to do. I'm hanging up. We've got a lot to do. I'll call back when we're in the car."

Before her parents could answer, she hung up. They were no longer in charge, she was, and she had things to do. "Sam, upstairs *now*. Pull the bag from under your bed and get the list out of it. Start filling it. We'll have lots of time to talk later."

Obediently, the boy raced upstairs. He'd never seen his sister look and sound the way she did now and instinctively knew not to argue.

As she entered her room, her thoughts traveled back to the chicken in the oven. The mall was twenty minutes away, and they had two hours to get there. She wanted to sprint out of the house and head to the mall, but they needed to eat. If things were as hectic as they sounded, their next meal could be slow in coming. They'd take the time to eat before they left.

Pulling the extra-large all-white duffel bag from under her bed, Lucy dug out the packing list. When invited into Anvil several years ago, her parents were each issued a similar heavy-duty bag. They were told that if something ever happened, this bag and a small personal bag were all they would be allowed to take with them. Since then, the bags and packing lists had remained all but forgotten under the beds, waiting for the end of the world.

The Anvil

The huge bag was similar in size to the ones hockey players used for all their equipment. She looked at the list and saw that most of the items were obvious: six sets of clothing, including at least two sweatshirts, and toiletries. Some things were more surprising. They were supposed to bring all their schoolbooks and at least two books for personal reading. She paused, trying to make sense of it, and then logic hit her. Over a thousand people were heading to the shelter. If they each brought two books, they would have an instant library. She continued down the list, not worrying about if each item made sense to her. They were also supposed to have a bag or backpack that held what they wanted for the trip.

As she packed, her eyes fell on the photo of her and Marcus next to the bed. They were dressed up for prom. She picked it up and stared at it until she felt a tear forming. She tossed it in the bag and continued packing. If she let her mind get off task, she wouldn't be able to resume.

She flipped the list over and glanced at the prohibited items, including weapons, fireworks, pets, and anything requiring refrigeration. She tossed the checklist down on the bed, not interested in the rest of the prohibited items, and heard Sam call.

"Lucy, come here. I'm done."

She went to the boy's room. "What do you still need help with?"

"Nothing. I think I have it all, but I still have a lot of room."

Looking in her brother's bag, it appeared like it was all in order; she took his list and quickly quizzed him, and found it was complete.

"Add one more set of clothes and two more books. Is Bear in there?" she asked, referring to the eighteen-inch tall, brown-and-tan stuffed animal that Sam had slept with since he was a baby.

"No, he wasn't on the list," he explained.

"Get him in the bag. Also, add a couple of other things that you want that will fit. I need to finish dinner. We need a good meal before we leave. When you're done, get Mom and Dad's bags out and fill them from their lists. I don't want to hear you complaining about having to touch their underwear."

"But I thought they weren't going to get there in time."

"They'll try. In case they do, I want their stuff there for them," Lucy explained. Taking her bag, she turned and headed downstairs. As she went, a framed photo on the wall grabbed her attention. It had been taken last summer in the park and was of the whole family.

After depositing the bag on the couch, she started the water boiling for the macaroni and cheese. Then, she took a minute to walk around the house, collecting several framed photos of the family, which she placed in the bag, between layers of clothing to protect the glass. When she finished, her bag was stuffed and she had trouble closing it.

As she was finishing, Sam appeared, carrying his parent's bags. "I brought them all down. Mine is full now, but there's a lot of space still in Mom and Dad's."

"Good. Come and eat, and think about what else might be useful for us to have. It would be kinda stupid not to fill them all the way."

Sam said, "I'm going to pack all the candy and snacks we have into one of their bags."

Shaking her head, Lucy looked at her brother and asked, "Why would you do that?"

"We're going to be stuck in this shelter for a long time with over a thousand people. Right?"

"That's what they told us."

"Well, I saw a movie about prisoners who traded cigarettes and candy for things they wanted. They were like money. I figure, if there's room, it couldn't hurt to have a bunch of candy. Right?"

Putting her arm around her brother, she pulled him close. "For a dumb little brother, you're kinda smart."

When they finished eating, Lucy washed the dishes and then put them away. She'd no idea if her parents would be returning home but, if they did, she wanted them to see that she'd been responsible.

Chapter Six

Lucy Wilson backed the car out of the driveway. They'd rushed to pack and eat and had kept their minds from dwelling on what was happening. Now, as they drove away from the house, possibly for the last time, the depth of the situation became apparent.

She wanted to call Marcus. Hearing his voice would be comforting, but he was at work.

"We're never coming back, are we?" Sam asked, the grief thick in his voice.

"I don't know. Whatever is happening might be over in a couple of weeks. We don't know what's going on yet."

"The day after tomorrow, my science class is going to meet early and try to see the comet. It's so big and close that we'd be able to see it without a telescope, even in daylight," Sam reminded his sister.

"I know. That's all everyone is talking about. The Menesa Comet is passing closer to us than any other on record."

After a few seconds, he said, "Maybe it'll hit the Earth. Maybe that's why we're going to shelters."

"Maybe. I don't know," Lucy answered, her voice weary.

"Are all my friends going to die?" Sam's anxiety increased as he considered this possibility.

Lucy felt inadequate to answer her brother's questions. She was struggling with the same thoughts. With tears running down her face, she said, "I'm worried about that too, but try not to think about it until we learn what the problem is. This might not be as bad as we're imagining. Let's call Mom and Dad. I told them we'd call when we were in the car."

Reaching for the console above the car's radio, Sam scrolled through the menu until he found the address book and selected his mother's phone number. The car had automatically connected to Lucy's phone, and in a few seconds, the ringing sounded over the car speakers.

Answering on the first ring, Marie Wilson asked, "How are things going? Any problems?" Concern was evident in her voice.

Sam replied immediately. "Hi Mom. We're in the car."

Lucy gave her brother a look that he was familiar with, and he stopped to let her talk.

"No, Mom, no problems. We had plenty of time, so we had dinner at home. We don't know when we'll get food again. We got our bags packed."

Their father's voice came through. "Good job. You have plenty of time, so don't rush."

"We packed your duffle bags and have them with us," Lucy informed her parents.

"You do? Okay." Alex sounded a bit confused.

Catching that, Sam said, "You said that you would try to meet us. Right?"

There was a brief pause. "Sure, son. We hope to, but we don't know if that will work out. But we promise to do our best."

"Well, if you do, we have your stuff, so you won't have to stop and get it."

"Okay. Good thinking."

Changing the subject, Lucy asked, "Do you guys have any idea what this emergency is?"

Marie replied, "Since we got off the phone with you earlier, we went to a lounge with a bunch of TVs and have been listening to news stations. We don't hear anything that sounds concerning. The only unusual thing is the comet that everyone is looking forward to."

"Sam wondered if maybe the comet was going to hit us. That's the only idea we've come up with," the teenager said.

"We don't know. If so, someone is doing an amazing job of hiding it from everyone," Alex answered.

"So, what's the plan when you get off the ship? How and when will you get back to the US?" Lucy asked.

"We dock in St. Maarten the day after tomorrow. First thing in the morning. We're leaving the ship and heading to the airport. I booked a flight leaving at 10:00 AM. It lands in Miami at 1:00 PM. We then leave Miami in the afternoon and will be back in Chicago at 7:00 in the evening. Then there's a two-hour drive home. We can be back to our house in just about 48 hours from now," their mother explained.

There was a long silence, and Marie anxiously asked, "Are you guys there? Did that make sense?"

"Yeah, we're still here," Lucy answered. "That just seems way too long. After that, you'll still need to locate us."

"We know guys, we know," Alex acknowledged.

"Okay. Well, I can see the mall. I need to disconnect, but we'll text you and let you know what's going on and try to talk to someone about your delay," Lucy informed them.

"Okay. Watch out for each other. We love you both and are very proud of you," Marie said, her voice full of despair.

"Love you too," the kids said together, and Sam disconnected.

Both remained silent as they circled the mall. Halfway around the complex, they spotted three large buses sitting together away from all the buildings.

"Lucy, can we just go home?" Sam asked with a slight tremble in his voice.

"No, but I want to too."

As she drove, she let her mind drift to Marcus. When would she see him again? Was he safe? What would he think when she disappeared? She didn't know what this situation was and didn't want to go without him.

They approached a four-way stop and needed to turn right to go down a hill and enter the lot where the buses were parked. Lucy had her mind on many things, and one of them wasn't the stop sign.

Without stopping, she turned to the right. At the same time, a van approached from her left. That van was planning to go straight through the intersection, which it did ... without stopping.

Chapter Seven

TIRED FROM WORKING ALL DAY, THE DRIVER OF THE VAN WAS an emotional mess. His kids were in the back seat, scared and arguing, and his wife sat next to him crying. He seldom came to this side of town and wasn't familiar with the mall. All he knew was that he had to find some buses that would take him and his family away from the lives they'd built.

At the last minute, Lucy heard the sound of brakes locking up—right before the van impacted her door at over thirty miles per hour. Something hard slammed into her side, and she felt extreme pain and heard the sound of her brother's scream as glass from her window exploded all around her. The car slid sideways, pushed by the van. Lucy had been in the middle of a right-hand turn, which elevated her left arm away from her side. If not, the arm would've been broken, as her door was crushed inwards over a foot. She stomped on the brake, trying to stop her movement. Her eyes clamped shut until the sliding vehicle came to a stop.

Her first concern was Sam. She twisted her head and body and, at the same time, yelled his name. Even his short name didn't make it out of her mouth before she shrieked in agony.

Fiery stabbing pain came from her ribs. The attempt to call out and twist around had been a colossal mistake.

"Lucy! Are you okay?"

Fighting to breathe, she waited for the pain to subside. She was glad Sam was talking and therefore alive. Finally, she was able to get out a few words. "Sam. Are you hurt?"

"I don't think so. Nothing hurts too much. Just kinda sore. You don't look good. What's wrong?"

"I hurt my ribs. I'm sure it isn't serious," she said, hoping to reassure her brother but not believing it herself. This injury wasn't minor; it was a big problem.

She gently felt skin where it was the most painful and checked her hand, glad to see that it hadn't picked up any blood. As she was checking her injuries, Lucy was startled by someone looking in through her shattered window.

It was a man with a scraggly beard and a dingy ballcap. He looked terrified. "I'm so sorry. Are you okay?"

"I think so. Hurt my ribs pretty bad," she answered with a grimace.

"How about him? Is he hurt?" the man asked as he looked at Sam.

"I'm okay. But my sister is in a lot of pain."

The man nodded. "I don't want to just leave you, but I need to get down to those buses in the lot there."

"That's where we're going too," Lucy explained.

"Oh, you are? Okay. Will your car make it?"

Nodding, Lucy said, "I think so."

"Okay, I'll see you down there."

Moving slowly, Lucy turned the wheel and managed to get the car heading back towards the parking lot. She drove slowly, afraid of hitting a bump and the pain it would bring. All the while, Lucy took short, shallow breaths, trying to keep her ribs from moving. Still, she felt each breath.

While driving, it became clear that her car was severely

damaged. There were strange, loud sounds when she turned to the left.

As they approached the buses, they could see the sign in the front window of each one that read "ANVIL". Lucy took a parking spot close to the buses and noticed many other cars parked nearby.

She tried to get out of the car, but the wrecked door wouldn't move. Trembling in horror, she thought about how much pain she'd experience if she had to climb out Sam's door. Before she could complete the thought, she saw Sam; he had gotten out and now ran around the car to her window.

He also tried unsuccessfully to open the door. "I'll be right back."

"Sam, don't go anywhere," Lucy said in little more than a whisper, but the boy was already gone. She closed her eyes and didn't fight the tears that started flowing.

Soon Sam returned with the same scraggly-looking guy who had been driving the van that struck them. "I hear your door is stuck. Let me see."

He grabbed it and pulled. The crushed metal groaned and creaked as the door slowly opened. Lucy was glad they were getting on the buses because there was no way the door would ever latch again. "Can you get out?" the man asked.

"I don't know."

Turning her body carefully, Lucy felt the pain ramp up again as she did. Ignoring it, she continued until her feet were out of the car.

"Let me help," the man said, and he stuck out his arm.

She grabbed it and slowly pulled herself up to a standing position while taking rapid puffing breaths, fighting the searing pain. Once standing, she was glad to be out of the car and upright.

"Are you hurting anywhere else?"

Shaking her head, Lucy answered, "No, just the ribs. I think they might be broken."

He nodded. "You should go to a hospital. But if you're supposed to be on one of these buses, you can't."

"I know. Can you help with our bags? I can manage myself, but I can't lift the bags right now."

"Sure. Glad to help. But first, we need to brush some of the glass shards off of you."

Starting with her hair, he carefully removed most of the shattered safety glass. Then, using a tee-shirt from Lucy's back seat, he wiped the remaining glass from her clothes.

They unloaded the four bags and their backpacks. Lucy took her pack, and Sam and the man, who hadn't yet provided a name, took the large bags.

As they walked, they saw soldiers in uniform directing people to the different buses. They were tagging bags and loading them into the compartments under the large vehicles.

Two soldiers were looking at them. Each had a holster on their right hip. One held a tablet computer and the other had an open case with a long strap over her shoulder.

As they approached the first soldier, Lucy saw that he was relatively short and seemed to be only a few years older than her. He asked, "Can I get your names, please?"

Trying not to let her injured state show, she said, "Last name is Wilson. We're Lucy and Sam. Our parents, Alex and Marie, will be joining us later." For the first time, she wondered if they'd be allowed to go without their parents.

"You only get to take one bag each," the young soldier said.

"We know. These are our parents' bags. They told us to bring them."

The soldier looked down at the tablet computer, dragged his finger up and down the screen a couple of times before responding. "Okay, I found you. Everything looks good."

He looked at his partner. "Cooper, give me four luggage tags and ID cards for eighty-seven."

The other soldier reached into her case and withdrew

what looked like four keycards attached to yellow lanyards. The number eighty-seven was in big bold letters on a plastic yellow card. Below the eighty-seven were smaller numbers. Lucy's was 87-0816 and Sam's was 87-0817. They also received four yellow luggage tags.

Looking at the Wilson kids, he said, "I need to ask, do you have any weapons, pepper spray, anything flammable or alive in any of the bags?"

Sam answered, "No. Nothing like that."

Nodding, the soldier said, "Good, keep these lanyards on at all times. Secure these tags to your bags and then take them over to the third bus. You can sit anywhere you want. You won't be seeing the bags again until you reach the final destination. Keep your backpacks with you."

"Do you know where we're going?" Lucy asked.

With a sympathetic look, he said for at least the twentieth time today, "They haven't told us anything other than to get you people organized and loaded on the buses. I think I heard you're going to a military base, but I'm not sure. We don't even know what this Anvil project is."

They dropped their tagged luggage in a pile that a team was loading under the bus and headed for the vehicle, carrying their backpacks and wearing their lanyards.

Lucy looked for the family that had hit them and saw they were headed to a different bus.

It would be the last time they saw them.

Chapter Eight

LUCY CAREFULLY STEPPED ONTO THE BUS AND ALLOWED HER little brother to choose their seats. She told him that he could have the window seat. This made him feel good, and Lucy would have the extra room that the aisle seat provided.

Looking to his sister, Sam asked, "Should I put our backpacks above?"

She glanced at the baggage rack above. "Keep them down here for now. You'll be wanting the stuff in it, and we don't want to have to keep getting it down."

Not happy with the answer, he took his seat and stuffed the bag by his feet. Lucy stood for a few seconds longer, dreading the pain that would come when she had to twist and bend to get seated.

While standing, she regarded the other passengers. The bus was about half full. She was surprised to see how many other kids there were. Almost all the other people were in groups, which she assumed were families, and all but one of them had kids with them. Looking at a boy who was about her age and sitting two rows back, she saw that his lanyard was light blue and had the number seventy-two on it.

Boldly, she took a couple of steps farther down the aisle

and, while holding her lanyard out, smiled. "Any idea what the colors and numbers mean?"

He returned the smile. "No. We were discussing that. I've seen other yellow tags like yours, and they all have the same number."

Lucy nodded, returned, and slowly took her seat, the pain ripping through her flank as she turned and lowered herself to the padded seat cushion. She looked at her brother, who asked, "Are you okay? I can see you're hurting."

Lucy waited for the agony to subside before answering. She considered downplaying the injury so he wouldn't worry but decided that they were in this together, and she needed to be honest with him. "I think I've broken some ribs. It hurts a lot when I move." She stopped to take a few more shallow breaths. "But I'll be okay. We'll get through this together," she assured him and dug through her backpack until she found the bottle of Ibuprofen. She took out four tablets, which she swallowed without water.

"How about you text Mom and Dad and let them know what's going on? Please don't mention the accident or my ribs. They don't need something else to be worried about."

Sam nodded, pulled out his phone, and began updating their parents. As he was working on it, a soldier stepped on the bus and, in a reassuring tone, said, "Everything is going fine. We'll be leaving in about ten minutes."

By this time, there were few seats left on their bus and, when Lucy looked out the window, she could see only a couple of families left to load.

After a brief wait, the driver got on board. He started the engine and left the parking lot. Sam continued to send text updates to his parents over the next hour and a half as they traveled to their unknown destination. As they drove, there were only hushed conversations and the occasional sound of sobbing.

It was getting dark. Lucy had used the mapping app on

her phone to determine that they were heading to an airport. She suspected that their actual destination was Grissom Air Reserve Base, an Air Force facility located in Kokomo. She wondered if they would prohibit the use of phones. Lucy suspected that whoever was in charge wanted to, but didn't wish to risk a confrontation with hundreds of stressed civilians who were starving for information.

When the base's sign became visible, she switched out of map mode and texted her parents: "Arriving at a military base in Kokomo. I suspect we'll be flying from here. I worry they'll confiscate phones. The more I think about it, the more it makes sense they would."

Almost immediately, she got a response back from her mom: "K, keep us informed. We love U."

Lucy typed back. "I wish U were here."

"Me 2, but U can handle this."

Lucy was pleased with her mother's confidence and hoped she was right because she sure wasn't feeling confident. What Lucy wanted to do was to curl up and cry. But she couldn't. She needed to be strong for Sam. As she was putting the phone away, she saw someone ahead, waving the bus through a guard gate.

They proceeded down an access road and out onto the flight line. There were military aircraft parked nearby, and private planes were visible on the opposite side of the airfield.

The bus came to a stop in front of a large hanger. Its massive doors were closed, preventing anyone from seeing inside. There were two other buses here, and they were finishing unloading their passengers. Three soldiers were waiting as the buses approached. When their vehicle stopped, the door opened and one of them stepped in.

"Ladies and gentlemen, please listen closely. These instructions are important," the soldier said solemnly. "When you exit the bus, you'll proceed in an orderly line to the door to the left of the hanger. Once inside, you'll see a registration area.

Proceed there. After you've registered, go to the center of the hanger and pick up a boxed meal. There are cots in the back of the hanger if you want to sleep. Listen for your lanyard color to be called. When it is, you'll proceed immediately to the front of the hanger, and we will show you to your aircraft. Does that all make sense?"

When he saw many nodding heads, he continued. "Unless any questions you have are related to these instructions, please know that no one here can provide further information. We're instructed to organize you and get you to an aircraft that will take you somewhere else. Also, we're prohibited from asking your questions, so you already know more than we do." There was another pause, and then he turned around and exited the bus saying, "Follow me."

Lucy stood cautiously, and with her backpack in hand, guided Sam so that he was in front of her. She didn't know what was going on and wasn't going to lose track of her brother. The pack was heavy and painful to carry with her injuries, but she wasn't about to ask Sam to carry it for her. They stepped off the bus into the cooling night air. She'd made sure Sam had stuffed a sweatshirt into his backpack and was now glad that she'd thought of it.

They entered the expansive hanger and saw several hundred people wandering around. The place smelled stale, with a faint scent of petroleum. Old fluorescent lights provided barely adequate illumination. The walls had peeling paint and there were letters and numbers in strange combinations on the concrete floor.

There was an area near the left wall with a new sign which read Registration. Several people from an earlier bus were finishing up the process, and her fellow passengers got in line behind them. Six soldiers were serving as registration workers, so the line moved relatively fast. Soon, Lucy found herself standing in front of the registration team member.

"Names, please?"

"Lucy and Sam Wilson."

Looking up from the computer screen, he asked, "Are you alone? It looks like there should be four of you."

"There's supposed to be. Our parents were out of town and are meeting us at our destination."

"Is that something they've worked out? I don't have any information about it," he inquired with a creased brow.

"That's what they told us." Lucy suspected that things would be better if no one knew how far away her parents were until they reached the final destination.

"Okay, I guess. Let me see your lanyards. I need the smaller numbers on them."

He took the four lanyards and linked the numbers on them to their names on the computer. After a few additional questions, he said, "Okay, go grab a meal and listen for someone to announce your aircraft. We'll call it by the color on your lanyard. It'll probably be a few hours."

"Thanks." Lucy turned and walked away, again thankful that no one was asking too many questions about her parents.

They approached the center table and saw several hundred generic white boxes. The siblings looked, but there were no labels on them. Lucy grabbed one and handed it to her brother.

"No thanks, I'm not hungry," Sam said.

"Take it and stuff it in your backpack. We don't know when we'll get food again," Lucy directed him.

Without arguing, her brother took the box. "Where do you want to go?"

Lucy looked around. There were a bunch of cots near the back and scattered chairs in other places. "You can pick."

Sam thought for a minute. "I want a cot. He said it would be a few hours. Let's take the back corner." He headed toward the back.

The hanger seemed mainly clean, with a few faded grease stains on the concrete floor.

When they reached the rear, they pulled a couple of old canvas cots and chairs together. Lucy figured that they could give up the chairs if the place got too crowded but, for now, there were more than enough.

Sam dropped his pack on the cot. "Okay, if I wander around a bit, sis?"

Lucy thought for a minute. "Don't go outside and keep your phone with you."

"Will do. Should I ask if there's a doctor that can look at you?"

"No, I'll be okay until we get where we're going."

After thinking for a few seconds, she called to him again. "Hey Sam, while you're looking around, see if you can learn anything. Ask a few questions, if you can."

He nodded and walked off. Lucy was thankful to be alone. She turned so that her left side was facing the wall, and no one could see. She raised her shirt and exposed the ribs, and was shocked at what she saw: deep purple bruising more than twice the size of her palm. She gently applied pressure until the pain got worse, then slowly inhaled, filling her lungs as much as she could tolerate. As she did, she was sure she felt something in her ribs moving or grinding.

Lucy took a seat on a cot. Lowering herself was agonizing. She then texted an update to her parents, leaving out the most exciting part of their adventure. When she finished, she opened the white box. Inside was a sandwich on wheat bread; it looked like turkey. Lucy shook her head; she despised wheat bread. There was also a bottle of water, a bag of potato chips, and an oatmeal cookie.

She took the water bottle and cookie and stuck them in her backpack. She put the sandwich back in the box and she tossed it on the other cot. Sitting back, she opened the bag of chips and forced herself to relax for the first time in hours.

Taking out her phone, she looked at Marcus's photo. She

knew the rules but couldn't stand the idea of leaving and not telling him something.

Sending a text, she said: "I just wanted to tell you that I love you and miss you. Don't ever forget."

She put the phone away, unhappy that she hadn't said more. It was then that she noticed that she was still in her running gear and had never taken a shower. With much difficulty, she got herself lying on her right side. She closed her eyes and let the tears flow down her cheeks, allowing the stress of the last six hours to consume her.

In but a few minutes, she'd cried herself to sleep.

Chapter Nine

Sam decided to try to learn something useful as he started roaming the hanger. He was counting the number of different colored lanyards. So far, he'd seen six. Also, he'd noticed that there was another large wave of people working their way through registration.

He assumed that they'd come on additional buses. The boy approached and saw five of the six lanyard tag colors present in the new arrivals and believed the colors were indicative of everyone's final destination. In his mind, he pictured dozens of locations like this around the country, actively sorting people.

After wandering for a while, he noticed a group of about twelve people in chairs pulled into a loose circle. He walked closer; they were deep in conversation. Most importantly, however, there was a variety of lanyard colors. Sam assumed that meant that they weren't all together before arriving here.

Feeling bold, he strolled to an empty chair in the circle. "May I join you, or is this private?"

"Take a seat, Yellow," a middle-aged man said, noticing Sam's lanyard.

A tall thin man spoke. "We're all just sharing ideas. Trying to figure out what's going on and killing time."

Sam nodded. "That's what I figured."

A young, pretty woman in the group spoke up. "We've all been sharing ideas. You haven't heard any of them. You're a fresh perspective. What have you figured out?"

Feeling put on the spot in front of strangers, he wanted to get up and head back to his sister. Instead, he took a chance and shared his ideas, "The big number on the lanyard tag is our final destination. The colors match the numbers, like all yellows are one number, and all greens are another. The colors allow for easy identification." Sam paused, looking around the circle to see how far off he was.

There were several nods, then a teenaged girl with a green lanyard and the number 98 looked at him. "So, where do you think they're taking us?"

"Sorry, I don't have any ideas about that. It'll all depend on what the big problem ends up being."

A young African American mom in the circle said, "That's what doesn't make sense. Nothing is going on in the news. No Ebola epidemic. No new wars. Nothing."

There was a pause, and Sam decided to test his theory. "That might not be true."

He wasn't sure who asked, but he heard someone say, "What do you mean?"

Every eye was on the twelve-year-old boy. He spoke hesitantly. "There's something unusual in the news. Everyone is talking about it. The comet."

"The greatest astronomical event of a generation is what they keep saying," someone responded.

"Son, are you saying that you think it'll hit us?" one of the men asked.

"I don't know, but it's two days away, and we're being rushed to shelters," Sam pointed out.

"That's if you call this rushing," someone said with a chuckle.

As they spoke, a loud commotion started and they heard yelling from the registration area. Everyone in the circle jumped to their feet to see, but the hanger had become rather crowded, and they were too far away. Two men from their group headed over to see what was going on.

Sam and the others re-took their seats and waited for them to return.

Sam heard his phone chime. He took it out and saw a text from Lucy. "U OK"

He was about to respond when the men returned. One of them spoke. "Some guy freaked out. He was yelling and demanding information. He was face-down on the floor with his hands zip-tied behind his back when we got there."

The second guy added, "The soldiers have been nice, but they aren't taking any crap from anyone."

Taking out his phone, Sam typed: "Fine here. Guy at registration causing trouble."

After another half hour of conversation, Sam headed back to his sister to report on what he'd learned.

As he sat on a cot, he could tell that his sister had been crying, but decided not to mention anything. As he started describing what he'd learned on his walk, there was an announcement.

"Green and Purple will be loading in fifteen minutes. Start toward the exit. Only the first 150 of each will fit on the aircraft. Additional planes will be loading soon. Unless you want to wait longer, be one of the first 150 in your line."

"I wonder how long it'll be for us," Sam said.

"No idea. How about we try to get some sleep? I was out for a little while before the commotion earlier," Lucy stated.

Looking around, he saw that many of the cots were filled with people sleeping or trying to. He wasn't sure if he wanted to sleep, but there was nothing else to do. He'd seen several

The Anvil

groups of people playing cards while he was exploring, but they hadn't thought to bring anything like that.

He reached into his backpack and pulled out a small battery pack and cable, and plugged in his phone to charge. After returning the devices to the pack, he stretched out. He lay there trying to fall asleep but heard someone nearby snoring.

He wasn't sure how long he'd been asleep when an announcement rang forth. "Red and Silver, line up for your aircraft. Loading will begin in ten minutes."

He looked over at his sister, who appeared to be sleeping. He soon drifted off to sleep again.

"Yellow and Brown, your aircraft is arriving. Be lined up and ready to load in ten minutes."

The announcement woke the Wilsons. They sat up and looked at each other. As they gathered their belongings, another announcement came over the PA. "Green and Orange, your aircraft will load after Yellow and Brown depart. Get ready but remain out of the way until Yellow and Brown have departed."

"Lucy, when I was wandering around, there were no Orange tags. They must've all come in since I got back. How long was I asleep?"

"About four hours. Also, if every aircraft holds about 150 people, then 600 have already gone and, yet, this place is much more crowded than before," she pointed out.

They headed over to the departure doors and got in line. There were uniformed soldiers getting everyone organized.

"There's only room for the first 150 on each aircraft. However, there are two planes for Brown. You'll see luggage stacked on the aircraft. Don't look for yours. There's a good chance it'll be on a different plane."

After a few minutes, the door opened and Yellow was escorted outside. There were three military transport planes parked in front of the hanger. The rear ramps were down.

47

The planes were large enough that, if needed, someone could easily drive a couple of small trucks inside. As they ascended the ramp and into the plane designated for Yellow, they saw narrow seating attached to the plane's inside walls. All the seats faced the center of the aircraft. The new arrivals were aware of a poorly lit interior and strange smell, which was similar to what they'd noticed in the hanger, but much stronger.

"Move all the way in and take the seats closest to the front. Don't leave any seats unfilled," someone shouted to them.

In the center of the plane were about a dozen large rolling bins, each filled with the passengers' duffel bags.

As she sat, Lucy was immediately aware of how narrow and uncomfortable the seat was. She was pinned between her brother and a largely built man. It was no fault of his, but he pressed tight against her broken ribs. The pain was terrible, and each breath made it worse. She glanced at her brother and saw that he was also unimpressed with the seat, but he seemed to find the no-frills transportation interesting. She'd already taken a second dose of Ibuprofen and, while it helped a little, being pressed up against the person next to her was rather agonizing.

As soon as the last person was seated, an Air Force crew member started giving instructions on fastening seatbelts. After a couple of minutes, there was a loud rumble as the engines powered up. Lacking the insulation found in a civilian passenger plane, they found the transport aircraft's noise deafening. Sam had to shout so his sister could hear what he was saying.

After a brief wait for the engines to get up to speed, the plane was quickly airborne.

Chapter Ten

DURING THE FLIGHT, SAM DUG INTO HIS BAG, TOOK OUT THE boxed lunch and begin eating. Lucy decided that she was also hungry and took out the water bottle and cookie, and finished off both. She thought about the sandwich and decided that she wasn't *that* hungry yet.

Closing her eyes, knowing that she'd never fall asleep, she tried to relax. She debated texting her parents but decided not to. She believed that their ship was further out to sea and no longer in range of any cell towers since her last two updates had not received a reply. Instead, she pulled up several news sites.

She glanced through headlines, looking for anything to indicate a reason for the Anvil alert. But nothing jumped out. There were stories about the approaching comet and all the excitement that it was generating. People would be gathering all across the globe to see it. She wondered if Sam might be right about it hitting Earth, then pushed that thought from her mind. The idea was too disturbing. But she didn't see any articles to indicate anything else.

They'd been in the air for over an hour when she heard the plane's engine noise decrease and felt them descending.

Out of curiosity, she took out her phone and pulled up the map. It indicated that she was in southern Michigan. She continued watching and saw that they were approaching an airfield labeled Battle Creek Air National Guard. This destination seemed to make sense, considering how long they'd been in the air.

Lucy poked Sam to get his attention and showed him the phone. He gave her a questioning look, and she responded with a shrug; the movement caused her ribs to move, bringing renewed pain and reminding Lucy that she needed to be more careful.

The wheels touched down and the plane taxied for several minutes. The jarring landing generated a new wave of intense pain. Their speed decreased until it felt like they were moving at a crawl. Then the engine power increased briefly and the plane turned in a tight circle, and then stopped. As soon as the engine noise ceased, the Air Force crewmember who'd spoken to them earlier stood and walked to the back of the plane. He worked a hidden control, which lowered the loading ramp. He then yelled out, "Please unbuckle and exit the aircraft. Make sure you have anything you carried on with you."

The siblings stood and headed to the rear of the plane. Walking down the ramp, Sam was surprised to see that the sun was starting to rise.

The group was lead into another hanger. This one was outfitted similarly to the last one, with scattered chairs and cots. There was another large group of about 150 people, all wearing pink tags on lanyards. A soldier was speaking to them. "When these new arrivals are all inside, you'll walk out to the aircraft. Take the seat closest to the front and make sure to have all your belongings with you."

Another uniformed man approached the new arrivals of Yellow. "Please give me your attention for a minute. First, welcome to Battle Creek, Michigan. This isn't your final stop. In about twenty minutes, you'll be boarding three buses that will be taking you on the final leg of your journey. Now, that's all I know. I don't know where your destination is. Secondly, make yourselves comfortable. There are pizzas and drinks available along the back wall. When we announce your bus, please load quickly; we've got more Yellow and Gold people arriving soon and want to have you on your way by then. That's all I have for you now. Try to relax."

Lucy looked around and saw the last of the Pink group heading out the door. About seventy other people were milling about. She observed a mix of Gold and Yellow tags.

"Sam, follow me." She'd noticed a family of four watching the new arrivals. As she approached, she thought that they looked friendly, though maybe a little apprehensive. The adults seemed to be in their mid-thirties while the girl was about her age and the boy closer to Sam's. "Hi, we're Lucy and Sam."

The mother spoke. "Hello. I'm Megan Tanner, and this is my husband, Jake. These guys are Lauren and Ray."

"We were just curious since you're also tagged Yellow and weren't on our plane. We're still trying to put the pieces together," Lucy explained.

Jake nodded. "We had a van with soldiers show up at our house. They gathered three other families and us, and took us to a military base. From there, we flew here."

"We had a similar experience," Lucy said. "We got a text to meet at a mall in south-central Indiana, bussed to a military base and flown here."

Sam added, "We've seen eight different tag colors, but this is the first time we've seen Pink and Gold. In Indiana, there were planeloads of each color leaving and more people arriving all the time."

"Before we got here, there were several other groups that flew out from here. Pink seems to be the last one. Only Gold and Yellow have flown in. I know that there were at least three earlier busloads of Yellow that have already left. We just missed getting on the last one."

Lucy took a minute to process what they were learning. Small pieces were falling into place. She knew that they would eventually learn the whole thing, but it was interesting to try to connect the dots with nothing else to do.

Her thoughts were interrupted by Megan. "Where are your parents?"

Sam's head whipped over and looked at his sister. He was interested in what she'd say.

Lucy liked this family and felt comfortable talking to them. It looked like they'd be sheltering together, and friends were important. She decided to take a chance. Looking at Megan, she said, "We haven't eaten in a while. Sam is going to get some pizza for the two of us. Is it okay if these guys go with him? They might as well start making friends, since it looks like we'll be together for a while."

A questioning look appeared on Megan's face and she glanced at Jake, who shrugged and nodded at the same time.

Lucy looked at her little brother and nodded. He had an irritated expression on his face. He didn't like being kept out of the conversation. She smiled and quietly said, "Please."

The boy gave a reluctant nod and looked at the other two kids. "Wanna go get pizza?"

They glanced at their parents and their mother said, "Just stay together."

Once the kids left, Jake looked at the other two and indicated several nearby chairs. "How about we sit?"

The Tanners watched as Lucy sat slowly—with a grimace.

"Lucy, are you hurt?"

"Please don't tell anyone ... at least, until we've been at our shelter for a while." As she spoke, she raised the side of her shirt, exposing the dark purple bruising that now extended from her armpit to below her ribcage.

"My word!" Megan exclaimed. "What happened? You

The Anvil

might have some broken ribs. You need a doctor to look at that."

"I'm sure I broke some, and I'll get it checked when we get where we're going. Right now, we just need to keep going."

"How did that happen?" Jake asked, concern evident in his voice.

"Car accident on the way to the meet-up. It looks bad and hurts a lot, but I can keep going. I'm just careful how I move."

The couple both nodded.

"So, what about your parents?" Megan prodded.

"About two hours before they sent the Anvil text, our parents pulled out of the Port of Miami on a cruise ship for a week-long vacation."

There was a pause before Lucy saw Megan's eyes go wide.

"They called us and told us what's going on," Lucy continued. "Since we're also in the program, they told us to go and that they'd try to meet up with us. Their ship's first stop is in St. Martin. It arrives in about twenty-four hours. They have a flight booked out of there first thing and plan to be in Chicago by mid-afternoon tomorrow. I just need to let them know where to meet us."

Megan thought for a minute. "And nobody had questioned where your parents are?"

"None of these people know enough to question me. They know less about what's going on than we do. I just keep telling them that my parents will be meeting up with us. So far, they accepted my explanation."

"How do you plan to explain their absence when we arrive at the shelter? They'll push back more," Jake asked.

"When we get there, I plan to tell them the whole thing," Lucy advised. "They might be able to help with getting our parents to the shelter."

Megan and Jake glanced worriedly at each other, both wondering whether their new friend's plan would work.

"If there's anything we can do to help, just ask," Megan

said. She was about to say something more but was interrupted by the three returning kids.

Sam handed his sister a cup of watery lemonade and a plate with two pieces of pizza. It looked like it had been sitting out for several hours. Lucy didn't care and started eating. While she was eating, her group became aware of the sound of another aircraft approaching. Soon, a mix of people wearing Yellow and Gold tags entered. They were given the same speech that the Wilson kids had received.

A few minutes later, they heard a voice from the overhead speakers. "There are three buses here for Yellow. If you have a Yellow tag, please head to the west exit."

The group of six moved toward it. They weren't sure if there were enough seats for all the Yellow waiting in the hanger and wanted to make sure that they got seats that, if possible, were together.

As they exited, the cool morning air felt refreshing. They boarded and found seats together on one of the three large charter buses. Lucy didn't want to take the window seat. Sliding in would be painful, but it would allow Sam to sit across the aisle from Ray, whom he seemed to be getting along with. She was glad that he already had a friend.

Once seated, they noticed something strange about the windows. Someone had covered them over from the outside. No one could see out of the bus.

For the last several hours, Lucy had forced a single thought away, not letting it in; now, she did.

Marcus! What will happen to Marcus? Her hand drifted to the bracelet on her wrist again.

Chapter Eleven

THE BUS DEPARTED AND WAS SOON ON A HIGHWAY AND MOVING quickly. Lucy pulled out her phone to send another update to her parents. She was surprised to see that she had no service. Shortly, she heard hushed conversations on the bus. Others had also noticed that their phones weren't working. She poked her brother gently, interrupting his discussion with Ray.

"What?"

"Check your phone. Do you have service?"

Pulling it out, Sam showed Lucy the screen. She smiled drily. There was no reason to confiscate phones when they could jam them.

She put the phone away. "I want to thank you for helping out back there and taking a walk to get pizza with the others. I know you would've rather stayed for the conversation, but I didn't want everyone hearing it. I know you understand that."

Sam looked at her for a few seconds. "I understand. I just don't like being treated like a little kid."

"You aren't. You've been great all through this. I don't know what's going to happen, but we're in this together."

"Do you really think that Mom and Dad will be able to get to us in time?"

She eyed him closely and decided to be honest. "I hope so. But I think the odds are 50/50 at best. Hopefully, we'll know more within a few hours of getting where we're going."

He leaned his shoulder gently into his sister's arm. She leaned back. They were scared, but they weren't alone. After nearly an hour, they felt the bus take an exit, and Lucy again wondered where they were headed.

Her mind too active for sleep, she closed her eyes and rested. She was aware that Sam had resumed his conversation with Ray. As she thought, the driver made an announcement. "We'll be arriving in about ten minutes. Collect your belongings."

The bus made several turns and was soon on a dirt road. It passed through a gate with a chain-link fence and continued for several minutes before stopping in a large open area. There were three other buses already unloading, and the other two from Battle Creek were behind her bus. Apparently, these other buses had come from somewhere else.

A ten-person crew worked to remove the luggage from under the bus and stack it onto carts attached to small electric vehicles. The driver picked up a microphone. "Please remain seated. We'll be unloading as soon as the other buses are out of the way. Someone will be getting on board to give directions."

Lucy looked at her brother. "I guess we're here."

"Yeah. I'm not sure if this a good thing or bad."

"I know," his sister agreed with a sigh.

"What are we going to do if Mom and Dad don't get here?" Sam asked.

"I don't know. I really don't know." As Lucy said this, she took her brother's hand, and he responded by gently squeezing hers.

Soon the doors opened and a woman in her early twenties with Hispanic features and wearing a casual beige outfit stepped aboard. In a friendly voice, she said, "Welcome to

Grand Rapids. My name is Rachel, and I'm on the admission team here at Shelter 87. In truth, I arrived on a bus just like this last night.

"When you get off the bus, don't worry about your luggage. Someone will bring it in for you. Just follow the group inside, and you'll receive more instructions. The shelter will be closed and secured tomorrow at 6:00 PM. Until then, there will be lots more people arriving. Fewer than half of the shelter inhabitants are here now. There won't be any additional information about the event provided until then. Okay, let's go."

"What *is* this place?" someone called out.

"There's a bunch of abandoned gypsum mines in this area. They built the shelter down in the old mines," Rachel explained.

"Why aren't our phones working?" someone closer to the front called out.

"This is a secret facility. We can't have people sharing its location online. You'll have internet access from your rooms after they seal the facility, and there will be internal Wi-Fi available at a later date."

There was audible grumbling and complaining about this news, but everyone got up and started down the aisle and off the bus. The Wilsons joined those exiting and were soon standing in the comfortable spring air. They watched as the buses that preceded them left the area. They then saw passengers disembarking from the other buses that arrived with them. Lucy and Sam looked for the shelter but didn't see anything other than a smooth dirt lot, with no visible structures and a sloped hole in the ground.

The line of people headed down a large ramp that looked like it went deep underground. Between the bus and the ramp, a man was greeting many of them. He was a short stocky man, wearing a dress shirt, and appeared to have some degree of authority.

Lucy held her brother back until everyone was ahead of them and then moved forward. They watched as their new friends, the Tanners, went through the line and spoke to the greeter. Some of the new arrivals were going around the man while others stood in line to talk to him.

The Wilsons waited. When it was their turn, he looked at them and glanced around, probably looking for adults. Then, with a puzzled expression, he said, "Welcome to Shelter 87. I'm Gary Bison. I'm the site leader."

Lucy was relieved; he seemed friendly enough. "Hello, Mr. Bison. I'm Lucy Wilson and this is my brother, Sam. Are you the person in charge here?"

"Yes, for now, I am. We'll be appointing a senate that'll make all decisions, but until that happens, I'm all there is," he said with a slight smile.

"Good. We've got a problem that we need to discuss."

Gary Bison groaned inwardly. He'd heard this line repeatedly and there was little he could do for most of them. One of the most recent was a woman who was upset because they'd refused to allow her to bring her cat, Buggles, on the flight from her hometown. She'd incorrectly assumed that Gary would arrange for someone to go and get him.

"Miss Wilson, there're lots of people with problems and lots of logistics I need to work on. Can this wait a while?"

With a calm, cold edge in her voice that left no question as to her determination, Lucy said, "No, Mr. Bison. This *can't* wait."

He looked at the teen, sensing this might be more than he was assuming. "Where are your parents?"

"That's what we need to discuss," Sam interjected.

"Okay. Is this going to take long?"

"Probably," Lucy answered.

"Come over here." He led them to several crates that were waiting to be moved into the shelter. They sat on them and he asked, "What's going on?"

Lucy noticed the change in his voice and felt that she had his attention. Taking a deep breath, she said, "Our parents are Marie and Alex Wilson. They're part of Project Anvil, so by default, Sam and I are too. Correct?"

"Yes. That's how it works," the director of Shelter 87 answered.

"Well, two hours before the Anvil text went out, my parents pulled out of Miami on a cruise ship that won't stop anywhere until tomorrow morning. And that will be in St. Martin."

Lucy paused and watched Gary Bison's face drain of color before continuing. "They called us and told us what to do, and here we are. Now, we need to get them here. They dock tomorrow morning and have already purchased tickets on a plane returning to the US. Their plane is scheduled to arrive in Chicago at 7:00 PM tomorrow."

Gary didn't know what to say. These kids were here alone, and he wasn't sure what to do. "Do you mind if I call you Lucy?"

"Of course not."

"Lucy, all shelters have to be locked down and secured by 6:00 PM tomorrow. I don't know what we can do."

"Well, I've had over twelve hours to think about this," she said. "The best option is to have the Navy or Coast Guard pull them immediately off that ship. Today. If that doesn't work, have a military aircraft waiting there to pick them up in the morning and bring them here. The other option is to get an exception and keep the door open, or whatever it is, so they can arrive at 10:00 or 11:00 PM."

"I'm not sure if I can get anyone to take action. We're currently moving close to two hundred thousand people into shelters around the country. I'm not sure I can get anyone to focus on two that aren't where they're expected to be."

After thinking a minute, Lucy said, "Is there a communication center here? Let's see what we can do. I'll help in any way I can."

"Okay, let's go." The director stood and walked toward the entrance.

The Wilsons, with their backpacks over their shoulders, followed.

They boarded an electric cart, similar in size to a golf cart, and Gary Bison took them underground.

Chapter Twelve

THEY DESCENDED DEEP BELOW THE SURFACE AND SOON encountered several sets of massive steel doors. The open doors were over a foot thick. If closed, they would stop even the most determined from continuing down the tunnel.

The deeper they got, the colder it became. Lucy now understood why several sweatshirts were on the recommended packing list. The floors were concrete, and the walls and ceilings stone. There were painted lines on the floor and, occasionally, they saw a marker indicating how far down they'd passed. The downward slope of the vast tunnel eventually leveled off.

Rows of fluorescent lights hung from the ceiling and provided adequate illumination. Lucy was surprised that the walls of the tunnel were dry. She'd been in caverns before, and they'd all dripped with water. Along the ceiling were pipes of several different colors.

After ten minutes, they caught up with the others from their bus who were still walking. They passed the line of people and stopped at a table where the processing of new arrivals was occurring.

"Maggie, got a second?" Gary asked one of the people working at the registration station.

"Sure, boss, wassup?" asked a tall African American woman with a warm smile.

"Please get the Wilsons here processed, and then I need them in Operations as soon as possible."

"Sure thing. I'll get them taken care of now."

"Thanks Maggie." Looking at Lucy, he said, "I'll go and get started on a few calls. I'll see what I can get moving."

The Wilsons got off the cart and walked to the table as the golf cart disappeared down another passageway.

"Ok, guys, let me see your lanyards," Maggie instructed.

They handed over all four. Maggie entered the numbers into the computer. "Okay, the Wilson family. I've all your information here. Where are your parents?"

"That's what we're working on with Director Bison. We don't know yet," Lucy explained.

With a confused look, she said, "Well, when they get here, they'll be all set. You're assigned to Residential Area 6, or just Res6. Room 42. I wrote that in this folder. The yellow card on your lanyard will now open the door to your room. There's lots of information in here that you'll need about dining rooms, education, recreation, and work programs. There is also information about the basic rules and how the legal system works here. In the back, there are maps, which are also available on the computer terminals throughout the facility. "

She handed Lucy a thick folder and continued her presentation. "For the next two days, there will be a video playing every hour on the hour in Theaters B and E. It talks about all the features of Shelter 87 and how things will operate. You'll want to make sure to see it. Sometime in the next day or so, there will be a major announcement about the nature of the emergency and all the details. Make sure to explain this all to your parents when they arrive. Make sense?"

"I think so," Lucy replied and Sam nodded his head.

The Anvil

"Okay, follow me. I'll take you to Operations."

They entered the main passage and were immediately aware that the lighting was different. They could feel some warmth from the overhead lights, and there was a strange yellowish color to the radiated light.

"What's with the lights?" Sam asked.

Maggie smiled. "That's everyone's first reaction. The lights are supposed to mimic actual sunlight. Your body needs sunlight for Vitamin D production and overall health. Your room will have normal lighting, but all the corridors and some common areas have simulated sunshine."

"Sounds like they expect us to in this shelter for a long time," Sam mused aloud.

"That's what most of us are thinking," Maggie replied.

"Is it always so cold down here?" Lucy asked.

"You have heating controls in your room, but all the common areas are like this now. When they seal the shelter, they'll be bringing the reactor online. I've heard that the water used to cool the reactor will be circulated through all the red pipes and bring all the common spaces to a consistent 72 degrees." As she said this, she pointed to the ceiling and the several lengths of colored piping that ran the length of the passageway, two of which were red. "Until then, wear a couple of sweatshirts."

As they walked, Lucy was aware that this place could prove to be an underground maze. Fortunately, there were many signs and almost all the corridors had colored lines on the floor. These would help keep them from getting lost. The markings indicated that all the residential areas were the blue sections and Operations were green. She decided that they'd do some exploring as soon as possible. She wanted to familiarize herself with what would be "home" for a while.

Maggie swiped the Yellow tag hanging on her lanyard against the wall-mounted sensor and a door marked Operations opened.

As they entered, the Wilsons were surprised at how large the space was. Signs hanging from the ceiling showed all the departments in the Operations area. Signs included: Communications, Engineering, Security, and Administration. There were others, but these ones were close enough to read from the doorway. Thirty-some people were at work in this area.

They headed for Communications and saw Gary Bison. He was wearing a headset and was on a video conference. Lucy saw several people on the screen and the one speaking looked familiar. She wasn't sure who he was, but he was in a uniform and she knew she'd seen him on the TV news or online.

Maggie directed them to a round table, where they pulled out a couple of chairs and took seats. As she proceeded to sit, Lucy felt severe pain tear through her side; she fought back the tears and managed not to yell. She desperately wanted to finish this meeting and go to their medical center, but getting her parents here came first.

Gary Bison's call continued for several minutes. He then approached them, looking grim. "My superiors would be willing to send a Coast Guard helicopter to get your parents. Unfortunately, there are a couple of problems. First, the weather is bad in that area. Not dangerous for the cruise ship, but too rough to safely land a helicopter on her deck. Also, while they're close to 200 of these underground shelters, the Navy and others spent the last couple of years constructing a massive undersea shelter as well. It was supposed to be able to hold about three thousand people.

"They were in the process of moving people into it yesterday when there was a catastrophic incident. No one is sure what happened, but there was some kind of massive structural failure. It sounds like it's a complete loss. They built it off the Florida coast, and all available Coast Guard assets are involved in Search and Rescue. There's no one available to go into the Caribbean and get your parents off that ship. If an aircraft becomes available and the weather improves, they'll try."

Lucy looked at her brother when she felt Sam squeezing her arm; his expression was one of terror. Thinking for a few seconds, she finally asked, "What about getting permission to delay sealing up this facility?"

"They're discussing it, but I doubt it'll happen. It was a massive effort to secretly move two hundred thousand people to hidden locations in a forty-eight-hour window. Undoubtedly, many people noticed. We need to be buttoned up and hidden before anyone takes too much interest. We can't have people figuring out where everyone is and swarming the shelters when the you-know-what hits the fan," Gary explained solemnly.

"If the Coast Guard isn't able to get them off tonight, do you see any other way to get them here?

"Lucy, I'm sorry, but I don't see any other way."

Depressed, Lucy replied, "Please try to get them here. But if you can't, I have one more idea."

Chapter Thirteen

OVER AN HOUR HAD PASSED SINCE THE WILSONS ENTERED Operations. Now, they had help and a plan for their parents. As the meeting with Gary Bison came to an end, Lucy asked one final question. "Mr. Bison, is there a medical center here?"

Confused, Gary nodded. "Yes, we've got a state-of-the-art facility with excellent staff. Why?"

Standing, Lucy hesitantly raised her shirt enough to show him the bruising on her ribs. With wide eyes, he stood and said he would personally take her to Central Medical.

"Lucy," Sam said in a quiet but firm voice.

She glanced at her brother, indicating that she was listening. She already knew what he was going to say.

"You never showed me that. I didn't know it was that bad. It looks messed up."

She nodded. "I didn't want you to worry."

"You said that we were in this together. You should've told me it was that bad," he said angrily.

Knowing that he was right, she put a hand on his shoulder and felt his muscles immediately tighten up. "I know. I should've."

The Anvil

Gary led them the short distance to Central Medical, and the door opened as they approached. As they entered, the kids were surprised by the ultra-modern feel of the space. Everything up to this point had felt as if they were in tunnels with stone walls. Other than the lack of windows, this felt like any other hospital. It even smelled like one.

There was a registration desk with spots for up to four people at a time, and the waiting area could easily hold a dozen. Leading them to the desk, he pressed a button. Less than a minute later, a man in his mid-twenties appeared. He had a nametag that read Dan.

He smiled. "Are you here to be seen?"

"This is Lucy; she needs to be checked out," Gary said.

"Alright, we'll get you taken care of. You're only the second patient that we've had."

"You guys should be all set. I'll check on you later," the director said and turned to leave.

"So, Lucy, what is going on today?" Dan asked.

"I was in a car accident on my way here. I think I broke some ribs," she explained.

"Are you having any problems breathing?"

"No, other than it hurts when I inhale."

"Okay. Since you're the only patient here at the moment, I'll take you right back. I have you in the system, but we need more information." He handed her an electronic tablet. "Just fill this out and return it to me before you leave."

"My parents aren't here, and I don't have my insurance information. Is that a problem?"

"No. None of those things are a concern here."

He led them to the treatment area and, as they walked, Lucy saw large signs on the wall giving directions to different areas: Patient Rooms 1-50, Surgery, ICU, Imaging, and Maternity. There were others that the teen didn't catch as they walked past. Lucy was thinking about this as she walked. This medical center seemed much more elaborate than she'd have expected.

An hour later, she left the medical center feeling like a celebrity. A dozen members of the medical staff had visited with her, not that it had been necessary, but she was only their second patient and they'd been bored; the previous patient had sprained her ankle stepping off a bus.

The medical team took X-rays and confirmed that Lucy had three cracked ribs, which would prove very painful until they healed. Fortunately, there was no additional damage. They gave her tips on how to support them when moving and, best of all, pain medication to use for the next week.

As they exited the medical center, Sam asked his sister where they were going.

"Let's go check out our room and then get something to eat. Okay with you?"

"Sure, I guess."

Consulting the map on the wall, they saw that the residential areas were divided between a couple of levels. There were also massive areas on the map marked as storage and others that said off-limits. Eight sections were listed as Training / Education. They saw the medical center they'd left and three cafeterias. Five different theaters and two gymnasiums were well marked. There was even a swimming pool and a large area labeled Hydroponics.

As the Wilsons headed to their next destination, Lucy thought about the map. The swimming pool bothered her. She was glad that it was there, but why have it? That reminded her of the size and specialties she saw in the medical center. They wouldn't add it to a shelter that was only needed for a few months. Something much longer was envisioned. She started to wonder if she'd grow old down here, which took her mind back to Marcus.

The Anvil

As they walked, they approached another descending ramp. An electric vehicle headed down the ramp with a long train of luggage carts connected to it. They headed down and noticed signs that indicated this was the route to the residential areas.

Passing the luggage carts, they saw lots of yellow tags on the bags and one that was blue. Sam pointed it out to his sister. "Someone in the blue shelter isn't going to be happy," he chuckled.

The Wilsons giggled at some unknown person's misfortune.

As massive as this complex was, it seemed to be laid out logically and was easy to navigate. The wall signs led them directly to Res6, and from there, finding their living space was simply a process of following the numbers. Many halls branched off the main corridor, but the signs clearly said which rooms were down each. They saw a branch leading to Rooms 40-48. After walking forty yards, they saw a door with the number 42.

Lucy indicated the door to Sam, who already had the yellow card at the end of his lanyard in his hand and pressed it to the sensor. The door clicked open.

When they stepped in, they saw that the main area was about the size of a standard hotel room. There were two small tan sofas and two matching recliners, a wooden desk with a computer terminal, and mounted on the wall was a midsize TV. On another wall was a digital clock.

They continued exploring and found four doors off this room. One led to a bathroom, the others led to bedrooms. The first bedroom had a queen-sized bed, two dressers, and a small closet. The bed was unmade, and bedding was neatly stacked at its foot. The other two bedrooms were smaller, and each had a single twin-sized bed and a dresser, as well as a small table and alarm clock.

The walls were modular and could be moved as needed to

change the sizes of the rooms. The whole living space had gray industrial-grade carpeting, which wasn't much softer than the concrete in the outer halls. Their quarters reminded Lucy of a hotel suite; she suspected the shelter layouts and furnishings were identical in every room.

After looking in both smaller bedrooms, Sam announced, "I want this one."

Lucy had checked both and found them equally unimpressive. "Whichever one you want is fine with me."

She moved to the living room and sat in a recliner. It was comfortable but, again, unimpressive. She looked at the desk with the computer. While she was in Operations, she'd learned that the computers all needed an access code and, after sealing the shelter, everyone would get access. They'd provided her the code early so she'd be able to communicate with her parents and get their plan in motion, but to get this special privilege, she had had to agree to keep this early access a secret.

She logged in and checked what she had available on the system. As she poked around, she found a setting for environmental controls. "Sam, I just found out how to turn up the heat."

"Good, make it warmer. I was afraid I'd freeze to death down here."

Smiling at the sarcasm, she adjusted the temperature in each of the four rooms to a comfortable seventy-two degrees. That was a good start, she decided, and continued to check out the computer and found lots of familiar programs and several for communications. It looked like she could video conference to other rooms in this shelter and even to other shelters if she knew someone there.

"Lucy, I'm hungry. Can we get something to eat?" Sam asked.

"Sure. Take a look at the map and lead us to a cafeteria."

Sam liked it when she trusted him with more responsibility. Lucy was always trying to stretch him a little, and he appreciated it.

They exited the living area and walked back the way they'd come, departing the residential area. There were signs on the walls that led to "Café B", the closest of three cafeterias available in the complex.

It was a spacious area with hundreds of seats and a standard cafeteria line. The food smelled good and the Wilsons got in line behind a family of six. Lucy got a chicken breast and rice, and Sam went with pizza. They had no trouble finding seats because the dining area was only twenty percent full. They ate quietly, both consumed with thoughts.

"Can we sit with you?"

Lucy looked up, startled. Lauren and Ray Tanner stood there, holding trays.

Before she could answer, Sam said, "Sure."

"We haven't seen you guys since we got off the bus," Lauren said. "Have you been to your room yet? What did you think?"

"Kinda boring. Like a hotel," Sam replied.

Nodding, Ray said, "That's what my dad said."

"Did you guys come to eat alone, or are your parents with you?" Lucy asked.

"Our luggage just arrived, and they wanted to stay and get things put away. Also, our parents told us about the situation with your mom and dad. They want you to know that if you need anything to contact them," Lauren smiled.

"Thanks. What do you guys think of this place?"

"It seems big, lots of things to do, maybe," Lauren responded. "I still can't imagine staying down here for a long time."

They ate in silence for a few minutes, and then Lucy suggested, "When we get done, how about we go exploring? See what all there is here?"

The other three agreed, and they ate a little faster, eager to see what secrets their new home held.

Chapter Fourteen

EARLY IN THE MORNING, WHEN IT WAS STILL DARK OUT, stored-up text messages started arriving on the phones of Alex and Marie Wilson. The texts didn't awaken them because they'd barely slept at all and were wide awake. Their luggage was packed, and they were anxious to get off the floating paradise and back to the US.

Their phones had been silent for over twenty-four hours, ever since the ship had moved out of range of the last tower on US soil. But when St. Maarten had become visible on the horizon, service had returned, and the messages from their kids started to arrive.

They read through the list of messages several times, wishing there was a way to contact them. Lucy had explained in one of the last messages that their shelter was in Michigan and that cell phones were useless underground. She said that she'd make contact once they heard that the flight had landed in Miami. Until then, she was working on a new plan.

When they'd disembarked the ship, they'd looked for, but had not seen any sign of Debbie Maxfield, the woman who was also cut off from her children.

Now, several hours later, they sat in the uncomfortable

seats on a half-full Boeing 737 airliner as it approached Miami International Airport. They'd just completed filling out their documents for US Customs and made sure their passports were accessible.

Looking at his wife, Alex could see she was anxious to speak to the kids. "I know you won't relax until you speak to them. But they're safe in the shelter, and that's the most important thing."

"I know, but I just want to be with them."

As they talked, the wheels touched down and the plane started slowing. They taxied for several minutes and came to a stop at the jetway. Exiting the plane, the couple followed the signs that led to the lines for US Customs; they hoped that they would get this completed quickly. Before leaving the plane, the aircrew had announced that phones weren't allowed in the customs area and customs agents would confiscate any phones that were used in the restricted zone.

When they got to the line, there were only a handful of people in front, and they quickly made it to the window, answered a few questions, handed over their forms, and were on their way. Just a few yards away was the baggage carousel. Since they were coming into the US from another country, they had to collect their luggage and then check it back in for their domestic destination.

As they waited, a vibration signaled a text message. Given they were still in the customs area and couldn't use their phones, Marie snuck a quick look. It came from a number that wasn't familiar: "Don't recheck your luggage on the Chicago flight. Call this number when you can. Lucy."

After waiting for what seemed an eternity, their bags appeared on the carousel. They gathered them and departed the area. Instead of re-checking the luggage, they continued until they found a bank of unoccupied seats. Taking out her phone, Marie dialed the number that had been sent with the text.

The Anvil

After a single ring, a male voice answered, "Eighty-Seven."

Marie was confused by the greeting. Drawing a deep breath, she said, "I'm calling for Lucy Wilson."

"Stand by."

Almost immediately, she could hear the line ring again, then Lucy answered. "Mom?"

Hearing her daughter's voice brought tears to Marie's eyes. "Are you okay?"

"We're fine. All checked in with room assignments."

"Great, tell us where you are. We can still make the Chicago flight and be wherever you are by midnight."

"Mom, can Dad hear me?"

"Yes, he's sitting close."

"All the shelters will be sealed by 6:00 PM today. There are no exceptions. I tried, but it won't happen. However, I've worked something else out."

"What do you mean? How are we getting to you?" Marie asked anxiously.

"Mom, pay attention. You can't get to us. Over the last day, the shelter leader here and I've tried everything from a Coast Guard intercept of the cruise ship to an Air Force fighter jet in Miami to bring you here. We couldn't get any of that to work out.

"Now listen. There's a driver in the Ground Transportation area. She's waiting for you. She'll be transporting you to a shelter that's a couple of hours away from where you are now. They're expecting you. In a couple of days, there will be video communication available between the shelters. We'll be able to stay in touch."

"No! We need to be together. As a family," Marie cried.

"Sam and I want that too, but that isn't going to happen."

Alex took the phone from his wife. "Lucy, can we call you back in a couple of minutes? We need to discuss this."

"Yup, we'll be here."

75

Alex disconnected and took his wife in his arms. The news crushed his spirit; to be permanently separated from the kids was something he couldn't handle. The family was his life and, if he felt this way, he knew Marie was just as devastated.

After a few minutes, Marie spoke. "I don't want to go to a shelter. Not without the kids."

Alex thought before answering. "If we don't, we might well die."

"I don't care. I don't want to go without them."

Alex wanted to disagree with her, but he felt the same way.

After some additional conversation, they redialed the phone and waited to be transferred to Lucy.

"I'm here," she said in greeting.

"Lucy, we aren't doing this. Without you guys, we aren't going to a shelter. We're glad you're safe, but we're heading home and will be there about midnight. Maybe whatever this is won't be as bad as they think."

"Okay, Dad. If that's what you think is best. Sam and I will be leaving here in a few minutes. We'll probably get home before you," Lucy said.

"What? *No!* You can't leave the shelter. We need for you to be safe." Marie felt her heart racing as she envisioned the kids leaving the safety of the shelter.

Nodding his agreement, Alex said, "That's right. You need to stay there."

There was a brief pause. Finally, Lucy spoke, her voice calm and firm; there was an edge to it they'd never experienced before. "I'm sorry to say this, but this isn't your choice. Either you get to baggage claim and head to the shelter, or Sam and I are leaving here and heading home."

Alex and Marie were stunned into silence. Lucy had never spoken to them like this before.

While they recovered, Sam added, "Lucy's right. We've already discussed this and agree. You go to the shelter ... or we'll meet you at home."

The Anvil

Lucy was thankful for Sam's interjection; some of the weight came off her. It wasn't only her being defiant; the tears in his eyes informed her he was in this with her.

"Guys, we're your parents," Alex stated. "We'll make the decisions—"

"No. I'm sorry, but we're past that," Lucy interrupted abruptly. "I'm telling you the way it'll be. In ten minutes, I'll call the driver. If you aren't in her van, Sam and I will be headed home. The driver is a soldier, and she'll be taking you to a store to pick up all the things you need for the shelter. I'll send you the packing list by text when we hang up.

"You don't have a lot of time, so you *need* to get going. The driver will let us know when you finished shopping, and we'll call you back. We love you, and I'm sorry about how this is going down." Lucy disconnected.

Alex and Marie sat in stunned silence, staring at the phone that Alex held.

Finally, Marie broke the silence. "I don't think she's bluffing."

"She isn't. I guess we all die together, or we all live but apart."

As they were talking, another text came in. It contained a detailed list of everything the Wilson parents would need for their shelter in Florida.

Reluctantly, the weary couple stood and headed for Ground Transportation. As they walked, Alex said with a shrug, "This may turn out to be nothing. We may all be home in a few weeks."

Marie shook her head. "No. It's much more than that."

"What do you mean?"

"Think about it. Imagine you were organizing dozens of shelters, with thousands of people in them. You had to coordinate how everyone would get to the shelters and, of course, stock those shelters with needed supplies and equipment. How long do you think it would take?"

"A couple of years, I guess. If you had enough people working on it."

"Exactly, and when were we recruited into Anvil?"

"Just over two years ago."

"Exactly. Anvil was never a contingency plan. They knew something was coming, and they've known for a while."

Alex loved how his wife's mind worked. She had a knack for putting pieces of a puzzle together and making sense of random facts. What she said made sense.

As they entered the ground transportation area, multiple chauffeurs held up electronic screens with people's names on them. There was also a single woman in a military uniform. She was a short brunette in her mid-twenties with a focused expression. She had her phone out and would glance from the screen to the crowd and back again.

The Wilsons approached her and she locked her eyes on them, then visibly relaxed a little. She put her phone away after a final glance at the picture of her targets on the screen. "Mr. and Mrs. Wilson?"

"That's us."

"Good, I'm Corporal Evans. I'll be transporting you. I'll take your bags for you." She reached out and grabbed the luggage.

"Thank you, Corporal. Where exactly are you taking us?"

The corporal chuckled. "The same place I've been taking everyone for the last three days. Out into the middle of nowhere. Day and night, I've been shuttling people out there, by some abandoned phosphorous mines. I've seen other vans and even charter buses." She opened the back of her all-white unlettered van and loaded the luggage into the back.

As they got in, she handed them each a lanyard with a plastic card hanging from it. It was silver and had a green stripe running diagonally across it. There was a large number 16 printed on the card and smaller numbers at the bottom. "Keep these with you at all times."

The Anvil

As the vehicle got in motion, she asked casually, "What is it about you guys that's different?"

Alex and Marie looked at each other, curious.

"What do you mean? Why do we seem different?" Marie asked.

"Well, several things. You're the first people I've picked up at an airport. I'm supposed to take you shopping first. Also, there was some extra urgency about making sure I got you quickly, and you're the only ones that don't have kids with you."

Chapter Fifteen

THE VAN PULLED OFF THE MAIN ROAD AND CONTINUED FOR over a mile. It was a rough dirt road and was descending into what looked like a giant hole. From the view out the window, it was clear that it had been dug out many years ago. When they reached the bottom, there was more than enough room for them and the two charter buses that were turning around and preparing to depart.

The senior Wilsons stepped out of the van and looked around. They each carried a large new duffel bag that they'd purchased after leaving the airport. Alex and Marie had filled them with the items from the list Lucy had provided. Their original luggage, which they brought off the ship, remained in Corporal Evans' van. She'd agreed to get rid of it for them.

They saw that there had been heavy industrial activity here at one time. Off in the distance were the rusted skeletons of some kind of machinery.

The people who arrived ahead of them entered what looked like a large cave opening into the hill.

The Wilsons took a minute to thank Evans for the ride and her assistance with the shopping. As they were talking, three people approached: a tall, slender Hispanic woman with shoulder-length hair and two teenage boys.

The woman asked, "Are you Marie and Alex Wilson?"

Alex nodded. "Yes, we are."

"Good. I'm Abby Kosta, and I'm the site leader here at 16. These guys will take your bags to your room. Please follow me."

As the van departed, Alex asked, "What *is* this place?"

"Way back, it was a very productive phosphate mine. It closed over twenty years ago and has sat abandoned since; now, it'll be our home."

"We're thankful you could make room for us," Marie said with a grateful smile.

"I got a call from Washington yesterday. They told me to find a place for you. We knew that there would be a few who were in Anvil that wouldn't show up. So, we all overbooked—just by two families in every shelter. Of the 300 families intended for Shelter 16, I had five that didn't show up. As such, I had room available. I spoke to your kids briefly. They're in 87 in Michigan. It is a little larger than this facility and is a good place for them to be."

As they walked into the mouth of the large cave, they saw that it had unfinished rock walls, and the tunnel gradually sloped downward. After 50 yards, there was a massive blast door that looked to be about a foot thick. It was wide open, and they passed through. From there, the walls and floors were made of smooth, finished concrete.

"You're the last to arrive," Abby informed them. "That big door will close soon and remain shut until the emergency is past. If anyone chooses to leave, there's a smaller exit to use."

"Do you expect people to want to leave before it is safe?" Marie asked.

"The psychologists predict that if this is a long-term event, five to ten percent will leave in the first couple of months."

"Months? Do you know how long we'll be down here?" Alex asked, baffled.

"No, I don't. There'll be an announcement tomorrow about that."

"What are we supposed to do until then?" Marie asked worriedly.

"I'm taking you to registration. They'll get you assigned to your quarters. Everyone here will have some kind of job to do. Am I correct that you're an anesthesiologist?" Abby asked Alex.

"Yes, that's correct."

"In the next 24 hours, please report to Central Medical and coordinate your work schedule with them. Also, there's a listing on the computer in your quarters of available positions. I suggest that you, Marie, look for something that might interest you. There's also an introductory video for everyone to watch. There's more information about that in the registration handout that you'll be getting."

As Marie walked, she wondered how she could best use her accounting background in an underground shelter.

A young man in his early twenties approached. Abby glanced at him and smiled. "David, what are you doing out this way?"

"I heard our other VIPs were arriving and wanted to see who they were," the new arrival answered with a broad smile.

"That's funny," Abby chuckled. She looked back at the Wilsons. "Everything was going smoothly—too smoothly with getting everyone moved in here. Then two parties made me shuffle things up. In both cases, I got a call from Washington, insisting that I move things around because there was an emergency need to house another couple. Four days ago, it was David here and his mother and, today, it was you."

He smiled and held out his hand. "I'm David Cowan, but everyone calls me DJ."

Chapter Sixteen

Following the Tanner family, Sam and Lucy entered the theater. The six of them had spent much of the last day together exploring the shelter. They'd learned their way around and even had a few surprises.

They encountered a large hall with glass windows on one side, where they could see into a massive chamber about the size of four football fields. Inside were thousands of different plants. They recognized tomatoes, beans, and melons, but there were dozens of other varieties that they couldn't identify. The illuminated chamber had strange lights that made the room look sunlit.

Further down the hall was a set of double doors that read "Hydroponics", which led inside the vast space. Each of them took a turn, trying to open the doors with their card. None worked.

That evening, Sam and Ray explored more of their new home and found a door propped open, leading to a darkened hall. Neither boy noticed the "Authorized Personnel Only" sign and ventured down it. They found several locked doors that their key cards wouldn't open.

At the end of the hall was another closed door with a sign.

The single word read "Crematorium." Shocked, the boys went running back to find their older sisters.

This morning, they met at 8:00 AM for breakfast before heading to Theater A.

At 9:00 AM, a major announcement about the scope of the disaster was scheduled. Everyone would hear it on the PA systems, but all the theaters would be live-streaming the information for those wanting to see the speakers.

The previous evening, Lucy spoke to her parents after they'd settled into their new home in Shelter 16. She learned that they were getting the information at the same time; as such, they assumed that this had to be going to all the shelters simultaneously.

Sam made sure to point out to his parents that he shared a four-person living area with only his sister. His parents admitted that their living space was considerably smaller. They hoped that no one would notice all the extra room they had since their parents had ended up in a different shelter.

They'd arrived at the theater early, wanting to make sure that they could sit together, and everyone was glad they did. There were three hundred seats in the theater and almost all were filled, and there were still twenty minutes before the broadcast. While there was some small talk, palpable nervous energy kept most people quiet. Lucy, too, was quiet, nervously playing with her bracelet and thinking about Marcus stuck on the outside.

Eventually, the large display at the front of the room lit up. The viewers could see four men standing together at a podium. Three of the men were in suits and one in a military uniform. The lectern bore the familiar seal of the President of the United States.

President Daniel Anson spoke first. "Good morning, ladies and gentlemen. This message is going out strictly to the Anvil shelter inhabitants. With me today is General Draper, the Chairman of the Joint Chiefs, Thomas Williams from NASA, and Dennis Roberts from the Department of Homeland Security.

"First, I need to clarify something. We have heard from some of the shelter leaders regarding concerns about Anvil being a military operation. That isn't the case. Anvil needed the stealth and manpower that the Department of Defense could provide to get you to the shelters quickly and efficiently. But that phase of the operation is over.

"Your shelters aren't managed by military personal but by a governing council. A team of security officers working with the local council will maintain law and order within the shelters, not military personal.

"Now that we have that clarified, this is the situation. As all of you probably know, the Menesa Comet will make a close pass on Earth tomorrow morning. What you don't know is that while most comets are composed primarily of ice and rock, this comet is extremely radioactive. We've known about its deadly properties for some time, and our best scientists have been unable to understand why this would be. It'll be passing close enough that the radioactive debris from the tail will be poisoning the Earth's atmosphere. We developed Project Anvil to provide shelter from the radiation that will wipe out almost all life on Earth. Dennis Roberts, the Anvil project director, will now discuss this a little more."

As the situation became clearer, Lucy grew aware that her little brother had taken her hand and was squeezing it harder and harder.

"Thank you, Mr. President. I have been managing Project Anvil for the last two years. There are 183 shelters scattered around the United States. They average 1200 people per site. That's a total of 219,000 citizens protected ... assuming everyone made it to their designated shelter, which we know didn't happen.

"Now, this is the hard part. We expect that the radiation will be at dangerous levels for about twenty years. That means each shelter has provisions for everyone to remain safe and underground for an extensive amount of time."

The whole theater came alive with people talking, some yelling, and many crying. The thought of having to remain underground for so long was staggering. Expecting this reaction, Dennis Roberts paused, giving his audience time to digest the dire information.

Sam glanced at his sister and saw she was transfixed by the screen, and tears were in her eyes; her whole body was trembling.

"Please listen. I know this is a lot to take in, but there's more you should know. The shelters are now all sealed, and no one else can enter. In a week, anyone wanting to leave will be allowed to. If someone leaves, however, they can't re-enter. We know this is horrifying news, but it isn't just about your survival, but that of the entire human race.

"24-hour news coverage will be available to anyone wanting to see what's happening to the outside world. There are counselors available in every shelter, and you're encouraged to speak to one if you feel it'll help.

"Additional information about your facility will be accessible on the computers in your quarters. We've now enabled shelter-to-shelter communication. Additionally, tomorrow evening we'll be turning on cellular repeaters in each shelter. This will allow you contact with the outside world. However, we will continue to block GPS signals, so those on the outside won't be able to find the shelters. Around that time, there will be a press conference announcing the crisis to the general public. Now, General Draper has an announcement."

There was a pause while General Draper replaced Denis Roberts at the podium.

"Ladies and gentlemen, while Mr. Roberts was in charge of Project Anvil, I was dealing with another key component of the plan to rebuild the human race. We constructed a massive facility similar to your shelter, but much larger. We nicknamed it the Ark. A new technology is available, by which we can put people into what is a cross between suspended animation and a drug-induced coma. There are 10,000 people with key skills in medicine, engineering, manufacturing, agriculture, and many more subjects sleeping now. When radiation levels are safe, they'll awaken with all the equipment, tools, and technology needed to rebuild. They'll assist you and your offspring when you come out of the shelters to rebuild the human race."

The room was much quieter as the general finished his speech. Everyone was thinking about the people that would be sleeping for twenty years.

Chapter Seventeen

STEPPING OUT OF THE SHOWER, LUCY'S BOYFRIEND, MARCUS Ditmore, grabbed his towel. He was glad to have the sweat from another baseball practice washed off, but he was exhausted. He awoke an hour and a half early to be at the school today. People from all over Armstrong had gathered on the football field to try to catch a glimpse of the Menesa Comet as it streaked past Earth in what was being called "a once-in-a-lifetime event". Many were calling the pass a near miss. Online, he'd seen more and more people referring to all the excitement as Comet Craze.

Fortunately, it was still mostly dark at 6:12 AM when it streaked overhead. Unfortunately, it was a cloudy morning so, while they could see it for the nine seconds it was visible, it was nothing more than a bright blur. It had hardly been worth the effort of getting up so early and being at school much longer than usual. Now, after a full day at school and baseball practice, he was tired. Maybe a little more tired than he would've expected.

Despite all that, his mind was troubled by something more: the strange disappearance of his girlfriend, Lucy Wilson. Lucy had missed several track practices, as well as a few days from school. Also, she was one of the few students who wasn't on the football field at six o'clock this morning.

Marcus had tried to call her several times over the last couple of days, but it kept dropping into voicemail, and he was becoming concerned. He'd even stopped by her house, but there was no one there. The last he'd heard from her was a strange text that seemed to have a hidden meaning.

Marcus and his mother were the only ones living in their house, and his mom almost always had dinner ready in the evening. However, tonight she had texted that she'd be late getting home from the hospital, where she worked in the emergency department. It was busy, with an unusually large number of people coming in with general illnesses, most of them elderly. Because of that, the teen had put a frozen pot pie in the oven before taking his shower. He had the TV on, but had muted it when he took his shower.

He removed his dinner from the oven and, as he was setting it down to cool, his phone rang. He smiled and felt relief from his worries upon recognizing the ringtone and hurried to answer the call from his missing girlfriend. As he reached for the phone, he was aware that the TV screen displayed the words "Breaking News".

"Lucy? Where have you been? Are you alright?"

"Yeah, Marcus. I'm fine." She was still unsure how to tell him the news.

Something in her voice was off. Something was wrong. "Well, where have you been? Your track coach is ticked. I've called you a bunch of times."

"I'm not completely sure where I am, but I'm in Michigan somewhere. I can't go into details, but my whole family and many others were whisked up and rushed to government underground shelters. They just enabled cell signals to get out. I haven't been able to call until now."

"Is this a joke?"

"No, I'm completely serious."

"Why are you in an underground shelter? What's going on?" His confusion increased.

"Things are bad, really bad. It looks like there will be lots of radiation covering most of the earth. It came from the comet. I don't know who picked my family, but there are underground shelters, and we're locked away until it is safe to go back out. I wish you were here. I really need you …" She struggled to finish the statement as her crying began.

"What? That can't be right. Where are you? I'll come to you."

"You can't. The shelters are locked down, and no one gets in or out. They won't even tell us exactly where we are."

He paused to digest what she'd revealed. "How long will you be there? I want to see you."

"They're saying it could be 20 years."

"No way! Locked underground for twenty years!" With tears running down his face, and fear in his voice, Marcus asked, "What about the rest of us? What do we do?"

It was several seconds before Lucy answered. She wasn't sure what to tell him. "I don't know. I don't even know where I am. I don't know what you should do. I'm so sorry. I wish you were here."

They listened to each other crying.

Marcus was silent as he considered the situation. Then, he asked somberly, "I'm scared. Do you have any idea how long we have out here? How long to live?"

"I don't think anyone is really sure. A week? Maybe more. That's just what I've been hearing. It could be wrong."

They talked for a few more minutes. Lucy couldn't answer any of the other questions Marcus came up with. Eventually, they ended the call, both still in tears.

He poked a fork at the still hot pot pie, then sat it down, his appetite gone. Picking up his phone, he texted his mother: "Your sick patients are all suffering from radiation sickness.

There's global radiation poisoning from the comet. We're all screwed. Call me when you can."

He glanced back at the TV and saw the President was speaking.

Several minutes later, Marcus's mother read the text. This was the first she or any of her colleagues had thought about radiation poisoning as the cause of all the illnesses.

It would only be twenty more minutes before the hospital got official word to expect cases of radiation-related illnesses.

Chapter Eighteen

MARCUS WOKE TO THE SOUND OF THE PHONE ALARM. GETTING to his feet proved a mistake, and he dropped back on the bed, waiting for the nausea to pass. He was aware of it before going to bed, but it was worse this morning. When feeling confident enough that he wouldn't vomit, he stood and walked to the kitchen. Grabbing a granola bar from the cabinet, Marcus ate it slowly, hoping it would help settle his stomach.

After his time on the phone with Lucy the night before, he'd spent time on his computer, researching radiation poisoning. If this was coming, he wanted to know what to expect. Evidently, the feelings of weakness and nausea were some of the expected early signs. So far, the website had been correct.

The teen made his way to the kitchen and found his phone on the counter. He looked at the screen and saw several messages. The most recent was from his mother. His mom would be staying at the hospital because of the increasing flood of radiation-related illnesses but wanted to make sure her son was okay. Marcus thought about her question and figured that he was as okay as possible given the situation.

The following text was an automated message sent from his school. It informed him that school would be closed today.

The Anvil

"Probably forever," the teen muttered. Marcus wasn't concerned about the cancelation of school. He had no intention of going anyway.

The last message was from Lucy, wanting to know how he was feeling.

Marcus decided to reply later; he was still trying to understand how he felt about Lucy right now. Marcus loved her deeply, but part of him was angry that she and her family made it to safety while he and his mother were left to die. He knew it wasn't Lucy's fault but, nevertheless, it made him mad. At the same time, Lucy had contacted him as soon as she could, wanting to ensure he knew what was happening and to give him advice. Unfortunately, that advice had all the value of a cup of water being thrown on a raging forest fire.

Still, Marcus planned to follow the suggestions. What else could he do? He took time to glance through social media feeds. All over the country, people who'd gone to the shelters were back online at once. They were posting about those shelters and their experiences and these conversations were attracting lots of followers. Those outside the shelters wanted to know how to get to one. Many of the posts were also very angry.

He sat on the couch, turned on a TV news station, and spent fifteen minutes watching story after story talking about the illnesses flooding hospitals worldwide. There were supposed experts, making predictions about how bad the situation would become. As he watched, the tears returned, and he didn't fight them.

The last story he watched was about a mob of angry people who were claiming that the government had known about the imminent destruction of life on earth and had kept it a secret. Smiling wryly, Marcus turned off the TV, thinking about secret underground shelters and knowing that all the ranting was the truth.

He dressed quickly and went to the kitchen drawer where

his mother kept an extra credit card. It was for him to use in case of an emergency. He then headed for his car. Lucy had provided some suggestions last night, and he would take her advice.

Assuming that word about the crisis was still spreading, he needed to move quickly. Marcus went to the grocery store and was surprised to find it packed with shoppers, even though the store had just opened. He grabbed the last available shopping cart and started filling it with easy-to-prepare products that wouldn't require refrigeration. Once the cart was heaping full, he checked out and filled the trunk of the car. Returning to the store, he filled the cart a second time, unaware that most of it would never be eaten.

When heading to the parking lot, he could see the line to get inside was growing. He'd considered making a third trip into the store but felt fatigued, and the nausea was returning. He headed for the gas station and waited in line for over fifteen minutes before being able to top off the car.

At home, he stepped from the car and gazed around. Everything *looked* normal. There was nothing to indicate that the air around him was full of gamma radiation, slowly destroying all the cells in his body.

Taking his time, he carried the loot from his car to the basement. He set up a folding camp cot and lay back, thinking how being in the cellar might offer protection from the radiation.

He called his mother, but the call went to voicemail. "Hey, Mom. I went to the store and bought a bunch of food. I figured that the stores would eventually stop getting deliveries and would run out. There was already a long line when I left, so I think I was just in time. Call me when you can."

He disconnected and made another call to Lucy Wilson.

"Hey, babe. How are you doing?" Sorrow was evident in Lucy's tone when she answered.

"Alright, I guess. A bit nauseous and weak. I can feel that something isn't right. School was canceled today, and I don't think it'll be open tomorrow either."

"Did you go to the store like I suggested?"

"Yeah, I got a ton of stuff. There were long lines. I'm glad you said to go first thing. Do you guys hear the news reports?"

"We have several news stations on at all times. That's all anyone is watching."

"It sounds like it's getting bad quickly. What am I supposed to do?" He started crying again, which made him feel weak.

"I don't know. The people leading our program are saying that the radiation levels are even higher than predicted. I hear that most hospitals are already overwhelmed."

"I'm worried about my mom. She's been at work for over twenty-four hours. All I get is an occasional text from her. How am I supposed to get through this without her and you?"

"I'm sure she's swamped," Lucy answered simply, ignoring the question. She had no answer.

"I got set up in the basement, as you suggested. Do you really think it'll make a difference?"

"Some. You're getting less radiation because you're partly below ground, but I think it'll only help a little. It might give you a little more time. You would need to cover the basement with twenty feet of dirt, or with sheets of lead, to protect you fully. Then, you would need enough food."

"Well, that isn't much help! I can't get twenty years' worth of food, can I?"

Lucy flinched at his anger. "The more you protect yourself down there, when you can, the more time you'll have; it helps a little. You *can't* give up!"

A few minutes later, they disconnected, planning to talk again in the evening.

Several hours later, Marcus angrily folded up the cot and

threw it back on the shelf. He headed up the stairs and took a seat on the couch, and turned on the TV. He decided that hiding in the basement only to add a day or two to his life wasn't worth it. The couch was much more comfortable. If he were to survive, he needed a cave and twenty years of food, and that wasn't possible.

Chapter Nineteen

Two days later, Marcus took a drive into town. It was the first time he'd left the house since the trip to the grocery store.

Since that day, he'd spent most of his time watching the news and becoming more resolved to accept the hopelessness of his situation. There were many broken items in the house from his fits of anger, when he'd *needed* to throw something. But those outbursts were over now.

He'd spoken to Lucy a few times, but the calls had seemed unproductive and always reminded him that his girlfriend was tucked safely away while he was left at home, slowly dying from an invisible enemy.

The teen glanced down at his shirt and noticed a bloodstain, considered changing into something cleaner, but then decided that would be too much trouble. He wasn't sure if the blood was from one of his bloody nose episodes during the night or from his mother.

His mom had stumbled home a day ago, physically exhausted from working so long with almost no rest. That allowed the radiation poisoning to impact her harder. She'd worked practically non-stop for two-and-a-half days. Marcus had helped her to bed, and she'd been asleep almost the entire time since.

Early this morning, he'd heard a noise and found her trying to sit up. She was extremely weak and had thrown up blood. Marcus cleaned her up and decided to see what was going on in town while he could.

Marcus drove toward town, aware that there was almost no other traffic. Most of the downtown businesses were closed. Ahead, a truck and a car had collided in an intersection. They sat there, blocking part of the roadway. There was no one around, and Marcus had the impression that this wreck hadn't happened recently.

It was shortly after that when he saw the first body. He couldn't tell if it was male or female because the upper half was obscured by a parked car, but the pelvis and legs were visible on the sidewalk.

"No one is even removing the dead," he thought aloud, knowing this was a very bad sign.

Approaching the Community Center, he could see more activity. Several people were outside it and a few cars were coming and going. Feeling curious, and hoping to encounter someone he knew, he turned into the parking lot. It had only been a few days, but he was longing to talk to someone other than by phone.

He parked in the congested parking lot, exited, and headed over. While walking, he felt the nosebleed start again; not caring what anyone might say, he grabbed a couple of tissues from his pocket and shoved them in his nostrils, and kept walking.

Marcus entered the Community Center gymnasium through propped open doors and was shocked: there were dozens of cots and all were occupied with the afflicted. Many weren't moving and some had sheets covering them. The smell in the gym was horrible. When he'd read about the smell of death, he'd never understood what that actually meant in terms of intensity or foulness, but it permeated this large room. It reminded him of a cross between dirty feet and a dumpster on a hot summer day, but much worse.

He saw Mr. Sawyer, his English teacher. He was sitting on a chair along the wall. He ambled over and sat next to him.

"Hey, Mr. Sawyer."

"Marcus. How are you doing?"

"Same as everyone else, I guess. I just stopped in because I saw all the activity. What's going on?"

"The hospital is impossible to get to because there are so many people trying to be seen. A couple of the local doctors set this up. A place for people to go. They're doing everything they can, but that's very little, so I decided to help out. They have me making runs for food and supplies, but it's getting harder and harder to find anything useful. I don't know how much more I can do; every time I get back, I have to rest longer and longer before heading back out."

"My mom is home, sick in bed. She can barely walk. Should I bring her here?"

"I wouldn't. Let her be comfortable in her own bed. There isn't anything here that will make a real difference."

Looking around the room, Marcus regarded all the people on the cots. "Most of these people are fairly young. I would've thought this would hit the elderly worst."

"It did. There aren't any elderly left."

Marcus sat a couple of minutes longer, thinking about the last statement. He was tempted to offer to help out here for a while. Then he thought of his mother at the house. "Good luck, Mr. Sawyer. I need to get back to my mother."

The teen got up from the chair and headed back to his car. Halfway across the parking lot, he vomited and could taste the blood. He leaned against another car, waiting for a wave of dizziness to pass. Again, tears ran down his cheek and reminded him how hopeless the situation truly was.

Exhausted, he drove home to check on his mother.

Chapter Twenty

LUCY LEFT THE THEATER AND ENTERED THE HALL. TYPICALLY, the four theaters in Shelter 87 would show movies, old sporting games, and recorded TV programs. They would also function as classrooms, churches, or could be used for group meetings. Since sealing the shelters, all but one of the theaters were committed to covering the disaster and what was transpiring on the surface. The one exception was dedicated to children and had 24-hour cartoons.

Lucy had spent much of the last few days in the theaters, catching up on the news in what remained of the world. She needed a break from the constant focus on the death of the world she knew. It was all anyone was talking about. She, and many others, were having problems sleeping, their minds fixated on death and destruction.

She had already heard that there had been a handful of suicides within her shelter, and she suspected there would be more.

Every time she checked on the destruction's progression, a smaller and smaller view of what was happening was available as more news stations went off the air; now, a week after the comet had gone by, there were only a few still broadcasting.

Her thoughts, and those of everyone else in the shelter, kept going back to the last official government broadcast. They had said that global radiation levels were significantly higher than anticipated, and it might take much longer than expected for the world to be habitable.

Taking out her phone, she called Marcus; it had been two days since she'd last talked to her boyfriend, and he had sounded very weak then.

That morning after she last spoke to him, she awoke to find a text from him. It had come in several hours prior. "I am very sorry. I have been angry because we aren't together, and I am left out here. The truth is I love you very much and am so thankful that you will have the chance to survive this. Take good care of your brother, and please don't forget me."

Since that message, he hadn't responded to texts, and when she called, all she got was voicemail. Lucy knew what that meant, but she kept calling, just in case. After hearing Marcus' recorded voice again, Lucy slipped her phone back into her pocket, dropped to the floor, and wept as she played with the bracelet on her wrist. Eventually, she headed back to her quarters, planning to check for messages on the computer.

Lucy and Sam had enrolled in school, and she was hoping her schedule would soon be out. Something to occupy her time would be nice. Sam had already learned that he would be meeting with his class in two days for the first time.

She'd also applied for several jobs within the shelter. Everyone was required to help out. The teen hoped that by applying early, she'd have a better selection. She wanted something in either medical or administration; she didn't want to be cleaning or serving food.

As she approached their quarters, her cell phone sounded with a text. She saw that the message was from her mother. "Got time for a vid call?"

"Sure. Will be on in 1 minute," she texted in return. She

was thankful that her parents had never mentioned the force and defiance she had used to get them to go to their shelter.

Entering the room, Lucy went to the computer and logged in. She pulled up the video conferencing program and selected the shortcut she'd made for her parents. There was a brief pause before her parents were visible on the screen, crouched together in front of their computer's camera.

"Hi, Mom, Dad."

"Lucy, great to see you," her father said.

"How are you doing, sweety?" her mother asked.

"Marcus stopped answering his phone," She began sobbing, paused and drew a deep breath. "I'd been talking to him every day. Listening to him die. I think he was mad that I was safe and he couldn't come here. He hasn't answered the phone for the last few days." She started sobbing again.

"Honey, he loves you. He's just frustrated and frightened," her dad said soothingly.

"No, Dad. He's dead!" The crying returned.

Her parents gave her time to let the despair pass.

"Sorry. I've been doing a lot of that lately," Lucy said somberly. "I really don't know what to think. Everything I hear on the news channels doesn't seem real. Everyone here is kinda in a fog, except for those that are crying all the time."

On the screen, her mother nodded, "It's the same here. Do you have counselors there? We've got a few, and they're encouraging everyone to find time to talk to them."

"Yeah, we've got some. One of them is this tall basketball player-looking guy. Every time I notice him, he's crying. I've got no interest in talking to him about my feelings."

"I understand, but remember that they're there if you need them," her dad advised. "And you can always get on with us anytime you want."

Lucy gave a quick nod in response.

Marie asked, "Is Sam there? I wanted to see how he is."

"No, he's off with Ray and some other kids he met. They

were headed to the gym to play basketball. Oh, did you know that we've got a pool here? It isn't open yet but should be in a week or two. Do you have anything like that?"

"A pool? No, our shelter is smaller than yours. We only have about nine hundred people. They call us a Level 4 shelter. We've got a gym but no pool," Alex stated.

"Nine hundred? We've got fourteen hundred. We're a Level 3. They told us that Level 1 could house 2500 people, but there are only a few of them." Lucy took another deep breath. "You guys know that I always try to be honest, right?"

"Of course. You always have been," her father agreed.

"Well, there's something I've been keeping from you. Only because I didn't want you to worry, but it's really bothering me, and I need to tell you."

Her mother had a familiar look of concern. "What is it?"

Rolling her chair back from the computer's camera, Lucy stood. When she did, her parents could see that she was moving with significant discomfort. She raised her shirt and showed them the deep purple bruising.

"Lucy! What happened?" Alex asked, stunned.

"When Sam and I were heading to the mall, a van blew through a stop sign and slammed into my door. Sam wasn't hurt, but I ended up with three fractured ribs." She felt instant relief from her guilt as she released the secret.

"Lucy, why didn't you tell us? How bad is the pain?" Marie asked anxiously.

"You guys were on the ship, trying to figure out how to get back to the US. I didn't want you worrying about it. Sam helped me a lot. After we arrived here and got the plan in place to get you to your shelter, I went to the medical area, and they x-rayed it. They gave me pain medication, which helps, but they say it'll be several weeks before it stops hurting."

Her father appeared confused. "You traveled all the way to

the shelter *without* telling anyone? If it had been even a little worse, you could've died."

"We were trying to stay under the radar since we were traveling without you. I figured that if I told anyone, they'd send me to a hospital, and I wouldn't make it to a shelter. Then I was even more likely to die."

"Well ... I guess that makes sense. I bet the pain was terrible," her father said.

"It's been five days, and it's still terrible, but there isn't much I can do. I just need to give it time."

They spoke for several more minutes before disconnecting. Lucy promised to have Sam call them when he got back.

Heading to her bedroom, she grabbed a pillow and held it against her injured ribs to brace them, and slowly lay down on the bed. She didn't want to see any more news stories about the world dying, so she lay back thinking about everything else ... until she eventually fell asleep.

Chapter Twenty-One

10 YEARS LATER

ALEX AND MARIE WILSON SLEPT SOUNDLY IN THEIR QUARTERS. They'd lived for the last ten years in Shelter 16, under what had once been part of the state of Florida. The only thing slightly unusual tonight was the ten-year-old boy sleeping in the adjoining bedroom.

Kevin Torez was born shortly before he and his mother, Wendy, had arrived at the shelter. Working in the medical center, Alex saw that the young mother was all alone and he and Marie had sort of adopted them, helping and guiding them as best they could. Alex and Marie had become the unofficial godparents to the young boy and were quite attached to him.

Keven occasionally got to spend the night with his godparents when his mother was working a night shift.

Suddenly, a screeching alarm ripped them from their peaceful sleep. The Wilsons sat upright in bed, confused, something never heard in all the years they'd occupied the shelter. Above the loud, piercing alert, a mechanical voice blared, "Fire, Level 4, Section 12, Kitchen 3. Multiple sensors activated. Evacuate Levels 3 and 4. All personnel evacuate Levels 3 and 4."

Young Kevin Torez ran to his godparents' bedroom, "What do we do?" his quivering voice loudly asked.

"Get dressed, just in case, but for now, we sit tight," Alex Wilson explained.

"Why?"

"Everyone from the lower levels will be coming up. The corridors will be crowded. If we go out there, we'll just be in the way."

"What about my mom? She's working in Kitchen 3 tonight."

"I know. She should've been one of the first to get out. When we see her, she can tell us all about what happened."

"Then why are we getting dressed?"

"Just in case. There's a fire somewhere, and we need to be ready in case they call for us here on Level 2."

Obediently, the boy rushed to comply and, in less than a minute, he was back.

A new voice boomed through overhead speakers. "All firefighting teams report to Level 4, and security teams to Level 3 to assist with evacuations."

This voice was familiar and belonged to Randal Clarence, the current head of the Senate, the elected body that governed life within the shelter. They worked with the shelter operations staff and security officers and served as a jury the infrequent times one was needed.

Alex tried to appear calm but was anxious about the situation. He knew the firefighting teams had been trained for this, but they had never actually fought a fire in the shelter. Alex also knew that Kevin's mother, Wendy, was in the middle of what was going on, and she wasn't the kind to run from danger. As he thought about this, he was aware of something else: there was a faint smell of smoke. He glanced at his wife and saw the concern on her face; she smelled it too.

Several seconds later, Kevin asked, "What's that smell?"

Alex was confused, then realized that Kevin had lived his

entire life in the shelter; he didn't know what smoke smelled like.

The automated voice interrupted Alex before he could answer. "Smoke detected on Levels 4, 3, and 2. Everyone evacuate to Level 1. All personnel evacuate Levels 2, 3, and 4."

Alex hopped up. "That's us, Kevin. Stay with me. We need to go."

Marie opened the door to the hall and they moved partway down it, toward the main passageway, and found it blocked.

For several minutes, people from the lower levels moved upward, and the corridor became blocked. The smell of smoke was much more noticeable than it had been in their quarters. No one was coughing, but panic was increasing steadily. They heard someone yelling for people to move. A voice shouted back that the hall on Level 1 had become packed with people. There was nowhere to go.

In the meantime, the smoke continued to thicken.

Young Kevin felt bodies pressing against him. Short for his age, they were all so much taller and they blocked his view of what was ahead. He squeezed Alex's hand tighter, fearing that they would become separated.

The blaring mechanical voice returned. "Smoke detected on all levels. Evacuate to main access tunnel. Proceed to main access tunnel." There was a pause and then the voice resumed. "Main tunnel doors open ... main tunnel doors open."

In less than a minute, the packed hoard of bodies began to proceed as the ones in front began to ascend the ramp and head into the cold radiation-filled winter night.

Fortunately, for the Wilsons, more than half the shelter's population was ahead in the pack. They made it as far as the main access tunnel before the pack thinned out—enough for them to congregate in an underground area that was still safe.

Looking at his wife, Alex said solemnly, "I should get to Central Medical. They'll be needing everyone's help. Will you two be okay here?"

Marie agreed. "We'll be fine ... go."

Pushing his way through the crowd, Alex disappeared from view.

As the crowd continued to thin, tension decreased, but only for a moment. Then, an even greater problem arose. A new alarm sounded, with far faster speed and urgency. The automated voice returned. "Smoke and heat detected in Reactor Cooling Room 1. Coolant pressure decreasing."

The alarm continued to blare and the warning was repeated every thirty seconds. After several minutes, the alarm stopped, and all the lights went out.

Not only was it now pitch black, but the complete lack of sound was worse; everyone held their breaths. The constant mild hum from the pumps that circulated hot water away from the reactor and all through the shelter was gone. There was no shelter heating and no reactor cooling.

Those that ended up outside, waited for the smoke to clear enough to return to the safety of the shelter. During those four hours, most of them received a lethal dose of radiation. They wanted to get back inside, but the tunnel was still filled with people because the lower levels were still smoke-filled. Among them was a thirty-one-year-old kitchen worker who had been one of the first evacuated—and, therefore, one of the first to step outside.

She stood in the chilly Florida night, wondering where her ten-year-old son Kevin was.

Chapter Twenty-Two

MINUTES BEFORE THE WILSONS AWOKE TO THE FIRE ALARM, Melony Jones sat alone in the reactor control room. She'd just finished video-chatting with her boyfriend. He liked to contact her and talk each evening before heading to bed. That was part of why Melony enjoyed the night shift. She was alone, and things were more relaxed.

Glancing at all the indicators on the console, she saw that, as always, everything was running fine. In all her years in this job, she'd never seen a light that wasn't green on that console. She felt that she had the easiest and probably the most boring job in Shelter 16. The reactor was twenty-five yards down the hall from her, on Level 5, the deepest part of the shelter. It sat in a secure room and was the size of a railroad car. The design allowed it to run for twenty-five years with almost no human intervention. Sometimes, she felt like she was nothing more than a glorified babysitter.

When she'd first arrived at Shelter 16 as a fifteen-year-old kid, she didn't know the first thing about nuclear reactors. A few years later, when she finished school, she wanted to pick a different and interesting job. The formally trained professionals who came to 16 to manage the reactor, trained the next generation. Now, Melony and her team were as knowledgeable, if less experienced, than their trainers.

She opened a novel on her tablet and started to read. Almost immediately, the blaring fire alarm interrupted her reading. She was used to unplanned emergency reactor drills, but never did they involve setting off alarms throughout the shelter. She listened to the alert: a fire was on Level 4. The reactor room, control center, and mechanical section were on Level 5. Few people had access to Level 5, and it sounded like the fire was directly above. However, Cooling Rooms A and B extended between the two floors and contained the massive pumps that moved water through the system.

From the console, she could pull up information beyond her area of responsibility. She accessed the fire control systems and looked at which sensors had activated. From that, she knew exactly where the fire was and where it was spreading.

Rechecking the panel, she saw everything involving the reactor was still green. Now, she needed to decide what to do. Level 5 was well secured. It was doubtful that fire could reach her, but the large water lines that brought in cold water from a nearby river and pushed out hot water that had cooled the reactor, passed through Level 4.

Usually, the first step in any emergency regarding the reactor was to disable the automatic systems and take manual control. However, Melony's panel was still all green. There was no reactor crisis at present. She gazed back and saw the fire was still spreading toward Cooling Room A, and she made a snap decision.

Melony pressed the intercom button on the panel and began flipping switches to disengage the automatic controls.

"Operations, is that you, Melony?" a male voice from the desk-mounted speaker.

Recognizing the voice, she answered quickly. "Yeah, Dan. It's me. What's with the fire? Should I be concerned?"

"They're saying they have it surrounded, and it should be

under control soon. The problem is there's tons of smoke, and lots of people are down. Not sure how bad yet."

"I'm activating Alert Level Yellow. All systems are still green, but I'm moving to manual control," Melony reported.

Dan switched to a more formal tone. "Reactor control reporting Alert Yellow. All systems to manual."

Minutes later, she saw the first light on the panel change from green to red. Thermal sensors in Cooling Room A were showing a rapid climb in temperature. The cooling rooms each held two sets of large pumps for moving water through the system and maintaining the reactor's thermal stability.

Before she could report the problem, there was another alert on her panel. There was a water pressure decrease in Cooling Room A, quickly followed by a blinking light showing that the reactor temperature was slowly climbing since the water to keep it cool wasn't flowing as it should.

Hitting the intercom button again, she felt her heart race. They always trained for the "what if" situation, knowing it would never happen ... and, yet, it had.

While waiting for Operations to come online, she began diverting all cooling to Cooling Room B.

"Operations," a different voice said.

"Reactor Control. Activating Alert Level Orange. Cooling Room A is offline. It looks like the fire may have gotten in there," Melony stated gravely. The time for a friendly chat was gone.

"Confirming reactor Alert Level Orange. Cooling Room A offline."

A single cooling pump room should easily keep the reactor at a safe temperature, but that wasn't happening. Even with the pumps in Room B running at 100%, the reactor temperature continued to climb.

For several minutes, Melony heard reports coming in, stating that people were evacuating the shelter, but she couldn't think about that. All her focus was on getting the reactor temperature down, but nothing she tried worked. The temperature was approaching critical. There were only a few lights on her control board that were still green.

She hit the intercom button again.

The response was immediate. "Operations."

"Alert Level Red." Melony fought to keep her voice calm. "Reactor temperature is approaching critical. Attempting emergency cooling."

Entering commands into her terminal, the valves that controlled the flow of the heated water that ran through the facility to maintain a comfortable temperature all closed. This caused the hot water from the cooling chamber to head directly back to the river, without circulating through the shelter. It was a more effective water flow and increased the cooling efficiency of the system.

The reactor temperature stopped climbing but didn't decrease. It was still in the critical range, and damage to the system was likely if she couldn't get it cooled immediately.

Scared and alone, Melony wished one of her team members was here, but she knew the fire prevented them from coming to help. Feeling nauseous, she made a decision and contacted Operations again.

"Situation is still critical. Bring emergency generators online. Prepare for reactor scram."

Scramming a reactor was the emergency process to immediately stop the nuclear reaction and shut down the system. It was a sudden traumatic shutdown compared to a proper power down that could take hours to complete.

This time, there was no immediate response, but she was aware of hushed, anxious conversations in the background.

Another voice came online. "Please confirm you're preparing an emergency reactor shut down."

Melony swallowed hard. Her voice caught in her throat, but she forced herself to answer. "Y-yes, but we need the emergency generators online first. The reactor will still need cooling while shut down." Trembling, Melony waited for a full 30 seconds for a response.

"Reactor Control, Operations, propane generators are now online."

Melony flipped several switches that changed the cooling pumps from reactor power to emergency generator power and sighed with relief as they switched over smoothly. She raised the plastic shield that covered the large red button labeled Reactor Scram and pressed it.

Dozens of control rods quickly descended into the reactor core, decreasing the fission reaction. As the nuclear reaction dropped to a fraction of what it had been, the turbines that created 16's power slowed to a stop and the whole facility went dark.

Six seconds later the emergency lighting came on. Several terrifying minutes passed by as Melony waited and finally saw the reactor temperature slowly dropping.

Collapsing to the floor, Melony wept while wondering what she could've done differently.

Chapter Twenty-Three

SHELTER 16 SEEMED LIKE A COMPLETELY DIFFERENT PLACE since the night of the fire and near-meltdown of the reactor. The unpleasant, acrid smell from burned material remained in the air. The smoke smell would be nearly impossible to remove since it had permeated carpets and furnishings. Some walls still had smoke stains. Clean-up was moving slowly.

The feel of the shelter had significantly changed. Since the reactor wasn't operating correctly, it wasn't providing heat to the living spaces. The temperature throughout the facility had dropped by close to twenty degrees.

Job schedules changed, and Level 4 was still off-limits as emergency repairs continued. Critical work on the reactor and cooling system was ongoing, which led to frequent power outages.

The loss of life changed the sound of the place. Fifty-two people died from smoke inhalation that fateful night and eight more had passed since. Everyone who'd evacuated the facility for several hours made it back inside, and the doors were shut and sealed again. However, within a few days, the first person became sick, and more soon followed.

Within the next four months, twenty percent of the shelter

occupants, almost half of those who had left the facility, would be deceased.

Walking down the passageway, David Cowan was aware of the smoke smell. He was headed to Res2 to visit one of his students, Kevin Torez. The boy was home watching over his mother, whose health was fading fast.

As he approached the door, it opened and his friends, Alex and Marie Wilson stepped out.

"David, how are you doing?" Marie smiled.

David smiled in return, thinking again that he was glad that his nickname DJ had been lost soon after his arrival at the shelter. "Good enough, other than the cold. We got too used to the perfect 72 degrees. I haven't worn a sweatshirt in ten years, and now I've got two of them on."

The Wilsons nodded in agreement, both bundled up as well.

"Have you heard anything about the power problems? I heard a rumor that the reactor might be permanently damaged."

Marie glanced at her husband before turning back to David. She decided that a bit of truth would be good, given all the rumors circulating. "It is. The Senate met this morning; I spoke to President Clarence afterward. They can't get the cooling problems figured out. The sudden overheats and shutdowns are putting a tremendous strain on the system. Engineering says they can safely run and maintain it at about forty-five percent capacity, but that's all."

David's eyes grew wide. "What does that mean for everyone here?"

"Good question," Alex replied solemnly. "They're talking about evacuating several hundred people to other shelters. There are four that are fairly close. Nothing has been officially decided yet."

The trio stood in silence and, finally, Alex asked, "So, where were you headed before we dropped this news on you?"

"I just wanted to see Kevin. He understandably hasn't been in class, and I wanted to check on him."

Alex nodded. David was intelligent, charismatic and all his students loved him. He also served on several leadership committees within the shelter, and people expected that he would soon be serving on the Senate.

Marie sighed softly. "He's doing okay. Scared and struggling with seeing his mother the way she is, but lots of people have rallied alongside him, and he knows he'll be safe. We told Wendy that he was welcome to move in with us and that they should think about it."

"That's good. Kevin already knows and likes you. It would be good for him. Maybe good for you too."

"Well, whatever happens," Alex said, "we'll make sure he is taken care of."

Nodding, David started strolling away. "I'm going to have a chat with him. Let him know that we all miss him."

Before the Wilsons continued on their way, Marie said, "Sounds good. We need to get going. We've got a con-call scheduled with our kids in 87. Going to get to see the newest grandchild."

"Congratulations, that's great news. Is that your third?" David inquired with a warm smile.

"Yes, two boys and a girl now."

"Well, that's wonderful. I'll see you later."

David knocked on the Torez' door. It opened, and his student exclaimed, "David!"

The teacher walked in and gave the boy a quick hug. "Kevin, how are things going, buddy?"

The grin on his face dissolved. "Not good. She's really weak and sleeps all the time."

"Has anyone spent time with you, telling you what to expect?"

"You mean ... as she dies?" As he said these words, his voice collapsed to a whisper.

"Yeah. Has anyone explained that?"

"One of the doctors was here a couple of days ago, and he told me what would happen."

David nodded, glad the boy knew what was going on.

"Do you want to see her?" Kevin asked, his expression grim.

"Sure," David answered. Not certain that he did.

"Come on." Kevin led David across the living room that was identical to the other residential spaces in Shelter 16. The same furnishings and the same carpet. All the same. The government must have gone with the lowest bidder, he thought.

They entered the master bedroom and he saw Wendy Torez lying in bed with numerous blankets on top. Her face was deathly pale and her eyes looked sunken. Most of her once thick black hair was gone, and the one arm that was exposed looked like there wasn't any muscle left. She was literally just skin and bones.

"Wendy, are you awake? It's David."

The response was weak and difficult to hear. "Hi David. You caught me when I was awake. I'm sleeping most of the time now. This radiation sickness is brutal."

"Yeah, it looks rough," David agreed. "Is it painful?"

"Some, but they gave me good medications, and as long as I don't move much, it isn't too bad."

As they spoke, the lights suddenly went out. Everyone waited until the emergency lights kicked on. This concerned David because it was happening more and more frequently.

"I don't want to keep you awake. I wanted to see how you're doing and talk to Kevin."

"He's a good son. He won't leave, not even to eat. Every time I wake up, he's sitting here, holding my hand." Her voice was growing weaker.

David could tell she'd soon fall asleep.

"David, when I'm gone, please watch over him. He'll probably stay with the Wilsons, but he really likes you."

"Wendy, I will. We *all* will."

Two days later, Kevin would move his belongings in with the Wilsons.

Chapter Twenty-Four

Twenty-seven-year-old Lucy Wilson-Brown pushed the stroller containing her infant daughter, Kara. While they walked, her two-year-old son, Tyler, kept one hand on the stroller as he trudged along, just like she'd taught him. Lucy was fortunate to have her children this close together in age, at eight months and two years of age. In all the shelters, it was essential to manage reproduction. It was necessary to maintain a youthful population, but it also needed to be balanced to protect the food supply.

Every day, shelter inhabitants received three pills with their breakfast. Taking them wasn't optional. One pill was a multivitamin, the second was a supplement, which helped make up for the loss of natural benefits of being outside in the sunlight, and the third was birth control. There were different pills for the males and females. When a couple wanted to have children, their names went into the rotation; when their turn came up, hopeful parents could skip pill three. The system wasn't foolproof but worked quite well.

After Tyler's birth, Lucy and her husband immediately put their names in again and found themselves approved much sooner than expected. This was because of an industrial accident that claimed four lives and two other women who chose to remove themselves from the rotation,

If that hadn't happened, Lucy knew that she might never have received approval for another child. Soon after learning that she was pregnant again, leadership determined that radiation levels weren't dropping at the expected rate. Changes needed to be put in place to allow everyone to remain in the shelters longer than originally planned. Because of that, meal portions became a little smaller and, noticeably, fewer people received approval for childbearing.

Lucy continued walking, staying at a comfortable pace for Tyler, who'd rather walk than be carried. Lucy had left their home in Res7 with plenty of time and now approached the familiar turn. "Go knock, Tyler," Lucy instructed with a grin.

The toddler ran ahead, stopped at the correct door, and started banging and yelling, "Uncle Sam! Aunt T!" He managed to yell this three times before Lucy caught up to him and Sam answered the door.

Cradling his newborn son in his arms, Sam held the door open for his sister to get the stroller into the home—the same home the two of them had shared for their first six years in Shelter 87.

This infant was the latest in the growing generation known as the shelter-born. Since nobody was sure how much longer they would be in the shelter, there was speculation the shelter-born might someday outnumber the surface-born.

Sam's wife, Theresa, entered the living room from the bedroom, having heard the new arrivals. As soon as she entered, the toddler threw up his arms and started yelling again, "Aunt T, Aunt T!"

Carefully, she scooped up the nephew she'd come to love dearly and held him close, even though lifting him was still against her doctor's orders.

"I said I would have him able to say your name by the

time you had the baby, but it's taking a bit longer. I think he might always call you 'Aunt T'," Lucy said.

"That's fine with me. I'm just glad I get to hold my little buddy," Sam's wife said happily.

Theresa's deep fondness for Tyler was what made her agree with Sam's idea for them going on the parent rotation, something she wasn't sure she wanted to do before.

Glancing into the crib in the corner, Lucy saw a familiar brown-and-tan stuffed animal. "I see that Bear is still around."

Smiling, Sam said, "Did you think I would ever get rid of him?"

"No, but I'm surprised you passed him down to Oliver. You used to get so mad if I touched him."

"Well, I was about six when that happened."

Lucy changed the topic. "Are we still up for five o'clock?"

"Yeah, the satellite will be in a good position by then. We can talk for about eight hours if you want," Sam answered with a smile.

With an exaggerated shake of her head, Lucy said, "No thanks. Though, Mom and Dad would gladly look at the grandkids that long if we stayed on the line."

They shared a laugh and fell into small talk until loud chiming came from the computer. Immediately, Tyler ran to it, "Me talk!"

Everyone took a seat and Sam walked to the computer. The wide-angle lens would allow them all to be in the video. He patted the toddler on the head. "You'll get to talk, but you need to wait your turn." He pressed a button, and the wall-mounted TV lit up with Marie and Alex Wilson's faces.

"Hi guys!" Marie said cheerfully.

Everyone responded, glad to see the connection was working.

"Where's Chief today?" Alex asked, peering closely.

"He had to work," Lucy explained.

"Well, we've been looking forward to getting to talk to you

today. Having to wait for certain times is a pain. It was much nicer when we could just talk whenever we wanted."

"It was, but we need to be glad for this," Lucy stated. "As more satellites fail, and there are no replacements, the opportunities to talk will become fewer and fewer with time."

"Don't remind us," her mother sighed. "Now, let me see that new baby."

Holding his son, Sam stood. "Mom and Dad, meet Oliver."

Theresa walked over and stood proudly with her husband and son. She was an average height woman with curly hair and glasses. Although extremely personable, she had a perpetually somber expression.

"You guys have a wonderful-looking boy, congratulations," Alex grinned. He blinked away the tears that were forming as he regarded the grandchild he'd never get to hold.

Marie said nothing, the joy and the sorrow too much to allow words to form.

An awkward silence ensued as the grandparents cried and viewed the newborn. Eventually, Theresa had enough and decided to get the conversation restarted. She looked at her sister-in-law, clearly wanting help. Lucy nodded in the direction of her oldest, who was playing on the floor.

Theresa turned abruptly. "Okay, Tyler, your turn to talk to Grandma and Grandpa." She scooped up the toddler and placed him on her lap as she sat in front of the computer.

"Gama, Gapa," the child yelled in delight, glad to have his few minutes.

The excited greeting from their eldest grandson cheered the elder Wilsons, enough to bring them back from their sorrow. They laughed and enjoyed the three little kids as they listened to their parents talk about all they were doing.

Instinctively, Theresa knew when the time had come to end the conversation. "Tyler, want to take a walk with me?"

"Yeah, walk!"

Seconds later, Theresa left the apartment, taking the toddler noise and energy with her.

Looking into the camera, Lucy said, "So, how are things coming along there? The last time we talked was right after the fire."

"It's rough. We lost many good people, and there are about forty more that won't survive the month. Every shelter has a crematorium, but they were never intended to handle this volume. They're running around the clock. Our reactor is damaged, and they're talking about possible evacuations. Also, I doubt Kevin's mom will last more than a day or two."

"Will he be moving in with you?" Sam asked, concern lining his face.

"We're all he has. Actually, several people have offered, but he knows us the best, so I suspect that he'll be coming here."

"Poor kid. Glad he has you. You did great raising us. He'll be okay," Lucy stated.

"Thanks. That's kind of you to say," Marie said.

"If they evacuate, where would you go?"

"Nothing is decided yet," Marie shrugged. "They're still working things out."

Sam thought of something. "Not to be morbid, but I assume you also heard about how the radiation levels aren't dropping as anticipated."

His parents nodded.

"Well, have they said anything about how the loss of so many might impact how long you can stay in the shelter?"

"As you know, the original estimates were that we'd be here up to twenty years. They planned for enough food for everyone to stay for twenty, and then another five years of emergency rations in case something went wrong," Alex explained.

Sam nodded, "It's the same here. We were a little better off because we had more people choose to leave the shelter after the first month than was expected. They knew some would decide to take their chances, but we lost about fifty."

Alex nodded. "We had something similar, and now this. From what I hear, with some changes going in place and the decrease in population, they think that with the emergency rations, we can stretch things to about thirty-five years."

Sam lifted his newborn in front of the camera, "If that happens, this guy will be older than me when we get out."

Chapter Twenty-Five

Alex and Marie stopped walking as the passageway plunged into total darkness.

Marie started counting aloud, "1 ... 2 ... 3 ... 4 ... 5 ... 6." As she said six, the dim emergency lighting came on and provided ample illumination to continue. "They always come on at 6," she said with a wry smile.

The pair continued forward.

"Maybe, but it's happening more and more frequently," Alex stated with a frown. "There's been no improvement, and it's been almost a month now."

As they approached their destination, Training Room 2, they noticed a crowd gathering. When they got closer, they could see the doors were shut, and there was another group already in the room. Within a few minutes, the doors opened, and a large group of somber-looking people exited. The Wilsons had gotten to know most of them over the years, and several were crying as they walked by.

"Our group evacuates tomorrow," one of them said to Marie.

As they filed into the room, they were quiet, knowing what

was coming. The Wilsons took their seats and several members of the Senate stood in front of the assembled.

The Senate President spoke. "The damage done to the reactor isn't repairable at this time. In order to keep it running safely, we need to cut power output down to forty-five percent. Starting tomorrow, we'll be permanently shutting power off to most of Level 4, including the two kitchens there. The one on Level 2 will be the only one operational. Also, we'll be shutting power off to all of Level 3. This includes all residential spaces on that level, the gym, and classrooms 9-18."

He paused while the news sank in, then continued. "There are four other shelters within a few hundred miles of here which are willing to take some of our people. This group will be relocating to Shelter 104. It's about two hundred miles from here."

With that statement, the whole room erupted with concerned voices. Everyone clearly remembered what had happened to the last members of their community that went outside.

"Easy, easy," the President yelled. "Listen up! We aren't sending you out to die. You're part of this family. It pains us all very much to have to evacuate any of you, but we don't have any choice. You'll be traveling in two large buses. We've installed special shielding against the radiation. You won't have the same protection as in the shelter, but it should be enough. There are radiation sensors inside, and you'll be able to monitor your exposure. These vehicles are large but will be traveling as quickly as possible. The goal is for you to be there within three hours of leaving here. The condition of the roads will be the biggest concern.

"Now, this group will leave from this room tomorrow at 11:00 am. Be here before then with all your belongings. 104 is a Level 2 shelter, so it is double the size of this one. That means more amenities. And no, I don't know what they are.

"Before you leave, we have one more topic. The human

thyroid gland is more vulnerable to damage from radiation than any other part of your body. We'll be giving you a potassium iodide tablet for every member of your family when you leave here in a few minutes. Take it before bed tonight. It'll help protect your thyroid and help prevent thyroid cancer from your exposure.

"Lastly, we're genuinely sorry to see you depart. Tomorrow, we'll be saying goodbye to just over three hundred of you, and we'll all be weaker because of it. I hope you adjust and thrive as members of 104!"

When the meeting adjourned, the Wilsons waited as others filed out and approached the front. The Senate members were still there, answering questions. When he was available, they went up to Senate President Randal Clarence.

"Got a minute, Randal?" Alex asked.

Marie had recently completed a two-year term on the Senate. She would have to wait at least another two years before she'd be eligible for re-appointment. She considered Randal a good friend.

"Alex, Marie, come over here and have a seat." The Senate head led them off to the side. He sat on the edge of the stage and waited for them to join him. "I'm glad I'm getting to see you before you leave the meeting. There should be satellite coverage this evening. You should contact your kids and let them know about this move."

"We will. But Randal, we want to know why we're on the list to be evacuated. Our quarters aren't even in the sections you're shutting down. You know we have Kevin Torez with us now. He has been through a lot, and to put him through the relocation so soon after losing his mother is going to be a big strain."

"There are several reasons why you were selected. I personally added you three to the list for 104."

"Why?" Marie asked, her voice cracking with frustration.

"There are only four shelters close enough to send people

to safely. After that, it would be a full day or more in a vehicle. Even with the shielding, it would be a very dangerous trip.

"Those four shelters aren't excited about adding people who will be consuming their limited resources. It also means significantly impacting their child-bearing rotations. We've had separate negotiations with each, and they all want a lot in exchange for taking you in. In the case of 104, they insisted on a significant amount of supplies to cover what you'll consume. There will be three buses leaving here. Two will have forty people on each, and the other will be packed with supplies and equipment. They also wanted medical people. When I offered up an anesthesiologist, they were delighted. We've got three, and they have one. Their other died of heart failure several years ago. They've trained up replacements but want someone formally educated."

Marie's head slumped as she glanced at Alex, her despair growing.

Alex nodded. "I guess that's a reason, but why us? As you said, we've got two other anesthesiologists. Think about Kevin."

"I am. He's the main reason you're going. A couple of days before she died, I visited Wendy Torez. I'd always liked her. She made me promise to watch out for and do my best to protect Kevin."

Randal paused, watching the Wilsons nod in understanding; they knew she'd asked several others to make that same promise.

"What you don't understand is we aren't evacuating all of you so that we can continue on here without you."

"What are you talking about?" Marie asked, perplexed.

"If you do the math, the number of our people these other shelters are taking is barely half of what we'd need to relocate and bring our power consumption down to what is required. Even then, it is just a guess that we might be able to stabilize the reactor.

"The best case is that everyone doubles up in sleeping quarters, we lose most of our heating, and we continue a couple of years in miserable conditions. More likely, we'll have to abandon the shelter in six months because the reactor fails. Right now, we don't have any place to go if that happens. We didn't pick you to get rid of you. You're the ones we chose to *save*."

Chapter Twenty-Six

ALEX, MARIE, AND KEVIN ENTERED THE TRAINING ROOM carrying all their possessions. They'd spent the previous evening visiting with friends and co-workers, saying goodbye. They'd made many close friends in the ten years they'd been under the surface, and departing was difficult. Those that were staying were sad. It was clear to all that the ones departing were the ones who'd fare better in the long run.

The training room was getting full. Kevin spotted his friend and teacher, David Cowan, and headed to him. "David!"

"Kevin! I'm glad to see you! One more friend I know that I'll have in our new home."

"Will you still be my teacher when we get to 104?"

"I don't know. The leadership here sent all our records, skills, and current jobs ahead, and the leadership of 104 had to approve all of us. But I don't know if they'll need another teacher," David explained with a rueful smile.

"Everyone, please give me your full attention," a deep voice interrupted. "In just a minute, we'll be walking out of here as a single group. You've seen the maps with the large areas of the shelter marked 'Restricted'—that's where we're heading. You aren't supposed to see those areas until the radiation clears and it is time to leave the shelters. So, when we get to 104, *do not mention anything* you see as you leave. Don't wander away from this group and don't touch anything, okay? Now, follow me."

The group departed the room, preparing to leave their home behind. They continued down familiar halls until they got to a large set of double doors. There was a large sign marked "Authorized Personnel Only". They entered halls they'd never seen and saw doors as they passed. One door on the left had a sign reading "Jail" and one on the right read "Incinerator / Crematorium".

Having each spent two years in the Senate, Alex and Marie knew these places existed but had never seen them before.

There was another pair of closed doors with just a large "X" on them. They passed through and found themselves on a catwalk above the floor, in a massive room the size of a large warehouse. The ceiling was three stories high and there were rows upon rows of shelving taking up half the space. The shelving area had signs. Marie caught sight of a few, including: "Clothing", "Equipment", "Food", and "Weapons".

They continued walking to the opposite side of the enormous space where another sign read "Transportation". There were multiple levels, with a wide array of vehicles, many stored on large shelves, high in the air, some with wheels removed.

Pulled up front were five vehicles. Three of them looked like a bizarre cross between dune buggies and buses. They had oversized bodies with off-road suspension and big knobby tires. Mounted in the rear on each was a large bulb-like sphere with an eight-foot diameter. A team of people was loading large boxes into the bus farthest back.

The other two looked more like common four-passenger off-road vehicles, though much bulkier and with a smaller but similar sphere built into the rear. Each had a large blade, similar to a snowplow, mounted on the front and a winch on the back. There were four people gathered around each, all of whom looked familiar. They wore radiation-resistant suits and were holding helmets.

Alex watched as the crews entered the vehicles and put on their helmets. They were handed assault rifles, which they secured out of view. The crews then pulled the safety straps over their shoulders and latched them between their thighs. The restraints reminded Marie of getting on a roller coaster. They then drove away, down a nearby tunnel.

One of the people who had been helping get the two teams on their way called up to the group on the catwalk. "Those vehicles that just left aren't with you. They're preceding the next group that will leave in two hours. A similar group left two hours ago, headed for Shelter 104. Those are your scouts. Their job is to make sure you have a clear path so you can move at maximum speed. There's also a drone flying ahead of them, and it'll help them navigate around or clear obstacles. Their exposure will be much greater than yours will be, and they volunteered for this.

"A similar convoy to yours left at 9:00 AM, and they're almost to their new shelter. That one is in the opposite direction from where you're going. So far, no problems. Their scouts have found the roads mostly clear of obstructions.

"Some of these vehicles will be remaining at the destination, and others will be returning here. It all depends on what we arranged with each receiving shelter.

"When you board the buses, attach the safety harnesses and try to relax. Your driver and navigator will have headsets on so they can communicate with your scouts. There will also be two armed security persons on the bus. They're on board, just as a precaution. Don't let it concern you.

"There's one final issue. The shelter you're going to has agreed to take you in. That means that even though we're sending supplies, you'll still be a drain on their resources, and some of their people are having to change living spaces to make room for you. Please tread lightly and be thankful when you arrive. We aren't sure how well their residents will receive you."

The departees had something new to consider: would they be *un*welcome in their new home?

"Now, head down the stairs to the left and start loading the first two buses; the third is for cargo. Someone will tell you which bus to get on. That's just to keep families together."

As they moved forward, the group became anxious, thinking about entering a potentially unfriendly environment. They approached the bus and saw that the elevated suspension was so high that a stepladder was in place to help everyone board. They also noticed the entire body of the bus was tightly enclosed in what looked like a thick grey blanket; every inch of the outside was covered, including the windshield. They turned their baggage over to those that would load it in the compartments below.

Marie was the first of the trio to board. The first thing she saw was two seats in the front where the driver would typically sit. The one furthest from her, as she boarded, had a traditional steering wheel; the other had a wide array of equipment and several computer screens. The entire inside, including the windshield, was covered with the same material as the outside. They couldn't see out of the bus. A large video screen was mounted where the windshield would have been.

There were individual bucket seats for every passenger with a three-point restraint system. Marie took what would've been a window seat, if the interior and exterior coverings weren't completely obscuring the windows. Kevin sat next to her and she adjusted the restraint system to his smaller size. Alex sat across the aisle from them, next to a man who was about his age. Alex recalled that he'd played basketball with him a few years ago, but his name didn't come to him.

Four large computer screens hung next to one another from the ceiling and were visible to all the occupants.

When the last of the passengers and the security guards had boarded, two final people came aboard. Each held a helmet with a microphone attached. The first spoke in a friendly voice. "Good morning. My name is Deb, and I'll be your pilot today. Andy here will be my navigator. For those of you who have ridden in a vehicle before—I use those terms because this won't be anything like the driving you remember—once we're in motion, we won't be able to answer questions. We'll be too focused on our tasks.

"Our lives depend on how quickly and safely I can get us to 104. Now, we're in this together, so the screens will show the same things we're seeing, and you'll be able to hear our communications. If we hear any screaming from back here, we'll shut it off, and you won't know what is going on.

"Keep your seat belts on, and don't get up for any reason. We'll be traveling at speeds over a hundred miles per hour and, if you're out of your seat, you'll fall and may be killed. If that happens, we won't stop. Other than for a fire, we won't stop or slow down, no matter what happens back here. There will be at least one occasion when we'll have to go off-road for a bit. Our scouts are clearing a path and will be giving us step-by-step directions. There's a drone overhead helping, and you'll see its view on one of the screens."

Deb paused to determine if her passengers were absorbing the information she was dumping.

Satisfied they were, she continued in the same friendly voice. "The radiation shielding surrounding the exterior and interior should adequately protect us. Nevertheless, speed will be the most critical factor. See this device?" She pointed to a small black box affixed to the inside radiation shielding on the wall by the door. "This will record how much radiation is accumulated inside during the trip. The medical staff at 104 will use the data from this and determine what, if any, medical care we need upon arriving.

"Now, one last thing. No one in our shelter has ever driven one of these before, and no one expected the maiden voyage to be a two hundred-mile dash. I've spent over eighty hours in the simulator practicing for this. The manufacturer put these vehicles through their paces, and we'll be operating within guidelines, but just barely. I tell you that because, as I said, we're in this together. Any questions?"

The forty passengers stared back at her with open mouths and wide eyes, and didn't ask anything.

Chapter Twenty-Seven

With everyone strapped in, the power came on as the engine started. The video screens for the passengers came to life. Of the four screens, the ones on the far left and right showed an angled view, forward of the bus. The second from the left was a straight-forward, wide-angle view. It almost felt like looking out a windshield. The last screen showed instrument data, including speed, time, odometer, and internal and external radiation; this screen would be alternating between the instrument settings to the drone's view from overhead.

They began moving slowly up the access tunnel and audio from the pilot and navigator rang forth through the speakers. "16-40-5 ready for doors."

"Doors opening 40-5. Good luck."

Alex sat thinking about the meaning of the numbers he heard but came up empty.

On the monitors, they could see and hear the massive doors ahead opening. The second bus would be two minutes behind them. The pilot had lots to be focused on and didn't need to worry about the other vehicle's position.

"Continue on exit path as planned. Slow speed ... the road conditions have deteriorated."

On the screen, the Wilsons recognized the place where they'd been dropped off years earlier. There were small craters in the dirt roadway that had developed over time and the capable off-road bus wasn't even trying to avoid them. The passengers hardly noticed anything as the suspension absorbed the effects of the rough terrain.

The screen showing instrument data changed, displaying the view from the overhead drone. They watched their vehicle head toward the highway. Two minutes later, the view of instrument data returned. After several miles, the bus approached the on-ramp of a two-lane divided highway with a freshly painted line across the pavement.

"Stop at the line and reset the odometer to zero," the navigator instructed.

The bus came to a stop. "Odometer at zero."

"Accelerate and remain in the left lane for sixteen miles."

Watching the monitors, the passengers saw the speed increase rapidly, until they reached and held at one hundred miles per hour. Scanning the other screens, Marie noticed that the internal radiation was in the green but close to yellow. External radiation was in the middle of the red.

Kevin watched the monitors closely, particularly those looking out the front at angles. Curious, he often asked questions. "Is that a house?"

"Yes, that was someone's house."

"Is that a car?"

"Yes. That was called an SUV."

"What did that mean?"

Calmly and patiently, Marie answered all his questions, glad for something to take her mind off the race across the dead world.

"Coming up on mile sixteen ... maintain speed and move to the right lane before mile twenty," the navigator instructed.

Two minutes later, they saw a disabled truck sitting in the left lane. They passed it without slowing down. It was hard to be sure at this speed, but Alex thought he saw a corpse on the ground next to the truck.

"Maintain speed for twenty-one miles and move back left during that time."

Fifteen minutes later, they heard, "In the next mile, decelerate to forty and, at the X, cross over to the oncoming lanes."

On the screens was a large X painted on the pavement and the bus left the highway and crossed a wide, overgrown median with no difficulty.

"Stay in the right lane and accelerate again for nine miles. Between miles nine and eleven, get over to the left lane."

Minutes later, there was a collapsed overpass blocking the side of the highway they'd been on. Alex wondered how much additional radiation exposure the scouts received while mapping out this route. The high-speed ride continued with occasional lane changes and an eventual return to the correct side of the highway.

The internal radiation level was out of the green and had moved into the low end of yellow. Everyone had their eyes glued to its continual advancement, wondering how high it would go before they arrived.

"At mile 87, decelerate to thirty. We'll be going over debris in the road."

The passengers felt the speed bleed off and, on the forward-facing screen, was a large sign which had originally been mounted to a highway overpass but had now fallen and was lying across the highway. At the decreased speed, they passed over it with relative ease and then returned to their previous velocity.

Alex focused on the view outside. At first, the world seemed dead; there were no signs of life. There was merely a once vibrant society slowly rotting away. Then he realized that wasn't entirely true. There was living vegetation. Most of the larger trees looked dead, but others had visible leaves. Along the roadside, there were smaller living plants; the radiation hadn't destroyed everything.

"Somewhere in the next three miles, get to the right lane and exit the highway and go into the field at the X."

Without warning, the screen to the far right went dark.

"We lost camera three," the navigator stated.

"Understood. Not stopping," the pilot replied.

The bus slowed and, at the painted X, proceeded across a field. Ahead of them, everyone could see flattened grass from the tire tracks of another vehicle. Marie understood that they were following in the tracks of their scouts.

"Stay in their tracks until they exit on the street and then go left."

They entered downtown where the remains of familiar businesses were identifiable. Recognizing a familiar gas station and restaurant logos on dilapidated buildings was hard on Marie and she struggled with seeing what had become of the places she'd grown up with.

The sights made Kevin even more curious and the questions returned. Seeing large yellow arches, he pointed. "What was that place?"

"It was a fast-food restaurant. They were in almost every town."

"What's fast food?"

Again, Marie answered everything he asked, appreciating his fascination with the outside world.

"Remain on this road for six miles and then turn left. The road is clear but curvy. Keep the speed below fifty."

After a few more turns, they left the paved road and continued for a mile before coming to a dirt clearing.

Realizing that they were arriving, Alex took one last look at the internal radiation sensor and saw that it had crept further into the yellow range.

"104 from 16-40-5," the navigator announced.

"Go ahead, 16-40-5."

"We're arriving. Doors, please."

Now, Alex understood the numbers a little. The first in the series was the shelter number.

The bus moved to a ramp that slanted into the ground, and they descended fifty yards, then stopped at a large metal door that started opening slowly.

Chapter Twenty-Eight

THE NEW ARRIVALS PARKED IN AN AREA SIMILAR BUT LARGER than the one they'd departed from. Identical vehicles to the ones they saw when they were at Shelter 16 were in rows on multiple levels.

Six people in radiation-resistant suits, with air tanks on their backs, approached the bus and scanned it with handheld radiation detectors. After several minutes, the one in charge signaled that all was clear. He then boarded the bus as the others backed away. Removing his glove, he waved a scanner over the radiation sensor on the wall of the bus, nodded, and stepped back off.

A well-dressed man stepped aboard. He was tall with Asian features and a friendly expression. "Welcome to Shelter 104. I'm Tony Chambers, and I'm the Senate President.

I'm looking forward to getting to know each of you.

"First, the important news. Each of you had a dose of radiation during the trip that's within acceptable limits, and there should be no need for any type of medical care unless you experience problems. Still, we need each of you to report to Central Medical sometime within the next twenty-four hours for a quick check-up.

"Now, we received your personal files yesterday, so we should be able to get you processed quickly. We're assigning a guide to each family. Your guides are volunteers who will assist you in getting to know the facility and answer any questions. Spend at least a day or two with your guides. We selected your guides based on whether you have children ... because they also have kids about the same age. They'll be showing you around and introducing you to the people in your residential area, your work area, and taking the kids to meet their new classmates and teachers.

"Please exit the vehicle, and we'll lead you to a room for in-processing. Don't worry about your luggage. It was tagged when you left, and we'll deliver it to your new residences."

They filed off the bus in a single line, with everyone curious how their arrival would be received. They passed down several halls marked "Restricted" and arrived in a larger corridor. The paint scheme and decor matched what they'd been looking at for the last ten years.

They entered a large classroom and waited to hear their names called. About half the others in the room were announced. "Wilsons, Marie, and Alex. Please come up."

A friendly young woman greeted them as they approached the table. "Hi guys. So, we have Alex and Marie Wilson, and Kevin Torez. Is that correct?"

"Yes, that's correct," Alex responded.

"Great. Here are your door passes. I'm sure you know how they work." She handed each a black plastic card suspended from a lanyard. There was a large 104 on the card.

"Sure, no problem."

"Okay, there are guides assigned to your family who will help you get acclimated. But the Senate President wants to talk to you first."

Marie looked concerned. "Just us?"

"Yup, but I'm sure it isn't a problem." She waved and caught the attention of President Tony Chambers.

He strolled over, and they recognized him from the bus. "Alex, Marie, and Kevin, I'm Tony. Could you step over here with me for a minute?"

As they walked to the far side of the room, Alex asked, "Is there a problem?"

"No, not at all. We're trying to make the integration of the new arrivals as smooth as possible and had an idea. We have an opening on the Senate and were looking for someone to assign when your situation came up. I spoke to the leadership in 16, and they recommended Marie. They said that you had already served there, so you're familiar with the processes. I think someone coming in from the outside might have fresh ideas ... things that you have already tried that we might not have."

"I guess that makes sense," Marie agreed with a quick smile.

"I'll let you have a couple of days to think it over. Once you're settled, we'll talk about it again."

They all shook hands with the Senate President and before he walked away, he said, "I'll let your guides know that you're ready."

"Well, that's interesting," Marie said softly. "Maybe this place won't be as hostile towards us as we feared."

Alex was about to reply when they hear their names called again. The woman who had signed them in was waving them over to the door. She was standing by four people, an adult male and female, and two kids close to Kevin's age.

"Wilson family, these are the Baxters. They'll be your guides," she said with a cheerful smile. "For the next two days, you should do most things together. That will speed up your acclimation to 104." With a nod, she left.

"Hi, I'm Cindy, and this is my husband Carl, and these are Morgan and Ben."

Alex introduced his family and they all stepped into the

hall. As they walked, small talk started, and Marie and Alex immediately began to like the Baxters.

Alex noticed a sign indicating the location of the pool and smiled. He would have to let Sam and Lucy know that Mom and Dad now had a pool too.

"We'll show you where your home is, but first, we're supposed to take you to the gym," Ben advised.

Confused, Marie was about to ask why they were going there when she saw the sign indicating they'd already arrived. They could hear music from beyond the closed doors.

The doors opened and, once they were inside, were swarmed by people—several hundred residents had gathered in the gym, excited to greet the new arrivals.

Chapter Twenty-Nine

23 YEARS LATER

Training room two in Shelter 87 had been reconfigured for the evening's Senate meeting. The Senate gathered once every other week unless something unusual required an additional session. The half-hour meetings usually went twice as long as planned because there was always socializing on both sides of the meeting time.

As Lucy headed down the passageway that led to the training room, she thought about the upcoming meeting. The Senate President had instructed everyone to arrive early and plan for the meeting to go late. While most of the others attending the meeting were coming into this blind, Lucy wasn't. Her husband, Chief, and son, Tyler, worked on the XTeam; an XTeam existed in each of the shelters. While everyone had heard of them, very few knew what they actually did. Tonight, that would change.

Her husband had been born with the name Randolph. He had picked up the nickname Chief in grade school, and that was all anyone knew him as.

Passing training room one, she saw some fellow council members entering the next room and unconsciously increased her pace. She entered just behind them, walked to her usual seat, and set down her tablet and water bottle.

At one minute before 6:00 PM, Senate President Billings entered the room. He took a seat and announced briskly, "This is going to be a long meeting, so let's get started."

Everyone sat quietly, wondering about the cause for the special meeting.

"Well, my friends, it looks like the time has come. It's time to prepare to leave the shelter."

Conversations immediately commenced; questions and concerns erupted from almost all present.

Billings raised his voice to restore order. "Slow down. Let me explain the details. We were supposed to be down here for twenty years and have stretched it to thirty-two. We're down to a single year's worth of food, besides what we can grow, and it'll take about that long for us to get ready to leave."

"But, what about the radiation levels? Is it even *safe* to leave?" someone called out.

"The radiation levels are higher than we'd hoped for. We expected to be leaving here when the radiation was close to what it was when we first took shelter. It isn't. It is no longer deadly but still in the unhealthy range—the low end of unhealthy, but still possibly harmful. However, having no food is far *more* unhealthy.

"Also, you all know that there have been an increasing number of scheduled power outages for maintenance. The reactor is now eight years past its service life. It's having increasingly more problems, and we can't keep it running safely much longer—another couple of years at most."

"It sounds like we don't have much choice," Lucy said grimly.

"So, what happens? What do we need to do to get ready to leave?" someone asked solemnly.

"Well, first, I recommend that the paternity rotation stops. We can't be venturing into a strange, possibly dangerous environment with newborns and women who are pregnant. There will likely be many physical obstacles to overcome. And everyone needs to be at their physical best," President Billings explained, scanning the crowd.

"That might make sense, but it won't make people happy," a middle-aged man at the far end of the table declared.

Billings nodded in agreement. "Beyond that, there's a complete plan, prepared long before the comet, for when the time comes to leave. We just need to dust it off."

"Why will it take a full year to prepare?" Lucy asked. "What do we need to do?"

Billings smiled. "Perfect questions, Lucy. Everyone, you all probably know our two guests: Chief and Tyler Brown of XTeam. Today is the day everyone learns what XTeam does."

Standing, Chief smiled at his wife, excited to share the biggest secret in the shelter. He was a couple of years older than Lucy and stood a little over six feet tall with a slender build and dark black hair. "First, let me explain that when this shelter was built and stocked, a tremendous amount of storage space and equipment was dedicated for when the time comes for us to re-enter the world. That equipment needed to be preserved and maintained.

"XTeam is the group that maintains that equipment and regularly practices the skills needed to survive on the outside. Over the next year, we'll be training everyone here on many things ... including survival, how to drive an ORV, or off-road vehicle, firearms, first aid, and even how to use a chainsaw."

A younger woman sitting next to Chief asked, "What's a chainsaw?"

"That's my point. Skills that were common to those who entered this shelter have been completely lost to all but a few," Chief explained with a smile. "We'll be fixing that. There will be lots of training sessions and physical conditioning. We even have a simulator to get everyone able to drive and a firing range for those who want basic firearm competency. Now, someone asked how long it would take to get ready. The plan was for us to do that in six months. However, seven months from now will be the start of winter.

"More than half of our population was born in this shelter. They don't know how to manage snow and ice. They've never functioned in heavy winter clothing and certainly haven't driven in it. Therefore, we'll wait until spring to open the doors."

Someone whose name Chief didn't know asked, "So, once we open the doors, where are we going?"

President Billings answered. "When the US Government built the Anvil shelters, they decided that the Senate would make all decisions while in the shelters. Once we leave, everyone is free to do as they wish. I personally think that we'd all be better off if we stick together, but there's nothing to force that. I think we need to put together options so that people can choose what's best for them."

There were murmurs of agreement around the table, but Lucy glared at Chief, who gave her an agreeing nod in response.

"Some of you might remember this from a few years back, when we still had shelter-to-shelter video broadcasts," Billings continued. "There's a guy down in Florida who survived the evacuation of 16 and is now in 104. His name is David Cowan. He talked about the team of sleepers that's out there waiting to awaken and rebuild. He claims his father was a big part of that project and that he's familiar with how it's set up and about where they're located. He sent a recorded message to all the shelters years ago, inviting everyone to meet near there to rebuild and be close to those that awaken. I've sent a link to that video to each of your terminals so you can review it on your own.

"Now, before we let the XTeam members go, are there any more questions for them?"

The woman next to Chief asked another question. "Can

you tell us a little about the off-road vehicles? We've all seen things in old videos, but what are the ones we'll be using like?"

Glancing at his father, who gave him a nod, Tyler replied, "There are a variety of styles. I'm going to play a brief video that will give you an idea of what we have."

He clicked a button on the desk and the screen on the wall lit up, showing a series of vehicles. As the ORVs went through their paces on the screen, Tyler explained, "This is a promotional video that the manufacturer provided and is available in all the shelters. We've got five different sizes, ranging from motorcycles to buses.

"After thirty-three years, we expect most of the paved roads to be in poor condition. So, we need something that can manage *any* kind of condition. The ORVs all have high-ground clearance and can pass over most obstacles.

"Also, these vehicles were designed to be light and fast, but other than the bikes, they all have radiation shielding installed. We'll be leaving the shelters but will still get reasonably good protection while traveling."

As each was showcased on the screen, Tyler provided details. "There are a few two-wheel bikes that can deal with tight fits and steep hills. They can carry up to two people and move very fast. Notice the large bulbous tank on the back? All our ORVs are propane-powered and have a pressurized fuel tank.

"Next is a four-passenger. These, along with the bikes, are good for scouting ahead of the larger vehicles. Then we have the larger twelve-person, which is just a larger version of the four-person. The seats are all removable, so it can also haul equipment."

The screen displayed a massive bus-like vehicle. "Most of the people will be traveling in one of these last ones. Again, it can transport people or cargo, or a mix. There's seating for forty people and it's fully capable of going off-road and dealing with most obstacles."

When Tyler finished his presentation, Chief turned to the audience. "Any questions about the ORVs?"

Lucy spoke up. "Why are they propane-powered and not gasoline?"

"Gasoline has a relatively short storage life. The chemicals break down when exposed to oxygen and evaporates. We couldn't store it for anywhere near long enough for it to remain usable. Propane, on the other hand, can be stored. It is also easy to find. The Anvil project provided us with the locations of all the commercial propane storage facilities in the country. Not all of them will still be usable after all this time, but we think most will. If needed, smaller propane tanks can be found in many private residents. Those tanks are the same ones the two-wheel bikes use and can be modified to fit all the ORVs. Dealing with the vehicles, maintenance, the propane, and storage tanks will all be covered in greater detail in the training sessions everyone will be attending."

Chief glanced around. No one said anything so, after a moment, he asked if there were any more questions.

"Chief, you said something about weapon training. Is there a reason to think that there's anyone hostile out there?" another senate member asked with noticeable concern in her voice.

"In all honesty, we've got no idea what or who is out there. We expected that some people would manage to survive outside the shelters, but the radiation was more intense and long-lasting than expected. We don't know. But we'll be prepared to deal with whatever we encounter. Before we open the doors for everyone, we'll be taking a few scouting trips … just to get an idea of what to expect," Chief explained.

"What about the other shelters?" the same person asked. "Have any of them opened up already?"

Senate President Billings responded. "With the satellites no longer functional, we've had limited radio communications with other shelters. We do know that we aren't the first to have to leave because of food. Also, there were shelters in Oregon and Florida that had to evacuate years ago because their reactors failed. We seem to be running in the middle of the pack on food management. Some shelters opened last year, and there are several more that, the last we heard, should make it another year or two."

Lucy thought about the exciting news and was looking forward to the end of the meeting so she could share the information with Sam.

Chapter Thirty

SAM AND HIS TWENTY-THREE-YEAR-OLD SON OLIVER HEADED back to the home Sam had lived in for the past 33 years; it was also the only home Oliver had ever known. The young stocky man, with a round face and light blonde hair, was of medium height. He had an easy-going temper and was more likely to listen to a conversation than participate.

Tonight, Oliver's girlfriend, Marsha, had joined them and they'd just completed an hour in the driving simulator. They enjoyed the virtual reality technology and were impressed with how realistic the experience felt. The trio had a good time improving their driving skills and already looked forward to the next session.

Short and stocky Marsha was a fun-loving person who could also be very serious when needed. She and Oliver had been close since childhood and, in the last year, become much closer. Marsha had an older sister, but she had died during childbirth eleven years ago from a previously undiagnosed heart defect. Marsha's sister never identified the child's father, so Marsha, at fourteen years old, took the baby girl and raised her as her own.

Sam and little Jenny had become very close, and he enjoyed teaching the child about the world beyond the shelter walls. Oliver was pleased with how close Jenny had become with his dad. The two of them would sit and talk frequently, and Sam seemed to never tire of the girl's questions.

As they walked, they could hear muffled popping sounds coming from a shooting range in a distant tunnel. Tomorrow night, Sam and Oliver had a time slot on the range. They were going with Sam's best friend, Ray Tanner, and his family. Having enjoyed the previous session, they looked forward to more time on the range. So far, most of the training they'd gone through had been enjoyable and a welcome distraction to the boredom of shelter life.

The atmosphere in Shelter 87 had changed since the announcement they would be returning to the world in less than a year. Physical conditioning was critical, and everyone was trying to get into one of the two gymnasiums. There were sign-up lists that were days long. A whole new range of training classes was available. The videos were viewable in the theaters or at home. Tonight's feature was one they'd already seen—about North American weather patterns and considerations for survival. Sam had insisted that they watch it, having seen it a week earlier when it first became available.

Sam enjoyed all the training and often went to extra sessions when possible, if for no other reason than to spend time with his son.

"Dad, how much do you remember of the outside world?" Oliver asked.

Like all the shelter-born, Oliver was always asking about what the outside was like. This curiosity made the required training that had begun ten months ago even more interesting for them. These younger shelter inhabitants enjoyed the training videos that showed different aspects of life before the comet. Learning skills, like transferring propane from one tank to another and changing a tire, appealed to the younger generation. But other lessons weren't as appealing, such as how deep to dig a roadside grave.

"I remember riding in a car, kinda like the ORVs we're learning about, and wishing I was old enough to drive. I also remember our home, and my school, and playing sports. There were lots of kids in my school, and I'm surprised how few of their names I remember."

Marsha nodded. "I guess you're looking forward to getting out of here as much as anyone. To get back to the world you had to leave."

"I'm glad we'll be getting out, but I'm not looking forward to seeing what's out there. I doubt it'll be anything like what I remember." They walked a little further and he said, "I'm not sure what you guys have planned this evening, but do you mind stopping in for a bit? Theresa and I want to talk to you both."

Marsha and Oliver exchanged knowing glances. They were prepared for this and knew the conversation was coming.

"No problem, Dad. We didn't have anything interesting planned. Jenny is doing some training with a group of her friends, so we have time."

When they arrived, they were greeted with warm hugs from Sam's sister Lucy and her twenty-three-year-old daughter, Kara.

"Theresa is in the bedroom. We just got back from working out, and she wanted to get changed," Lucy explained.

They took up seats in the living room, and the others stood.

Theresa entered. "How was driving practice?"

"Fun, like always," Sam answered, and Marsha agreed.

"Aunt Lucy, you should've joined us. From what I hear, you need the extra practice. The last time you drove for real, you crashed," Oliver said, then winked.

The room broke into laughter, except for Kara, who stared

at her mother. She'd never heard of her mother's experience when heading to the shelters.

With a red face, Lucy shrugged and turned to her daughter. "It was a small accident on the way here."

"Small?" Sam chuckled. "You broke most of your ribs and could barely move. I thought I was going to have to leave you behind."

"It was just three or four cracked ribs. I don't really remember. And I could move just fine, but I do remember that the pain was horrible. And, by the way, I've got more driving experience than any of you, and I've already done a dozen hours in the simulator."

The friendly banter ended and Sam nodded at his sister for her to start.

"It is unfortunate the Tyler and Chief aren't here, but they're conducting classes tonight. So, as you know, most of us will be leaving the shelter in about a month. The Senate has come up with five options that will be available.

"The first two are East Coast, Gulf Coast. The idea is that there's more food likely to be available in the sea, so it would be smart to set up in those areas. Those plans are unrefined and will develop once people sign up for one or the other. The third option is West. We've all heard stories of the sleepers and seen the broadcasts by David Cowan. Some people will be headed in that general direction to, hopefully, meet up with them.

"The fourth approved plan is to remain here in the shelter. There will be minimal power, and those staying will need to go and find food, but they'll sleep in the safety of the shelter. The hydroponics area is still producing, though not like it was.

"There's another option, which is to head out on your own. There's plenty of vehicle capacity, and if you have a group that can fully utilize an ORV, you're free to do your own thing.

"You guys all know the story about how Sam and I ended

up separated from your grandparents when project Anvil launched. We've always promised each other that when we get out that we'd go looking for them. Theresa and Chief are in agreement, and when the doors open, we're heading for Shelter 104 in Florida."

Lucy stopped so the news could sink in.

Noticing the impassive looks on everyone's faces, Sam said, "It appears this isn't a surprise to any of you."

His niece, Kara, chuckled. "None. We've just been waiting for you to tell us."

Kara was attractive, tall and thin with long brunette hair. She had a reputation for having a smart mouth that got her into minor trouble. When she was 18 years old, she married a boy named Scott. The teens had grown up together in the shelter and were inseparable. The marriage had gone well for two years, and then Scott was involved in a fight while working in shelter security. The assailant had struck him repeatedly and caused severe head trauma, which he didn't survive. Two days later, after a brief trial, the jury decided to banish the offender from the shelter. He was only one of four people to be kicked out in the thirty years Shelter 87 had been occupied. That had been three years ago, and Kara still struggled with fits of anger, though they had become less frequent.

"We certainly would like it if you all came with us, but we can't make you," Lucy stated, gazing from face to face. "Of course, for Marsha, your parents are welcome to join us if they want."

Oliver asked, "Does that include Jenny?"

Before anyone could answer, Kara replied brusquely, "Really, Oliver? That was stupid. Would anyone expect her to leave her kid here?"

While Jenny wasn't truly Marsha's child, she was the only parent the child knew, and most people thought about them as mother and daughter.

Lucy shook her head at her daughter's typical blunt comment, but everyone else laughed, and Theresa smiled. "That was a kinda dumb question."

Chapter Thirty-One

CHIEF AND TYLER LOOKED AT EACH OTHER, BOTH WITH excited expressions on their faces. They sat on a stack of pallets as they laced up thick-soled black boots. They'd already zipped up the heavy tan one-piece jumpsuits, which were designed with materials to decrease radiation exposure and had built-in pads for the knee and elbows.

The clothing and shielding in the ORV should protect them from most of the radiation. However, they also had multiple small radiation meters with them. They had one on the inside of their jumpsuits and another hanging on the outside. They attached one to the inside wall of the ORV and another to the outside. Later, when they returned from the first trip out in thirty-three years, there would be a clear picture of their exposure and how much the protective clothing and vehicle shielding had helped.

They headed to the staging area.

"Dad, these clothes smell terrible and are really stiff."

"I know. They're both brand new and over thirty years old at the same time—they've been sitting in airtight plastic bags waiting for us to be ready to go outside."

As they approached the staging area, they saw the four

quad-seat ORVs that were prepared for this trip and the six other explorers that would be venturing out with them. Only two of the vehicles would head out today and the other two would be here with crews ready if the explorers ran into problems and needed assistance. Each of the ORVs had its identification in large numbers on the sides and on the fenders. These were marked 87-4 for the shelter number and the number of seats. There was another number indicating which quad-seat vehicle it was. These were marked 1-4.

Each ORV would have two highly trained XTeam members. Four others had completed the training and volunteered to be the first to explore what remained of their world. Tyler and Chief were paired up with Tasha and Gary.

The teams would head in different directions. The goal was to accomplish multiple tasks and splitting up would give them a better assessment of the area.

"How are things looking?" Chief called out to the crew that was outfitting the ORVs.

"Looks good, Chief. Everything you wanted is loaded," a young Asian female responded.

Tyler peered into the cargo area and saw the tools, ration packs, water bottles, cameras, med-kit, and M4 assault rifles.

The explorers were handed a tactical vest with pouches containing a two-way radio, a semi-automatic pistol, a knife, a water bottle.

"I'm driving first," Chief informed his crew.

None of them was surprised or concerned. They knew Chief's personality and knew that he would make sure they all got some experience behind the wheel. They boarded the two vehicles, and the drivers typed a five-digit code on a keypad to start the engines.

When Chief had first told Lucy about the scouting trip and that he'd chosen Tyler to be on his team, she'd not been happy. Having her husband heading into the unknown was frightening enough, but having her son on the same team meant that if one of them faced danger, they *both* would.

Chief had explained that the risk of danger was low and that the drones, flying for the last few days, had not seen anything of concern. Also, it meant a lot to him to share Tyler's first experience out of the shelter and be able to undertake that adventure with him. Lucy still didn't like it but would never ask him to miss out on this opportunity with his son.

The driver of the second ORV nodded to Chief and they started down the access tunnel.

"87 from 4-1," Tyler said into the radio.

"Go ahead 4-1."

"Doors, please. Recon teams departing and headed for overlook."

"Doors opening. Be safe."

Tyler exchanged glances with Chief, knowing that a concerned mother and wife was sitting in Operations, listening to every word that came over the radios.

As 87-4-1 emerged from deep below the Michigan landscape, three of the team members had their first view of the open sky and were speechless at the vastness of the open air.

Fighting the wonderment, Tyler flipped switches on the console in front of him, and the two computer screens came to life as he contacted the two drones flying overhead. One would stay with each team, circling and providing pictures of what was ahead and assisting with navigation. After thirty-plus years, the last of the GPS satellites had long ago stopped functioning. To make up for the technological loss, a team sat in operations assigned to each recon team. They had maps of the area and could interface between the drones and ORVs to send navigational data directly to the onboard computers.

The four-foot diameter drones only had enough power for about three hours, so there was a second drone, mounted to one of two charging stations on the roof of each ORV.

The Anvil

Throughout the day, a nearly depleted aerial vehicle would be replaced by the one that had been charging on the roof.

The teams headed out together and only traveled a few miles before stopping at their first destination; it was an area of high ground on the northwest side of the city of Grand Rapids. From here, they had an impressive view of the city and surrounding area.

Before exiting the vehicles, Chief confirmed that the external radiation levels were as expected. When they stepped from the ORVs, the team member who sat behind the driver was Tasha. She took an assault rifle and the person seated behind the front passenger, Gary, grabbed a camera. They had decided that whoever was behind the driver was always responsible for security.

The two recon teams gathered at the side of the road, stunned by the view. It was an overcast day, but they could see for miles. The entire city and surrounding area were visible. A steady early spring breeze made it rather cold for people who had never experienced a temperature other than the constant 72 degrees in the shelter.

"I'd no idea I could see that far," someone murmured, awed.

"This is amazing."

"This air is so cold. It feels strange to breathe," Gary said.

Chief glanced at the other recon team's senior member and they exchanged smiles as they listened to their teammates experience the outdoors for the first time. He was about to instruct everyone to head back to the vehicle when he realized they'd all wandered off to investigate the surroundings. One had examined tones and another was breaking a dead branch into pieces, studying it as it snapped. Tyler had scrambled up an incline and was stroking the surface of a large tree.

It became evident to him that leaving the shelter wouldn't be as easy as simply heading out. This was an entirely alien world to more than half of their people. As he thought this, he heard a yell and saw Tyler fall, striking the ground hard.

The other team's members hurried in his direction, and another called out, stumbling. The leader of the other recon team figured out the problem first and shouted, "Freeze! Stop where you are and don't move!"

Everyone reluctantly obeyed. The second person to fall was quickly back on her feet and brushing herself off.

"Chief, go get your son and bring him back. Everyone else, *slowly* walk over here."

Chief assisted Tyler to his feet and saw a large laceration on his forehead. "You okay?"

"Yeah, my head hurts but nothing else. I think I hit it on a rock."

"You sliced it pretty good; let's get it cleaned up."

Taking the young man's arm, Chief led him back to the vehicle, where someone had already pulled out a medical pack. They looked at the open head wound and knew it would need sutures.

Shaking his head, his dad asked, "What happened? Why did you fall?"

"I'd been looking at the trees and starting back down the hill ... and my feet just got away from me and got tangled up."

Chief's peer had arrived and heard Tyler's explanation. He looked at the young woman next to him. "So, why did *you* fall?"

"I saw Tyler go down and the blood on his head, so I hurried over to see if he was okay . . . but stepped on a large stick, which rolled under my foot and took me down."

Chief's expression was one of concern. "This is a problem. Two-thirds of our people have never experienced anything other than the flat floors of the shelter. They don't even know how to walk out here."

Chapter Thirty-Two

GARY EXAMINED TYLER'S HEAD. "CHIEF, I HAVE THE BLEEDING controlled, but he needs a few stitches, or I can staple it now."

Tyler was quick to respond. "It can wait until this evening. We don't need to go back early, and I don't want it stapled out here."

"Sorry, Tyler," his dad frowned. "Staples, or we go back. You know we shouldn't leave it open all day."

Tyler appeared irritated. "Fine, staple it." As Gary got his equipment together, Tyler asked, "Are you sure you know how to do this?"

"I was in the same training class as you."

Tyler wasn't comforted but didn't complain any further. When the wound was cleaned, closed, and bandaged, Chief eyed Tyler critically. "Are you sure you're up for continuing? I don't want you out here if you aren't at your best."

"Dad, I'm fine. Not dizzy or anything. It's just a little cut."

Chief debated for a few seconds and agreed. "Okay, let's get moving. We've got several tasks to get done today."

The two ORVs departed and soon split up, with Chief heading south and the other team to the east.

When emerging from the shelters, the survivors would

need large amounts of propane to run their vehicles; as such, Anvil had been prepared with a list of all propane dealers in the country. There had been six in the Grand Rapids area, and the teams would each visit two. They needed to get an idea of what still existed and what they would need to do to access it.

Chief drove south through the city on an elevated highway. The road condition was poor but passable. There were only a few skeletons of vehicles that they needed to work their way around.

They took an exit ramp and traveled for several miles before arriving at their destination. Most of the main building had collapsed, but the warehouse area was largely intact and contained hundreds of tanks in various conditions.

Outside, dozens of larger horizontal propane tanks sat inside a fenced area. Some looked intact, others had ruptured. In the center was a single mammoth tank; it was horizontal, perched on concrete supports, and more than double the size of a semi-trailer. The decades-old company name, while faded, was still legible on the tank.

"87 from 4-1," Tyler said.

"Go ahead 4-1."

"Arriving first objective."

"Understood. Drone view shows all is clear. And, also, your mom wants to know how your head is."

Tyler felt his face flush as he realized that his mother had seen his fall on the drone camera. "It's fine. Nothing to be concerned about." He glanced at his father, who wasn't trying to hide his smirk.

Stopping near the building, Chief gave instructions to the team. "Tyler, investigate the smaller stuff in the building. Gary, check the outside tanks, then take photos of everything. Tasha, position yourself so you have a good view of the road. Everyone be careful. No more falls."

Departing with her assault rifle, Tasha headed for a small

collapsed structure. She positioned herself behind it, where she could see both her team and the road.

After radioing to Chief that she was in position, he responded, "Good, and remember, if something happens, don't shoot in the direction of the tanks."

She shook her head. Tasha didn't know Chief all that well, but she sure hoped he didn't think she was dumb enough to do that.

Tyler had to hoist himself onto the loading dock to get into the warehouse. The old metal stairs had rusted away so much that they wouldn't support his weight. When he got inside, he saw a large warehouse space that was about two-thirds empty, and the rest had neat rows of vertical pressurized tanks. He carefully inspected many of the tanks and found that most were in acceptable condition.

The remains of the building provided enough protection that the weather didn't destroy them.

He located a pressure regulator on a utility cart, cleaned years of accumulated dust from it, attached it to a tank, and opened the tank valve. The regulator showed that the tank was still full. He repeated this on several other tanks, finding that most were usable. As he was finishing, Gary entered with the camera and began recording the facility's contents, focusing on tanks that had rusted out.

"How are the outside tanks?" Tyler asked.

"Some have rusted out enough that the internal pressure split them open. Others look good. The ones that concern me are the heavily rusted ones that haven't burst yet. They could rupture if anyone bumps them. If someone were close, they could be seriously injured. And if there's an ignition source, when that happens, the whole place could blow. How about in here?"

"Similar, but most are okay. I checked some of them, and most seem to have held their pressure."

As Gary continued to take pictures, something caught

Tyler's attention. Where the empty area of the warehouse met the first row of propane tanks, there were numerous circles on the floor; the closer ones were clearest and the further less distinct. He dragged his foot across the closest circle, disrupting the dirt that surrounded the circle. Everything clicked into place. The circles were clean spots on a floor without the years of dirt and dust build-up. Taking the closest tank, he wrestled it a couple of feet to the side, and the spot where it had been was a clean perfect circle, identical to the others.

"Gary, need the camera here."

"What did you find?"

Tyler pointed out what he'd seen and done. "Over a long time, these tanks have slowly been disappearing. Looking at the spot I made, and the one next to it … the last to go wasn't too long ago."

As Gary took more photos, Tyler left in search of his team leader and found Chief finishing up his assessment of the mammoth tank.

"Hey, Dad. I found proof that there are survivors in the area."

"What did you find?"

Tyler reported his findings regarding the missing tanks.

Taking the microphone attached to the radio in his vest, Chief said, "87 from 4-1."

"Go ahead 4-1."

"We've got strong evidence that there are survivors in the area."

"Good news. Let us know as soon as you finish there. Your drone shows smoke near you. It could be related to your finding. We're going to have you check it out."

Chief and Tyler smiled at each other, relishing the idea of meeting up with survivors.

"We should be on the way in less than ten minutes. Send the location to the ORV."

"Already done."

"So, what else did you find inside?" Chief asked.

"Things are good inside. At least half of the remaining tanks are still pressurized and usable. How's the big one?"

"Looks good. The paint is much thicker, so the rust isn't as bad. Most of the refilling hoses have rotted, and I wouldn't trust the rest. The pumps and valves are in rough shape, but we expected that and have our own. If the other sites around the country are like this, we're in good shape for fuel."

When they finished the assessment of the site, Chief called Tasha back to the vehicle.

Circling around to the other side of the structure she had been using for concealment, Tasha stopped mid-step with wide eyes. There were human footprints in the sand—more proof of survivors.

Chapter Thirty-Three

Cindy and Adam played in the cold water of the stream. They laughed and ran, not caring that they were wet. The spring weather was overcast and not very warm yet, but the snow was gone and today was the one day a week where they were allowed outside for a few hours.

This was a great time to be a kid. They were the first generation in decades to get to play outside at all. Up until a few years ago, no one under twenty years old went outside. Even then, the only ones that did were the ones confirmed to be sterile. They couldn't risk allowing the few that could bear children to absorb any more radiation than could be avoided.

Next year, Adam and Cindy would be in their teens, and their fertility would be tested. This would determine their direction for life. Either you couldn't have kids and then became a scavenger and got to see the outside world for short periods, or you could have children but never went outside. Because of this, the ones that could reproduce did so continuously and most of the children were raised by the ones that could never have their own. This created a situation where the fertile were revered for their sacrifice to maintain the population. On the flip side, the sterile were adored for their constant

The Anvil

risk of life to go and seek the resources the community needed in the radioactive wasteland.

That had all started to change a few years ago when, on three occasions in two months, scavenger crews had returned not just with their typical hauls but with fresh game animals. Usually, the community only had fresh meat once a year. But now, the animals were slowly returning. When that had happened, the community decided to increase exposure to the outside gradually.

Glancing around, Cindy saw five other children playing catch with a ball and running across the grass of the old park. It looked like they were having fun, but she and Adam preferred the water; the other kids would have to get wet when they bathed before returning underground, into the relative safety of the old drainage system. Three adults were also enjoying being outside and were laughing and talking. A fire had been started near the remains of the old playground. It would allow the wet kids to warm up after bathing in the stream.

Suddenly, two distant whistle blasts sounded. That wasn't right; they should have much more time. Then, there were three much closer whistle blasts.

Looking back at Adam, Cindy saw the fear on his face, and they both started sprinting towards the parking lot. They all knew what three whistle blasts meant. Ahead they could see the others all converging on the center of the lot and jumping one at a time without hesitation, feet first, into the open manhole.

They practiced this regularly, but this was the first time the alert had sounded for real.

She approached the hole as the person in front of her disappeared. Fighting her natural instinct, she jumped blindly. Ten pairs of hands and arms slowed her fall as she dropped the twelve feet. They weren't trying to catch her, just slow her descent.

As soon as her feet splashed down in the three inches of standing water, she spun into position, arms outstretched to help the next person coming down. It was Adam, and he landed cleanly.

"That's twelve. Everyone accounted for," a voice announced.

Seconds later, they heard a grinding sound as the heavy manhole cover moved back into place, eliminating almost all the light.

The goal was always to have everyone back underground within twenty seconds of the whistle. Their best time in all the practices was sixteen, and today they'd done it in fourteen.

"Hey, Josh. Should we clear out?" a woman asked worriedly.

"Yeah, get the younger kids back to the community. I'll keep Cindy, Adam, and Margy here with me."

Chapter Thirty-Four

When everyone else had headed out, Josh spoke, "Margy, take Adam to the drain on the far side of the parking lot. We'll take the other and be quiet."

The parking lot had large drain openings built into the curb. These openings made it possible for those in the sewers to look out across the lot and into the park without being seen.

As they quickly moved the twenty yards to their position, Cindy whispered, "Thanks for letting us stay."

"You're coming of age. You need to start having more experiences."

They climbed into position and peered across the lot, curious as to what had caused one of the two lookouts to blow the whistle.

Less than a minute later, they could hear something approaching, and then a strange vehicle moved into view. It had four large knobby tires and sat high off the ground. There were four doors and the whole thing, except for the windows, looked to be encased in strange gray material. But that wasn't the strangest thing. The body was elongated and a large sphere took up the rear quarter. The sphere looked to be seven feet in diameter. On the front fender was a series of numbers.

Gently elbowing Josh, Cindy gave him a quizzical look when he turned to her.

"No idea. I've never seen or heard of anything like that," he whispered, awed.

The vehicle entered the parking lot and made a slow circle before coming to a stop with the passenger side facing the drain.

Reaching to his back, Josh removed the 9mm handgun. He was comfortable with the weapon but hoped he wouldn't need to use it. The doors opened and a woman exited and moved to the front of the vehicle. She was holding an assault rifle and began studying the surroundings. From the rear, a male exited, holding a device of some kind. After a brief conversation with the driver, he returned the device and took a rifle from the vehicle. They took up positions on either side.

The front passenger side door was open and the occupant studied something on a screen mounted to the dashboard. They could see that there was a bandage on his head. After a few seconds, the passenger shrugged, and he and the driver got out.

The driver was older than the other three, with graying hair and a complexion that had lost its youthfulness. That was strange. Josh had no idea how old the man was, but he was definitely older than his underground community members lived to be. All four were dressed identically, which was also strange to see. Even the occasional groups of thieves and small gangs didn't look like this; these people were something different.

The last two to emerge weren't carrying rifles but had holstered pistols. They surveyed the area and together started walking towards the fire.

Cindy whispered, "They saw the smoke."

Josh nodded.

Soon, the other two joined them at the fire and a conversation ensued. They were talking about the fire; all four were regarding it closely, especially the younger three.

"What's so special about the fire?" Cindy asked, baffled.

"I don't know. They're acting like they've never seen a fire before."

"Not, the older one," Cindy noted, "He's telling the others about it. But the other three seem fascinated. Now would be a good time to move in on them. They aren't paying attention to anything else."

"That's true, but we aren't going to. They're too heavily armed to confront, and I don't think they're a threat."

The younger girl was confused. "How do you know they aren't a danger?"

"I don't know, but I just don't think they're a problem. And we aren't going to do anything to change that," Josh declared.

The older man pointed to the blue bucket on the ground near the fire. Cindy had filled it from the stream when they'd first arrived.

The man who'd been seated in the back hung the rifle over his shoulder and picked it up. He dumped its content on the fire, extinguishing it. They then walked to the stream and engaged in another conversation. The younger three stuck their hands in the cold water and laughed as they splashed around.

There was something strange about these people, Josh thought again.

Soon they headed back toward their vehicle, stopping briefly as the woman bent down and picked up the ball that the kids had been playing with, but the ball held minimal interest for the four newcomers—nothing like the fire and the stream had.

They returned to the lot and seemed to be a little more focused than they'd been when in the park.

The older one called out, "Please come out. We won't hurt you. We just want to talk."

Cindy looked at her elder, and he shook his head.

"We know you're close. We just want to talk," he said again.

Receiving no response, the leader talked to one of his people, who went to the vehicle and retrieved an indistinguishable item.

They took the bucket and placed it upside down and put the ball and the unknown item on top. Climbing into their vehicle with the older man in the passenger seat this time, they headed out.

They waited a couple more minutes and then Josh said, "Tell Margy to keep watch. You and I are going out."

Cindy relayed the message and met her elder back at the manhole cover. The two fought to quietly move the 120-pound cast-iron disk out of their way. Since they'd not heard any alarms from Margy and Adam, they lifted themselves slowly from the storm drain and onto the parking lot.

Something flying high in the air caught Josh's attention.

This day keeps getting stranger and stranger, he thought. This was only the third time in his life that he'd seen a bird. If he hadn't been so focused on what was on the bucket and the fear of the outsiders returning, he would've taken a second look and pointed it out to Cindy. She'd never had the chance to see a bird and certainly not a drone before.

"Remember, if we have to run, there's no one to catch you in the hole. So, go in slow," Josh advised.

Nodding, Cindy visualized dropping blindly into the hole and having no one there to catch her.

They approached the bucket cautiously while looking and listening for threats. As they got close, Josh knew what the device was and found it interesting that they had left it.

"Is that a radio?" Cindy asked, curious.

"Yes, it is." Josh picked it up. He'd never used one but

knew that the community had used them until their last generator had died years ago.

"Hello."

Josh almost dropped the radio as the voice spoke to him.

"We don't mean you any harm. We just want to talk to you."

"They didn't say anything until you picked the radio up. They're watching us," Cindy observed anxiously.

They looked in all directions, trying to spot someone.

"We aren't there. We're parked up the street at an old bowling alley," the voice said.

Thoroughly flustered, Josh pressed the button on the side of the radio. "But you're watching us."

"Yes. We don't mean you any harm; we just want to talk. Maybe even trade."

"How are you watching us?"

"To prove that we mean you no harm, I'll show you. Look in the sky."

They looked up and, for a split second, Josh thought he was seeing the bird again. Then he realized it was something else. It was directly over them and descending quickly. When it was twenty feet away, it stopped its descent and flew a slow circle around them. They could hear the whine of the electric motors. Then, without warning, it accelerated and increased altitude and headed in the bowling alley's direction.

"We trusted you by showing you that. Meet with us and talk."

"Who are you?"

"We'll discuss that when we meet. Hopefully, we'll be friends."

Josh thought before answering. "There's a large parking lot where they use to sell cars right near where you are. Someone will meet you there in an hour."

Chapter Thirty-Five

"So, what are we going to do for an hour?" Gary asked.

"The second propane site isn't too far. Let's do a quick check of it," Tyler suggested.

Chief nodded. "That sounds good. However, the drone's batteries are getting low. I'm going to swap it out while you figure out which way we need to go."

He started entering commands into the onboard system, and the replacement on the roof powered up. After reviewing a diagnostic panel, he saw that everything was green and initiated the swap. The magnets that held the fully charged vehicle to the ORV's roof released and the aircraft lifted into the sky. Once it was clear, the new drone signaled the original, which then hovered above the vehicle. A small laser on the drone's underside activated and contacted a receiver on the charging station. Following the beam, the drone lowered precisely onto the charging station. As soon as the connection to the charging station was complete, the six electric magnets engaged, and the drone was secure and recharging.

"Drone secure. Let's go," Chief ordered.

Tyler started driving, getting more and more comfortable

with operating the ORV. As he drove, the drone flew ahead and before they arrived, they knew the situation was vastly different.

Upon arrival, they were amazed at the utter destruction. The evidence of a massive explosion was undeniable. The large central tank looked to be the source of the blast, and it had taken everything else with it when it blew.

They parked and Tyler, Chief, and Tasha examined the site. Gary had turned the camera over to Tasha so he could take his turn at security.

Working their way through the debris scattered over a hundred yards in all directions, the trio made it to the remains of the large tank. It was no longer on its concrete supports and rested at a strange angle. Tasha took photos of several large rusted blades that looked like they belonged to a power saw. Charred skeletal remains of several adults were also found.

Tasha spoke first. "This didn't happen recently. Several years, at least."

Chief nodded. "Probably even longer."

"I think they were trying to get to the propane in the tank and were cutting something when it blew," Tyler proposed.

"Good possibility," Chief agreed.

They took more photos and departed since there was nothing to be gained staying.

"87 from 4-1," Chief said.

"Go ahead 4-1."

"We're clear of objective two. This site was obliterated by a gas explosion years ago. We're going to be getting in place for our meeting."

"Understood. Keep us advised as to how that goes. Do you want 4-3 to head your way, in case they're needed?"

Chief knew the answer but wanted his son's perspective, and glanced at Tyler with a questioning look.

Tyler knew his father and understood this was a test.

There was no right or wrong answer, but his dad wanted to know his reaction. "No. They seemed frightened but not dangerous. We'll be extra careful."

Chief nodded. He also knew that the crew of 4-3 was looking for an opportunity to depart the shelter, but not today; tomorrow the two teams that had gone out today would be sitting on standby while the crews sitting idly today would get the fun of exploring.

"87 from 4-1, we're all set. We'll let you know if we need assistance."

They arrived back at the decrepit auto dealer and circled the property several times before picking the place to set up for the meeting. The team choose a clear space on the edge of the property; there was a wooded area on one side and the old automotive repair center in the back. The building looked stable and should be able to hold a person's weight.

In the center of the parking lot were several rows of neatly lined up, rusted vehicles. Chief assumed that these corroded hulks were new on the day of the comet and had never been used.

After a brief discussion, they decided that Tasha would take the roof and Gary the tree line. Both would have binoculars and their M4 assault rifles; Tasha also took a laptop computer with drone access.

After helping her get to the roof, Chief and Tyler sat back in the ORV and waited.

Chapter Thirty-Six

Tyler was finishing an energy bar when Tasha's voice came over the radio, "Two men approaching. They appeared suddenly in the middle of the lot. Among all the cars."

Chief nodded and turned to his son. "There must be a manhole there."

"Two more just appeared. Four in all," Tasha advised. "The drone shows six more out by the street. They aren't approaching, just waiting."

"Keep the info coming. Let us know of anything that changes," Chief radioed back.

"I can't see anything from my location," Gary advised.

"The second pair to appear in the parking lot are holding back. One has a rifle. He isn't pointing it in your direction. The group on the street has rifles or shotguns. I can't tell for sure from the drone angle."

"What about the ones approaching? Any weapons?" Chief asked.

"Nothing visible. One of them is the guy you talked to on the radio. The girl isn't there. What do we do?" Tasha asked.

"Continue to watch and advise. They're just taking

precautions. Same as we did. Stay alert but don't do anything unless I say so or they start shooting."

Chief and Tyler exited the ORV and moved to the front to greet their guests. They were each wearing a Bluetooth headset that connected to their radios. Usually, too much trouble to bother with, now they could hear updates from their spotters, and Gary and Tasha could monitor what was said. They recognized the man who had picked up the radio. Even though they had only seen him on footage from the drone, they were sure it was him.

Keeping their hands open, Chief and Tyler faced the approaching men. Concerned, Chief felt little comfort from the 9mm in his tactical vest. The last thing he wanted to have to do was reach for it. Trying to look and sound friendly, he said, "Thank you for meeting us. We don't mean you any harm. My name is Chief and this is Tyler."

"I'm Steven and this is Josh. He's the one you spoke to on your radio. I'm the leader of our people. We don't want any trouble."

Chief nodded. "Good, neither do we. We'd like to talk. Exchange information. Maybe find a way to help each other."

"Josh said there were four of you. Where are the other two?"

"You weren't sure if you could trust us, so you made plans in case there's a problem—the six on the street and the others in the parking lot. We also weren't sure if there might be a problem. So, we took precautions too."

Steven decided this was reasonable, so he asked the main question. "Who are you, and where do you come from? Your clothes match and look new. Your vehicle also looks new."

Chief had already decided to be honest if this question was asked. "The US government knew the comet was coming. There was nothing they could do, so they built as many underground shelters as possible. Just before the comet arrived, they rushed people into the shelters and they were sealed in. No one in or out until the radiation levels were safe again.

"The plan was for us to be down there for twenty years, but the radiation was much more long-lasting than expected. We're just venturing out for the first time. Today is our first trip out to survey the area. My family was sent to the shelter when I was nineteen years old, and now I'm fifty-two. Tyler here and the other two with me were born in the shelter and saw the sky today for the first time."

Steven had appeared amazed as Chief told the story. "So, how many people are in these shelters?"

"Some hold about a thousand people and the larger ones, a little over two thousand."

"How many shelters are there?"

"Close to two hundred, scattered all over the country."

"You guys are now coming out of the shelter. Does that mean it's safe? The radiation is gone?" Josh asked.

"We had enough supplies for twenty-five years. We stretched it to almost thirty-three. The radiation is better but still unhealthy. It would be great to spend another ten years in the shelters, but we have to come out. We're almost out of food."

"Where is this shelter?" Steven inquired.

"Are you planning to tell me where underground your people are?" Chief smiled.

Steven shook his head and smiled in return. "No. I guess that was a dumb question."

Chief nodded. "It's a short drive but a very long walk. What is your story? How did you survive?"

"Our relatives were members of a large church in the area. When the news of the radiation came out, there was an emergency church meeting. They decided to try to save everyone aged thirty and under. They were immediately sent into the storm drains. Some of the tunnels run pretty deep.

"Those over thirty years old spent their final days moving

many tons of supplies into the storm system. There were several large food distributors in the area, and supplies were coming down faster than we could get them put away. Food, bedding, educational material, medical gear, and much more came. We had enough food to last many years. Fortunately, the comet came after the spring rains had ended. We had time to prepare for the following year when, some days, the storm drains filled with water.

"We set up a community, and it's awful down there but wonderful too. It's as much a family as anything. Only in the last few months did we start coming up for anything other than foraging."

Tyler and Chief were fascinated, listening to how these people had survived.

"Your story is as interesting as ours," Tyler stated. "All those people sacrificing themselves to make sure the younger generation had a chance is amazing."

"It certainly is. I would like to hear more." Chief waved the men to the ORV and removed an extra radiation detector from the cargo compartment. "From what we're seeing, if you spend less than half your time on the surface, you should be okay." He handed the device to Steven. "With that, you can monitor current radiation levels and accumulated exposure over a given period."

"We can *keep* this?" Steven asked, surprised.

"We've got another one. Consider it a gift from new friends."

He beamed. "We appreciate that very much."

"I've got a question if you don't mind," Tyler said.

"Anything."

"You guys were concerned about us, almost frightened to meet us. Are there other groups in the area that have caused you problems?"

"We know there are a few other groups of survivors in the area, but we almost never cross paths. We used to have CB radios and sometimes would hear from others, but we've been without a generator for several years.

"Then, a couple of months ago, one of our scavenger teams didn't return. We sent another out looking for them and found their bodies. They'd been shot. A few weeks ago, another of our teams was shot at but managed to get away uninjured. So, yes, we're a bit concerned about outsiders," Steven explained with a furrowed brow.

The two groups continued to share information for another half hour and, as things winded down, Steven asked, "Do you mind if we ask a favor?"

"No, go ahead," Chief smiled.

"When this all started, we had a couple of gas-powered generators. They made things bearable, but after a couple of years, we couldn't get gasoline that hadn't gone stale, and the generators became useless. We spent several years without electricity. We still had propane heaters, but they produced carbon monoxide, and so they're dangerous in the tunnels. Then, one of our elders began having stomach problems and was diagnosed with cancer. There was nothing we could do for him. The day after his fate was determined, he left. He just disappeared into the night. This happened only at about year nine, when the radiation was still extreme.

"Four days later, he returned, almost dead from radiation, but was pulling a wagon with a propane-powered generator, still in the original packaging. He told us where he got it and said there were several more on their loading dock. He knew he was dying and wanted his last act to benefit the community. He died the following day. That generator lasted us twelve years. The last few were rough, but we still were able to get power out of it.

"Now that the radiation has improved, we've been discussing trying to make a run to get another. However, it's a four-day round trip on foot. With your vehicle, you could do it in less than an hour."

Chapter Thirty-Seven

The large steel doors slid open and Tasha drove ORV 87-4-1 back inside. Everyone felt a little relief to be back home. But they also felt good about what they could do for the community living in the old sewer systems. They'd been able to get them two propane generators and several small electrical appliances. They could also now monitor radiation levels and begin returning to the surface. Anyone from 87 that remained in the area would already have good friends.

Members of the medical team were waiting to meet the crew to collect the radiation detectors and vehicles to assess their exposure. The four explorers would be headed to Training Room 6 for debriefing, but there was one thing they needed to do first.

Lucy stood waiting. It was clear that she was relieved to see them back and in one piece. "Tyler, let me see your head."

"Mom, it's fine. After debriefing, I'll go to medical, and they can check it. But we aren't taking the bandage off here."

Lucy looked at her husband, who replied, "It'll be fine until after the debriefing."

Agreeing reluctantly, Lucy gave them each a hug. "I'm glad you're both okay."

Tyler hugged her back. "Mom, it was amazing. It's a whole different world up there."

Noticing the other members of the survey team, Lucy turned to Gary. "What was your opinion of the outside world? It was a whole new experience for you too."

Shaking his head, he answered in a disappointed voice, "I didn't like it at all. It was cold, and there was the wind that made it even colder. All there was is broken and wrecked stuff everywhere. Even walking was dangerous. I would just as soon never go out there again."

Walking around on the uneven surfaces had made him feel like a stumbling child. He hadn't been sure before but, now, he was determined to be one of those who stayed behind when most others left the shelter.

Lucy gave her husband a curious glance.

"The inside has provided us protection from everything: temperature changes, weather, dirt. It even made walking overly safe. Leaving the shelters will be a big adjustment for everyone," Chief explained. He looked at the other team members. "Tasha, did you feel the same way?"

"Well, I understand all of what Gary is saying and felt the same way at times. But I remember that first view overlooking the city. I realized how much more is out there than within the walls of the shelter, and I want to go see it all. Even if it might not be easy. We didn't observe any, but we know animals are still out there, and I want to see them. We met some people, and I want to meet more. I can't wait to get out there again!"

They continued to discuss their experiences while waiting for the other survey team to return, due in just a few minutes. After that, they had the first of two debriefings. The first was public and would be broadcast on video screens throughout the shelter to over a thousand people who were desperate to hear what the first look of the outside was like. There would even be an opportunity for shelter inhabitants to ask questions of the survey teams. The second would be with the leadership console and would be more detailed, and involve setting a strategy for tomorrow's additional exploration.

Chief only hoped that during the Q&A that Gary didn't share too much of his reservations.

Chapter Thirty-Eight

TWO MONTHS LATER

LUCY AND SAM AWOKE EARLY AND MET UP AS PLANNED. They strolled through the corridors and reminisced about their lives in 87. They remembered the wild twenty hours they'd spent together when they were little more than kids traveling here over thirty-three years ago.

At the time, they assumed they would be here for a few months at most. Now, here they were, decades later. In the morning, they would be leaving the shelter and returning to the world.

"This place seems so quiet. It's weird seeing it so empty," Sam stated, gazing around.

"I know. Almost a thousand have already left. I don't know how many plan to remain here permanently," Lucy replied.

They continued walking and entered Café B. Inside, most of their group was sitting and chatting. Chief and Oliver's girlfriend, Marsha, were in the kitchen area, opening dehydrated food packages and making breakfast. There were a few fresh vegetables from the week's allotment from hydroponics already on the table.

"So, did you have a nice walk?" Kara asked.

"Yeah, we did. It's strange, we've wanted out of here for so long, and now all I think is how much I'll miss this place," Lucy said with a rueful smile.

"We'll all be missing it as we suck up the toxic radiation outside," Kara said bluntly.

They all ignored the comment.

"I just want to ride in an ORV and see the outside, and I want to see rain and animals," eleven-year-old Jenny said excitedly.

"I remember playing in the rain as a kid. It was lots of fun," Theresa told the young girl.

Marsha set a container of eggs with bacon and sausage biscuits and gravy on the table, and everyone started in, sharing their last meal in the shelter.

After only a year, other than what they could grow, all the fresh food in the shelter was gone. Then, for a long time, there'd been a wide variety of canned and frozen options, but eventually, that was all consumed. Now all they had was dehydrated food, guaranteed to last on a shelf for up to thirty years. They just had to add water and it returned to a state similar to what it had originally been. The taste was only okay, and the variety was limited, but they'd all gotten used to it. Even though the packages were about five years past the thirty-year shelf life, most of them were still consumable.

The family ate quickly, everyone eager to get the adventure started. Kara and Jenny took care of the clean-up. Yes, they were departing, but they'd not leave a mess for those choosing to continue making 87 their home. When that was completed, they walked as a group to the equipment bays. The group arrived on the catwalk, above the main floor.

Tyler and Chief had been busy early in the morning getting the ORVs ready and all the equipment they were taking loaded.

Lucy was the first to speak. "Why are there three vehicles? We were entitled to a 4 and a 12. What's with the second 4?"

"We double-checked," Tyler answered. "When everyone

departed, there should have been ten 4s remaining, and there were eleven."

"That's true. I checked with the leaders of the teams remaining, and they were expecting ten four-person ORVs. So, Tyler and I decided it shouldn't go to waste," Chief added.

"Do you really expect us to believe that an extra four-person ORV magically became available," Sam asked, his expression clearly suggesting that he knew that his brother-in-law was up to something.

"All I can say is that those who are remaining have exactly what they're expecting," Chief said nonchalantly.

Lucy knew her husband wouldn't cheat someone out of transportation they needed, so she let the matter drop,

Looking down on the vehicles, they saw that they were labeled 87-4-22, 87-4-23, and 87-12-6. There was a pair of drones mounted on the eight-person and on one of the four-person ORVs. The other four-person had an M240B light machine gun attached to the roof, accessible from a hatch inside.

"Dad, what's with the 240? Do you think that's needed?" Kara asked with a creased brow.

"We're taking lots of stuff that we probably won't need. That gun is at the top of the list. I hope we don't need it, but if someone sees it, they may be less likely to cause us problems," Chief explained.

"Also, since we've all trained on it, and it was available, it just made sense to bring it along," Tyler added casually.

"Not everyone got training. You didn't let me practice shooting it. I just trained on the smaller guns," Jenny said, frustration evident in her voice.

"We know, and I know you don't like that. When you're older, I'll teach you to shoot it. But you're too small," Oliver advised the girl who looked upon him as a father.

Pouting, she stopped arguing, knowing it would do no good.

"Other than the one bag you're keeping with you, all the personal baggage has been loaded in the back of the eight," Tyler explained. "Now, grab your tactical vests. They're the same ones you trained in and have your names on them."

They slipped on the heavy-duty black vests, then checked the water bottles, knife, pistol, radio, and various pouches to ensure everything was where it belonged. As they were checking their gear, Chief saw Jenny standing back, clearly feeling left out. She'd passed the qualifications with both the assault rifle and pistol and had then learned that she shouldn't expect to carry either.

He reached in a nearby tote and pulled out one last vest and handed it to Marsha. She walked over to her daughter and held it out. The child's eyes lit up. Jenny took the vest and slipped it on, noting that there was no holster. However, someone had attached the radio, water bottle, and knife. The vest hung down to her knees even though the size was extra small.

The combat knife had been a significant source of discussion among the others. Jenny had gone through training and learned to use a knife appropriately, but there was reluctance to give one to someone so young. In the end, they decided to allow her to prove herself.

"Honey, we decided to trust you with the knife, but if there are problems, I'll take it. It stays in the vest unless you have a reason to need it. Understood?" Marsha asked.

Jenny understood. She hated feeling like a little kid. If they were going to trust her like this, she'd prove herself to them all.

They took a final look around. After a brief discussion about who was riding in which ORV, they boarded the vehicles and started the engines.

Chapter Thirty-Nine

Lucy, Sam, Chief, and Theresa were the only ones on the team who hadn't been born in the shelter, and they'd come up with a plan to acclimate the others to the outside world. They would take their time, initially stopping frequently, and explain what they were passing and the significance of what they were seeing. The four would also do all the initial driving as the others were too in awe of what they saw to be safe behind the wheel.

For the last several weeks, all the shelter inhabitants had to navigate random obstructions that Tyler had set up in the halls to help everyone get comfortable walking on uneven ground. These obstructions were to help build up the skills and balance for when they were outside the shelter.

The first stop was the same place Chief and Tyler had taken their survey team when they began their mission. The panoramic view was something they should all experience. There were hills, rocks, trees, living and dead for the family's younger members to explore. The sooner they all became familiar with the outside, the quicker they could move on.

Standing with Lucy and his wife, Theresa, Sam watched the others climb the hills and explore their new world.

"They remind me of people walking on ice, moving so they won't fall," he said wryly.

Lucy laughed. "Won't it be fun to see them the first time they encounter snow and ice?"

The others also laughed.

Jenny, who initially seemed unimpressed with the outside, was soon running up and down the hill, her youth letting her take the challenge without fear.

Oliver approached. "This isn't what I was expecting."

"In what way?" Marsha asked.

"The video of the outside showed almost everything dead, but there's lots of vegetation here."

Oliver was referring to the only views they had had of the outside since the comet. Those videos were distributed to all the shelters shortly after he was born and showed a dead world. They were recorded when the inhabitants of Shelter 16, including his grandparents, had had to relocate.

"We noticed that too when we were out surveying," his uncle responded. "I think the initial radiation destroyed almost everything; that's what we saw in those videos. However, as the radiation returned to safe levels, many plant species recovered … and have been doing so for years. It's a very encouraging sign for the future."

Thirty minutes later, they had had enough and were ready to move on.

Looking at the other surface-born, Chief said, "We can take hills, rocks, trees, and sticks off the list of things needed to be seen. Just a million other discoveries for them."

Soon, the three vehicles were on the road headed south.

In the lead ORV, Lucy drove while Chief worked on the laptop, studying the built-in database. The team that had set up Project Anvil had put lots of effort into deciding what information the people would need when they emerged from the shelters. They had detailed maps of the entire country, with information about most communities. These maps included every propane distributor, all the Anvil shelters, shopping areas, and other features that might be of value.

Chief was checking the information about a larger town that would be coming up fairly soon. It would have propane and large office buildings, and a good-sized residential area.

Their main goal was to get to Shelter 104 and, hopefully, find Lucy and Sam's parents. However, on the way, there were things to accomplish. One of them was helping the shelter-born learn about the outside world. That younger generation had grown up watching old recorded TV shows and movies but needed real-world experiences to put things into context.

After they'd been on the road for several hours, Chief announced, "There's a town coming up in about twenty minutes called Clinton. It looks like it'll be a good place to stop."

"Good, we're getting down to just half on fuel, and if there are problems transferring propane, we might have to try more than one fuel site," Lucy said.

"Well, I have three propane distributors on this side of town. One large and two small. We'll check out the large one first."

They took the exit and, with Chief feeding her directions, Lucy drove to the propane dealer, the sign for which had long ago collapsed to the ground.

Chief took the radio. "We're checking the larger tanks, 4-23; you assess the smaller ones. 12-6, spread out and take watch for anyone in the area. Put up one of your drones."

The other vehicles acknowledged the instructions and Lucy backed up to the large tank's main connection. She shut off the ORV and flipped a master switch to the 'Fuelling' position. This switch disconnected most of the electrical system and reduced the chance for a stray spark potentially triggering an explosion if there were a propane leak.

While Chief assessed the condition of the tank's aged valves, Lucy opened a compartment in the rear of the vehicle, exposing the fuelling connections. She also powered up the fuelling pump, the only electrical piece of equipment that could function when in 'Fuelling' mode. Its design eliminated the chance of a spark. She then attached a removable valve with a pressure regulator to the connection on the ORV and waited.

Using bolt cutters, Chief cut the padlock off the control box, then began disassembling the electronic pump controls. Connecting power to the old electronics was possible, but it was considered an overly risky option since the equipment had sat unattended for the last thirty years.

They both shut off their two-way radios, again to prevent a possible explosion from the electrical circuitry.

All shelter inhabitants had practiced this process on training equipment, so the procedure was familiar to them. Soon, he had the main tank valve exposed and was able to determine the size of the connection. He told Lucy, and she handed him the correct parts from what they had with them, and then connected a flexible hose between the tank and the vehicle. Chief fought with it, but eventually got the main tank valve open.

Lucy looked at the pressure gauge built into the valve she'd attached and did the math in her head and smiled. "There's plenty in there for all of us, if it checks out."

Next to the gauge was a pressure relief valve. She tore a half-inch square piece of propane reactive paper from a sheet and placed it in a tube. Then she attached the tube to the relief valve, opened it for three seconds, and was immediately aware of the sharp smell of propane.

After closing the valve, they compared the color of the paper in the tube to the guide in the compartment, which indicated that the propane in the tank was safe to use.

The pump built into the ORV worked at a specific pressure, so all they had to do was open the connection and activate the pump. While the fuel was flowing, Lucy walked twenty yards away, turned her radio back on, and let everyone know that propane transfer had begun and for the others to be ready.

Once the first ORV's tank was full, they removed the connection from the rear. They waited a full minute for any residual fumes to dissipate. Lucy then engaged the power, typed in her ignition code, and pulled away. As she moved out, 87-12-6 took her place.

In an hour, all three vehicles were full of fuel and ready to depart.

Chapter Forty

THE THREE-VEHICLE CONVOY MOVED ONTO THE ROAD. ALMOST everyone was feeling relieved. Their first refueling had been successful, improving their confidence in their ability to operate in this strange environment. The one person who wasn't feeling relieved sat in the far back of ORV 87-12-6.

Young Jenny was struggling with a wide variety of emotions. This outside world fascinated her, and she was excited and wanted to explore it. But she was also lonely. All the kids she grew up with had headed in different directions when the shelter opened. The closest person to her age was fourteen years older than she was, and was the only mother she'd ever known.

Anger was the other feeling Jenny was battling. Everyone had told her that she was part of a team, that they would be exploring the world together, but that wasn't how she felt.

During training, she'd attended every class available and participated in all the hands-on training. The instructors had commented regularly about how well she did. Other than Chief, she'd practiced fuel transfers more than anyone else and knew the procedure inside and out. Today, she'd asked to help but was told to stay with her ORV. Then, when it was her vehicle's time to refuel, they told her to get out and remain a long way away in case there was a problem.

No, she wasn't feeling like part of the team; she felt like an inconvenience. But she was also intelligent and knew to keep these feelings to herself. If she complained too much, she'd look more like a child, and that wouldn't help her.

They made a few turns and Marsha said, "Jenny, we're going to be checking out houses where people use to live. Make sure you stay with someone and don't go off on your own."

Jenny took in a deep breath, continuing to battle her feelings. More than anything, she wanted to ignore Marsha and not respond. She knew better, though, and forced out a reluctant, "Okay."

She peered out the window and saw the residential street lined with houses in various conditions. Some had completely collapsed, others were partly fallen, and some still stood and looked intact. They stopped in front of a pair of houses that looked to be in reasonably good condition and exited the vehicles.

"Gather here, please," Sam ordered.

As they gathered, Chief entered the first house.

"Just a reminder. Don't enter any house that's partially collapsed," Sam advised. "Also, why are some of the houses collapsed?"

Before anyone could speak, Jenny yelled, "Rain."

Sam nodded. "That's right. The roofs on the houses are good for about thirty years at best, and most weren't new when the comet passed. When a roof gets too old, it can no longer keep out the rain. The wood inside gets wet, rots, and eventually collapses. Then more water gets in and, eventually, the whole house comes down. Remember, the houses that are still standing may not be as strong as they look, so move carefully inside. No jumping around."

"We'll be checking these two out so everyone can see how

people lived back then. We need someone to stand watch out here with the vehicles. I'll do that for the first house, and someone can replace me when we do the second one."

Jenny felt the dread building. Any minute now, they would be telling her to wait outside with Sam ... but that didn't happen.

The group approached the house as Chief exited it. "Everything looks okay. There's one bedroom door on the upper level with the door shut. Don't go in there. Otherwise, stay with one of the surface-born and check the place out."

Theresa led her son Oliver, Marsha, and Jenny into the house. There was a strange smell: stale and old. That confused Jenny because those weren't smells, yet that's what they were. The first room of the house surprised the girl. The floor had a thick gray, dust-filled carpet. Much thicker than what she had seen in 87. There was a faded floral-print wallpaper. She was puzzled as to why the wall had pictures. The room was large, but other than that, everything was familiar. A TV on the wall. Couch and chairs and a shelf with books. Except for lots of dust, everything seemed normal.

Jenny went to the window and looked outside, interested in the ability to peer out from in the house. She took the curtain in her hand and examined it. "What's this for?" she asked.

Theresa walked over. "The window allows light in, but the curtain can control how much, and can be closed to keep someone outside from looking in."

Jenny shrugged, then nodded, satisfied with the explanation.

They moved into the kitchen, which was a little more interesting. All the appliances in the shelter were industrial-sized, and the shelter-born had seldom seen them, but this kitchen had the same stuff but in a smaller size. This generated questions that Theresa answered from childhood memories.

Marsha reached for the handle on the refrigerator.

"No! Don't open that," Theresa warned quickly. "All the food would've long ago spoiled and is still in there. The refrigerator is airtight, and if you open it, the smell could be horrible."

Marsha lowered her hand and stepped away from the fridge.

They examined the pantry's contents and asked Theresa more questions. Many she knew the answer to, and others she was sure that she once did. Eventually, they headed upstairs.

Climbing the stairs was slow and awkward, something unfamiliar to the shelter-born. Before reaching the second floor, there was a new smell. It wasn't too strong but was quite unpleasant.

The group walked down the hall. The door to the first room was closed. They could tell that this is where the smell came from. While it was new to them, even the eleven-year-old understood why Chief had closed the door and what the smell came from.

Three other doors were open. One was a bathroom and the others were bedrooms.

Jenny went into one and was glad that Chief had opened a window. Crisp, cool air was flowing in. There were marks on the far wall where water had run down recently and a wet area with mildew on the carpet. A single bed and a dresser furnished the room. It was just like she had in her room in the shelter. This was obviously the room of a young girl; Jenny wondered if she was the one in the room with the closed door.

There were toys, some of which she recognized, and a shelf with books. Several of the titles were familiar. She took one which she hadn't seen before.

Marsha saw her. "If you see a book or two that you want, you can take them. No one else is going to read them."

Jenny looked around the room at some other girl's belongings and then put the books back on the shelf. Taking them felt wrong.

When they finished in the first house, they exited and waited as Sam and Chief checked the second home.

When they stepped out, Sam stated, "No problems. They weren't here at the end."

Jenny felt relief; the smell had been terrible. She followed the others inside while Lucy took a turn outside, keeping watch.

The house was like the first, with a living room, bedrooms, and kitchen. She was interested in the excessive amount of space there was compared to her quarters in the shelter. Also, there were many decorative objects that served no purpose. She was hoping to find something new to examine in the kids' bedrooms.

Unfortunately, the kids here were much younger than she was, and both boys. There was nothing to interest her. Disappointed, she asked Marsha if she could go back outside.

"Lucy is outside; you can hang out with her until we come out."

Jenny headed down the stairs. It wasn't that she didn't find the old house interesting, but there wasn't much different from the first one, and the adults were investigating and talking about every little thing. Besides that, all the dust made her feel like she was always about to sneeze.

She stepped onto the sidewalk and saw Lucy seated in her ORV in front of the first house. She was about to head over to her when something caught her attention. There was a strange box attached to the side of the house she had just exited, and there was a glass covering like a dome sticking out from the box.

Curious, the girl walked over to check it out. Pushing her way through tall weeds, she eyed the dead digital display behind the glass. As she contemplated the device's purpose, she heard a noise in the backyard, which took away her focus from the electric meter. It sounded like someone or something running away.

She took a couple of steps toward the back and saw red liquid on the ground. She looked closer and noticed a narrow trail through the grass that something had trampled, and there was more blood. She took a few more steps, following the trail ... then realized what she should've done.

Chapter Forty-One

Tyler and his sister, Kara, sorted through objects in a closet. It was interesting, getting their first experience of what pre-shelter life was like, but they were getting hungry and wanted to get out of the dust-filled house.

"Do you think these houses are salvageable?" Kara asked.

Tyler nodded. "If they got their roofs replaced, I don't see why not. I don't know where we'll end up but seeing that there are some houses in this good condition is great news."

The conversation was interrupted by everyone's radios. "This is Jenny. There's movement and blood behind the house." There was excitement in her voice.

Everyone in the house raced for the door with Kara and Tyler in the lead. As they ran, they heard voices behind them. "What's she doing behind the house?"

"Jenny. Stay where you are. Wait for us."

They exited the house and turned toward the driveway, where they saw their mother running from the ORV with two assault rifles. She tossed one to Tyler, who caught it easily.

There was a scream from the back, and they ran harder. Kara had her 9mm in her hand and was aware of many additional feet behind her as she and Tyler ran ahead. As they rounded the back of the house, there was a crashing sound as Chief and Sam exploded through the rear door; it hadn't opened in thirty-three years and was a little slower moving than either of the men would tolerate. Marsha was right behind them franticly looking for her "daughter".

They all saw Jenny—crouching with her knife raised just as her training indicated. She could attack or defend, whichever was necessary. Seeing that she was uninjured, they approached cautiously. They were looking for threats in every direction, with enough firepower to stop anything out there.

She heard them approach and called out, "What's that?"

A pile of branches was on the ground with a collapsed section of fencing over it and, in front, was a freshly killed animal. For a second, Kara wondered if Jenny had done this and glanced at the girl's knife blade, but saw it was clean. She then noticed that the wounds on the animal looked like bites.

Lucy hastened over and placed a comforting hand on the girl. "Honey, it's a dead dog. It can't hurt us."

"No, something's moving under there," Jenny said, pointing the knife at the downed section of fencing. "I saw it."

Sam and Oliver holstered their weapons and lifted the rotted fence. As they did, they heard movement and whimpering. A scared puppy ran to its deceased mother, whining. It was short-haired with dark tan on the body and a white chest. Three of its feet were tan and the other was white. It had a crooked tail and the left ear was missing. There was no blood on the ear, so the disfigurement hadn't happened recently.

Lucy scooped up the trembling dog. She examined it, checking for injuries. Turning to Jenny, she said, "It's a boy, and I think his mother died protecting him from whatever you heard running away."

Returning her knife to her oversized tactical vest, Jenny asked, "Can I hold him?"

Reluctantly, Lucy gave the little mutt a last snuggle, then handed him over.

Jenny's eyes lit up as she gently took the dog in her arms, the way Lucy had instructed her. Fearful, the puppy trembled; it was his first time being held but he soon settled in and even licked Jenny's cheek.

"He's so sweet ... and smelly," Jenny declared. She looked around for Marsha, but she was off to the side, discussing something with Oliver and Chief.

Sam and Kara returned from searching the rest of the backyard, "Whatever it was that killed the dog is long gone. I suspect that Jenny's arrival scared it off and saved the puppy," Sam reported.

Marsha approached and Jenny asked, "Mom, isn't he great?"

"He sure is." Marsha reached out and felt a live animal's fur for the first time.

"Can I keep him?"

"That's what we were talking about just now. As long as you're going to be responsible for him, you can keep him. You'll have to give him a name."

"His name is Wilbur," the young girl announced.

Blunt as always, Kara responded, "Isn't that a pig?"

"Well, now it's a dog," Jenny retorted.

"There's a stream down the road we passed on the way in. We'll go there, and you can give him a bath," Chief said.

"I saw some old towels in the house we can use for his bath. Some of them were falling apart, but others seemed good enough," Lucy said.

As they turned to leave, Kara looked at Jenny. "You were upset because you couldn't have a gun. Well, now you have something much better. You're the only one with a dog."

Chapter Forty-Two

WILBUR'S FIRST BATH HAD BEEN BOTH EXHAUSTING AND amusing. The young dog wasn't impressed with the cold water but loved being wrapped up in a towel and dried off afterward. In the end, Jenny was almost as wet as the dog.

Now, the small convoy headed into the downtown area. They were looking for two things: a shopping district and a parking garage. Chief had picked this town because it looked large enough to have a parking structure.

While the radiation levels were in the tolerable range, they were still not desirable, so it was in everyone's best interest to find opportunities to reduce exposure. Getting underground for the night in the basement of a parking garage or large office building would make a big difference.

Arriving on the main street of the town, the team dismounted and split into groups again, heading in different directions. Everyone was excited to look around and Chief graciously volunteered to take the first watch with the vehicles. As the others departed, he launched a drone and set it to follow a repeating flight pattern above. He then enabled change detection in the sophisticated software; if the camera detected any change from loop to loop, it would alert him.

Theresa and Sam led Oliver, Marsha, and Jenny, and headed east up the street. Just as with the houses, some businesses were in good condition and others had collapsed. They stopped briefly in front of the ones that were still identifiable and taught the shelter-born about the purpose of the buildings. Some of the safer-looking structures they investigated. Sam and Theresa enjoyed watching the others exploring a clothing store. Much of the merchandise was partly rotted and falling apart. But, in the backroom, many of the products that had never made it to the racks were still wrapped in airtight plastic and were in good condition. In the end, they all left the store with a new outfit under their coveralls. They also made sure to radio the other teams to let them know to stop for new clothing.

The next surviving store was a hardware store that Sam thought the others would find interesting. The door had been forced open and then secured with a strap. Sam wondered if that had happened immediately after the comet or more recently. As the others looked at all the unusual items, he took Jenny, carrying Wilbur, and led her to the pet section.

"This is all for pets. You should be able to find a collar and leash for Wilbur."

Her eyes lit up. "So, I won't have to carry him everywhere." She examined the selection of nylon collars that had held up well over the years.

"Remember, Jenny. There's lots of broken glass on the ground and other stuff that could hurt him. You'll still need to carry him some."

She picked out a faded purple collar and matching leash.

"Get him a second collar that's bigger. He'll probably outgrow that small one soon."

She pocketed a larger one, and with "Grandfather Sam's" help, attached the other to her new fuzzy friend. Next, she picked out dog bowls for food and water and a small pet carrier, then hugged Sam and raced off to show the others what she'd gotten.

Sam smiled and began examining the store and enjoying the memories many of the store items recalled.

They were finishing up their inspection of the store when their radios spoke. "We have people in the area. It looks like there are three teams of two on bicycles. I think they heard our arrival and are looking for us. Some of them have rifles slung over their backs. Only one team is heading directly toward us, and it'll be several minutes before they get here," Chief's voice alerted them.

Lucy was the first to respond. "So, do we load up and clear out ... or intercept them?"

Chapter Forty-Three

The two-person team cautiously rode into the shopping area. This type of mission occurred every few months. Someone would report seeing or hearing something, so riders mounted up and went to investigate. Most often, it turned out to be nothing. There were a few exceptions. Once, they encountered a bear that had wandered into town. That was exciting and gave them one more animal to document as not being completely extinct. Another time, they were shot at by people on motorcycles. One small group had fled when approached. A couple of others had been friendly, and one even joined their community.

The recently married husband and wife team turned onto Main Street and were startled to see that fifty yards up the road was a strange vehicle. It was parked perpendicular to the road and was much bigger than a van and was the weirdest thing either had seen. The tires were large and the suspension raised the body quite high. There was an odd sphere in the back that looked like a large pressurized tank.

The most unexpected thing was what was accompanying it: a young girl standing by the front fender with a small dog struggling against a leash. The girl gave them a friendly wave

The Anvil

and their guard dropped a bit. Just as intended. They moved twenty yards closer and heard engine sounds behind them.

Two more vehicles came in behind them, next to one another. These were similar but smaller. On the roof of one was a person with a large gun who appeared to be deliberately pointing it away from them. They glanced back toward the first vehicle and the little girl and dog were gone. Instead, there was a woman with an assault rifle, again, not pointed directly at them. Using her free hand, she waved them forward. They glanced at each other and slowly complied. As they did, the couple detected movement to their sides, and other people emerged from inside the buildings. They too were armed, but not threatening.

Over the noise of the vehicles, there was another sound, radio traffic; these people were talking to one another. The couple couldn't help but be impressed with how cleanly they'd been intercepted.

Everyone met in the middle, including the little girl who had returned and was now carrying the dog. The woman who had waved them in was the closest, and she approached with a smile. It was clear that she was nervous, trying to hide it and not wanting to look too threatening while holding an assault rifle. "I'm Lucy. If you're friendly, we are too."

"We are. I'm Alan and this my wife, Jen. We live in the area."

Another member of their group said, "My name is Chief. I'm one of the leaders of this group. We're just passing through and were using your town for some training of our younger people."

A bit confused, Alan asked, "Training? What kind of training?"

"Five of our people were born after the comet. They've spent their whole lives in an underground shelter. Until today, they had never seen a store, a town, or even the inside of a house. Climbing stairs is unfamiliar to them. We've got a long trip ahead of us and want to get them acclimated to the new world that they'll need to operate in," Chief explained.

"Your story sounds interesting. Would you be willing to stay the night with us? We'd enjoy hearing more and telling you about what we've been through here. We could even show you the gardens we're planting."

"We really need to spend the night underground. This trip has had us out here all day, and we now need less exposure to the remaining radiation. We were planning the check out the parking garage in town. To see if it has a lower level," Lucy explained.

Jen shook her head. "You don't want to do that. The lower level of the parking garage is where a huge number of people fled when they learned about the radiation. The place is full of bodies."

"That's right, you don't want to go there," Alan added. "Our people are in the sub-basement of a large office building. It is where we were able to survive all this time."

Using a horn with a can of compressed air, Alan gave two loud blasts, which summoned the other two pairs of riders. They were equally friendly and interested in the team's vehicles and gear. They were fascinated as they watched the drone recovery.

Since there wasn't room for the six bicycles in the ORVs, the former Anvil team members followed the slow-moving bikes three miles to the building they lived under.

Chapter Forty-Four

THREE ORVs CROSSED THE MICHIGAN/INDIANA BORDER ON I-69 mid-morning the next day.

The surface-born had decided that their efforts in that town had been beneficial but that they would limit their exploration of new places.

They'd spent the previous evening in the basement of an office building with their new friends, shared information and discussed each other's plans for the future before falling asleep late in the night.

Since crossing the state line, Lucy had become quiet, lost in thought. The last time she was in her home state was the night of the Anvil activation. When she'd left Indiana, she was an injured teen, responsible for a younger brother and concerned she might never see her parents or boyfriend again. That was over thirty years ago and she remembered that night as if it were yesterday. She thought about Sam, riding in the vehicle behind her, and wondered what he was thinking.

Her attention was jerked back to the present when she realized that they were exiting the highway. There hadn't been any radio traffic and Chief was taking the exit. Looking in her mirror, she saw the other two ORVs follow. She was about to ask why they were exiting when she saw something familiar: the restaurant by the end of the ramp had partially collapsed, but she thought she knew it. Recognition clicked, and she looked left and right, sure of what she'd see. Yes, there was the commuter parking lot and the remains of the Shell gas station. Nothing looked at all the same, but she knew it well. Whenever her family had traveled, the kids knew that they were only twenty minutes from home when they saw the old colonial-style restaurant.

Lucy knew that Sam wasn't driving this morning. This detour was something Chief and Theresa had planned. Chief glanced over and saw the light come on as Lucy figured out where they were going. He also saw the color drain from her face. "Are you okay?"

"I appreciate the idea, but I'm not sure I want to do this."

"Theresa and I were talking and thought it would be good for both of you," Chief told his wife.

"Why us? You and Theresa have homes out here too."

"True, and if we were going anywhere near them, we'd stop there too. Yours is just on our way."

Lucy stopped arguing and thought about her home, and memories rushed back. Soon the dread faded and the anticipation grew. She stared out the window at the houses they passed, knowing that her home might have been destroyed by now. She tried to accept this possibility but found enthusiasm still increasing. There were several items from her childhood room she wanted—small things, like a necklace she'd gotten for Christmas one year.

Lucy also found herself thinking about Marcus again. She still thought about him from time to time. Now that they would be just a mile from his house, old feelings returned. Her hand unconsciously went to her wrist to where, for several years, a bracelet had been. Lucy still had it, packed in a bag with old family photos and other precious items she'd kept.

The Anvil

The ORVs pulled up in front of the Wilson residence and everyone got out. Lucy retrieved a digital camera from the cargo compartment and removed it from the case. Everyone gathered around Sam and Lucy and stood, silently staring at the intact house.

Kara was the first to speak. "You guys go in first; take as much time as you want. You can show us around when you're ready."

Sam nodded. "Okay."

Brother and sister walked up the driveway, looking at the rusted hulk of their father's pickup truck. It had only been a few months old the last time they saw it. Their mother's SUV would still be at the airport.

The garage behind the truck had collapsed, and a large tree limb rested across what remained.

Sam tried to remember what he might have had in the garage. His bike and old sled, and maybe a basketball?

"The walkway is gone," Lucy motioned. She was talking about the brick walkway between the driveway and the house. The whole area was overgrown, and there wasn't a single brick visible.

"Remember how Mom kept it so perfect? Never a weed," Lucy said softly, recalling many years ago.

Sam said nothing.

They reached the front door and turned the knob. The door stuck a bit but opened. In their haste to get to the Anvil shuttle, they'd neglected to lock it.

They stepped inside.

The others watched them enter.

Theresa said, "That has to be weird, going back and seeing everything the same ... but not the same."

"Knowing Mom, she'll be real quiet the rest of the day. Thinking about everything she's seeing now," Tyler said solemnly.

Chief and Kara agreed.

213

Everyone waited outside with growing anticipation of seeing their loved ones' pre-comet lives. Six minutes later, Lucy's scream of terror erupted from the house, startling them.

Chapter Forty-Five

Lucy and Sam had stepped into the house and then approached the living room. They stopped just inside the doors, taking the scene in.

"We were the last ones in here," Sam pointed out.

"Yeah."

They moved into the living room and Sam strolled to the far end of the couch and sat down. It was where he'd always sat when watching TV. The decades of dust in the cushions took to the air, causing him to cough and jump to his feet. "It sure isn't the same."

Lucy snapped a few pictures. If her parents were alive, she'd show these to them.

Sam moved to the kitchen counter. "This is where we stood when Mom and Dad called us about the Anvil alert."

"I was cooking chicken here for dinner when they called," Lucy said quietly. She glanced around the kitchen. Her attention caught on a glass sitting in the sink. Something about that bothered her, but she wasn't sure why.

Disrupting Lucy's thought, Sam said, "Lucy, look back here."

She followed Sam to the sliding door in the dining room,

on the backside of the house. Their screened-in porch was demolished. Part of the giant oak tree in the backyard had come down and crushed it.

"If it had come a few feet further this way, it would've taken the back off the house," Lucy noted as she took photos. Turning, she thought about going up to her room when she noticed a blank spot on the wall that didn't look right. It took a few seconds, but then she remembered there had been a family photo there. The night they packed to leave, she'd taken it with her.

"I'm glad they brought us here. It was a good idea," Sam stated with a soft sigh.

"Yeah, it was. It's weird being back, though."

"I know. Everything seems ... much smaller."

As she climbed the stairs, she thought about how she looked forward to showing Tyler and Kara her childhood home. Reaching the top, she was aware of an unpleasant smell. She turned into her room and froze.

Lying on her bed, on top of her comforter, was a mummified corpse. Beside it was a cell phone, and she recognized the case. She'd bought it as a gift. A breath caught in her throat when she glanced at the body's left wrist and could clearly see the thick gold chain and medallion—the sturdier twin to the one she still kept and cherished. The camera hit the floor.

The caught breath roared out of her in a scream that would leave her with a sore throat for several days. Racing from the room, she collided with Sam, driving him into the wall hard enough to crush the wallboard. Not slowing down, she descended the stairs three at a time, just as when she'd been a kid, and raced for the front yard. As she exited the house, she wasn't even aware of the hoard of family members with weapons racing in her direction.

She dropped onto the remains of the lawn, crying hysterically and vomiting.

Chapter Forty-Six

Chief reached her first and pulled her into his arms. "Are you hurt? Where is Sam?"

Just as he asked, Sam stepped out of the house, just as Theresa and Tyler were about to enter. Their guns were up and leading the way.

"Weapons down. There's no danger," he told them.

Confused, they lowered them.

He guided the group over to the vehicles and gave them a quick overview. While he was explaining, Chief was trying to comfort his wife. Lucy was babbling between sobs. "The bracelet. I bought the phone case. Now, he's dead on my bed. On my comforter. I loved him, and he's dead on my bed. I knew the glass was wrong. I did the dishes."

The more she talked, the more confused Chief became.

After a couple of minutes, Kara and Tyler helped their mother up while Sam led Chief into the house. They stopped in the living room.

"Did she ever mention Marcus to you?"

Chief nodded. "Yeah, he was an old boyfriend."

"No, he was much more than that. They were best friends

since the first grade. Soulmates, if there's such a thing. They started dating in high school and planned to attend college together. When she had to leave for Anvil, she didn't get to say goodbye.

"After the comet, she spoke to him several times a day while we were in 87. She tried to tell him things to do to protect himself from the radiation and later listened as he described his journey towards death. Then one day, he stopped answering his phone. We knew what that meant, but she still kept calling, several times a day for weeks. She was a wreck for a few months. Until about the time she met you."

"Okay, that makes sense. What happened in the house?" Chief asked, looking around.

"He's in there, a mummified corpse on her bed."

"He died in her bed?"

"On, not in. I think he wanted to be close to her in the end. His phone is next to him. Lucy bought him the phone case for their last Christmas together," Sam explained.

"She said something about doing dishes. What did that mean?"

"She'll have to explain that one. I've no idea."

The two men headed back outside. Sam gathered the others, and they left, heading for the neighbor's house.

Taking Lucy in his arms again, Chief said, "Sam explained everything to me."

"Why would he do that? Why die on my bed?"

"He probably wanted to be close to you at the end. I'm sure he never considered you might find him one day."

As comforting as Chief was, he was struggling too. The idea of a former boyfriend dead on her bed caused him feelings he knew were unneeded and unhelpful. He pushed the thoughts away. He would deal with those later.

After several minutes, her sobbing slowed, and he asked, "Do you want to go back inside? I'll go with you."

"No, I'm never going in there again. I just want to leave," Lucy answered woefully.

"Okay, the others are raiding your neighbor's garage for a couple of shovels. We can bury him if you want or leave where he is. It's up to you."

Lucy thought about it before answering. "I want him buried. I don't think I could leave with him still on my bed. I know it sounds silly, given he's been there over thirty years."

"It's not at all silly. If that's what you need, that's what we'll do. Do you care where we bury him?"

"Probably in the backyard. Make sure Sam is okay turning our yard into a cemetery."

Chief clicked his radio. "Sam, Chief. Can you come over?"

Sam joined them a few minutes later and went right to his sister, and took her hand, "I'm so sorry you saw that. I wish I'd gone up first."

She squeezed his hand back. "I never saw that one coming. And I'll never forget it."

"You okay with burying him in the backyard?" Chief asked him.

Sam thought for a moment. "Yeah, that's fine."

Squeezing the microphone on his radio again, Chief said, "Backyard. Start digging."

Sam regarded his traumatized sister. "Lucy, is there anything from inside that you want?"

Without a second thought, she answered, "No."

Getting up, Sam found Theresa and Oliver and took them inside. He still wanted to show them where he'd grown up. As they walked through the house, Sam shared his childhood with his wife and son. When it was time to go upstairs, he went first and entered Lucy's room. He retrieved the dropped camera and closed her bedroom door before having Oliver and Theresa come up. They spent a few minutes in his old room and then went to his parent's bedroom. He wanted to find something special that he could take to them.

After several minutes, he came across a box of paperwork on a shelf in a closet. Inside he found an envelope containing his parent's marriage license. He took it and photographed other items in the house to show them, and the three of them left.

Chapter Forty-Seven

THE THREE-VEHICLE CONVOY MOVED SOUTH ON US-75, leaving the Lexington, Kentucky area.

They were eager to get to Shelter 104 and see if their parents/grandparents were still alive. Nine years ago, the last communications satellite had failed, cutting off information about how they were doing. Alex and Marie would be in their early seventies now, if they were still alive.

So far, on their trip, they'd made relatively good time. They stopped for fuel mid-day yesterday and again late in the afternoon. That final stop had been on the north side of Lexington. They then continued into the city and eventually found an accessible building with a sub-basement to spend the night.

Most of the roadways were clear, with infrequent obstructions requiring them to detour. Chief's biggest frustration was that they had to stop every two and a half hours to walk Wilbur. So far, Jenny hadn't complained about doing the work and, because of that attitude, the others all volunteered to help with him.

Although a bit nervous at first, Kara had come to enjoy driving over the last couple of days. She looked forward to her turn and found she especially liked driving the large twelve-passenger vehicle. When Marsha had said this morning that she wasn't looking to another spell behind the wheel, Kara offered to take over.

Now, they were moving at a steady 45 miles an hour down the highway. They'd tried to go faster, but the roads weren't in great shape, and large debris could come up quickly at a higher speed. The ORV's design allowed for rugged terrain, but they couldn't afford an incident that might put one of them out of service.

Being more agile, the smaller four-passenger ORVs were in the lead, looking for any problems and radioing them back. She hadn't been watching her rear-view mirror closely since there hadn't been anyone else on the road. However, motion caught her attention. Her eyes went wide at what she saw, and she hit the transmit button for her headset.

"This is 12-6. I have motorcycles coming up behind me. Looks like four of them."

The surprise in Chief's voice was clear. "Interesting. Let them come up. If they look friendly, we'll stop."

"They're coming up fast and are spacing themselves out."

One of the ORV's design disadvantages was that the passengers couldn't see the road behind them because of the large pressurized propane tank. Therefore, no one else in the vehicle could see what was going on.

"Dad, the first one just passed. Something's wrong. There are two people on each bike. Neither even looked at me."

"Everyone be ready for anything," Chief ordered, his concern growing.

"4-22 ready," answered Sam, who was driving and currently in the lead.

As the third bike passed Kara, she was aware that the fourth was staying behind her and not advancing. Then, she saw the rear rider on bike three pull out a handgun.

The Anvil

"Guns! They're pulling guns!" Kara radioed, terror in her voice.

Tyler was riding in the rear seat of the middle vehicle with his parents. As soon as he heard the word guns, he was out of his seat and had the roof hatch open. Standing on his seat, he released the latch that locked the M240B in place.

By now, he could hear blasts of gunfire coming from several handguns and the sound of bullets hitting the light aluminum bodies of the ORVs. His heart was pounding; he knew it was up to him to protect his family.

The first bike he saw was in front of them and next to Sam and Theresa's vehicle. The rider on the back was shooting. Tyler released the safety and let a half dozen rounds fly. He wasn't exactly sure where he hit them, but the bike went out of control, swerving off the road, tumbling several times.

As he was swinging the gun around to the next target, he heard a bullet hit the roof rail, very close to his arm. Moments later, a tearing pain seared his left leg. He yelped and ignored the burning pain and pushed on.

There was a bike directly next to them and, from the roof, Tyler couldn't get the gun at the needed angle to hit something so close. To their rear was another bike whose rider was shooting at him. Tyler depressed the trigger again, and that bike also keeled over.

Kara saw the second bike go down and the one that had been shooting at them from behind, started passing her on the driver's side. "Hang on!" She yelled to her three passengers.

As the bike drew even with her window, the rider looked directly at her and started to bring his gun up. She tapped the brakes, just enough to make the bike pull up even with her front wheel. She gave the steering wheel a quick jerk to the left and then back. The ORV's front corner struck the bike and pulled back.

The driver lost control and swerved to his right, directly

into their path. The enhanced suspension handled the bike easily and the large vehicle's wheels rolled over it.

The remaining bike accelerated and raced past Sam, firing off a couple of wild shots as they passed. In a minute, he was out of view.

Kara triggered her radio. "12-6. No injuries." Her words were rushed and she was breathing fast; her adrenaline was keeping her alert and on edge.

Sam responded. "4-22. No injuries."

"4-23, one minor injury here. Nothing serious," Chief answered. "Let's get out of this area. Then we'll stop and assess the damage."

Everyone agreed.

Lucy was facing backward, looking at her son's leg. When he'd been standing on the seat with his head up the hatch, a bullet came into the passenger compartment and ricocheted off part of the vehicle frame before grazing his leg.

"Mom, it's fine. We'll check it out when we stop."

"Tyler," Lucy said, her voice quivering. Lucy hadn't been herself since the incident at her former home.

Tyler was concerned about this pushing further into darkness. He took her hand. "Mom, it isn't bad. It can wait."

They were interrupted by Kara on the radio. "12-6. Stopping now. We're leaking propane. Will evacuate."

ORV 87-12-6 came to a quick stop. As soon as the vehicle's movement ended, Kara killed the engine and tripped the battery disconnect. "Everyone out now and get away. Take rifles and leave your radios off until you're clear the area!"

The doors opened and Oliver, Marsha, Jenny, and Wilbur piled out. They moved quickly, far enough away that if the propane leak caused an explosion, they would be clear.

As they moved, the sound of pressurized gas leaking was loud, and the smell pungent.

Chapter Forty-Eight

The two lead ORVs turned around and raced back. They stopped one hundred yards from the disabled vehicle.

Kara sprinted toward them. "Who got shot?"

"Tyler, but he'll be okay," Chief replied.

Kara hurried over to her brother to see for herself that he was okay.

"Where's Oliver?" Chief asked.

"He went back to assess the damage. Now that we eliminated the chance of a spark, it should be safe," Marsha explained.

Before Chief could answer, they heard the high-pitched whine of electric motors spinning up. Turning, they saw one of the drones on the top of 4-22 rising into the air as Sam launched it. After the attack, they needed to know if there was anyone else in the area.

Chief walked toward Oliver, who was approaching. "Where's the leak? Did you get it stopped?"

"The valve that attaches to the tank was hit by gunfire and is cracked. I can't shut it off."

Nodding, Chief said, "We've got replacements for those valves, but we'll need the tank to be empty to remove it."

"Well, it'll be a while for it to empty; it was almost full. Also, it looks like they were mainly aiming for the tank. The shielding around it did its job, but it's dinged up. We need to check the other vehicles for damage."

"I'll go and do that," Tyler offered.

"No, you won't!" Lucy declared. "Marsha, please take care of his leg. He was shot and seems to have forgotten."

"Jenny and I'll inspect the others," Theresa offered.

Chief nodded again.

"Come on, kiddo." Theresa and Jenny walked back to the two smaller vehicles, followed by Wilbur.

Lucy was concerned about her son and followed Tyler and Marsha to get a med-kit and deal with the leg wound.

Chief eyed Kara and Oliver, the only ones without a task. "When that propane tank is empty, we can fix it fairly easily but it'll need fuel to get it moving. Once they check 4-23 for damage, how about you two take it? Find a residential area and get us a half dozen small propane tanks. If they're full, each can get an ORV 8-12 miles."

Nodding, Oliver said. "Sure, but where did people keep propane tanks? Their basements?"

"No, check the garage or back porch or patio. If the tanks were too exposed, they're probably junk, but if they had the protection of a garage, they could've survived."

"Sounds good. We'll be back as quick as we can," Kara told her dad.

Kara and Oliver approached the vehicle they would be taking. Jenny was examining something on the side.

"So, does it look okay? We need to take it for a ride," Kara asked.

"There's no fuel leak, just this one hole where the bullet that hit Tyler went in. There are lots of marks near the tank. It looks like that's what they wanted to hit here too," the eleven-year-old told them.

Oliver glanced at Theresa, who nodded her agreement with what the child had told them. "Good. Thanks, Jenny."

They walked over to see Sam.

"Oliver, you can drive," Kara said as they walked.

"Why? You said you like to drive."

"Yeah, but if something happens, I want to be on the 240," Kara smiled.

"Fine, I'll drive, but the last thing we need is you firing a machine gun."

Kara laughed.

They found Sam in the passenger seat, watching the drone view on the screen.

"Everything clear, Dad?" Oliver asked.

"So far, I'm not seeing anything moving."

"Good. Kara and I are making a run for small propane tanks. Can you widen the drone's circle to keep us covered?"

"No problems. I'll let you know if I see anything," Sam assured them.

They headed back to the vehicle and climbed aboard. Kara's eyes caught sight of the small pool of blood on the rear floor from her brother's wound. That was enough to refocus her as to how serious the situation truly was.

They headed back the way they came for a couple of miles and then took the exit. Oliver had to slow several times for tree branches and other debris on the side roads but passed over them with no difficulty.

Kara had two screens in front of her. One had the drone view and the other a map that showed a subdivision coming up. She kept her eyes focused on both.

The subdivision was just what they expected. Some houses looked good while others had collapsed, but most were in between. This time, however, they were looking at garages, not houses.

They exited the ORV and Oliver got a pry bar from the utility compartment.

It took three garages before they found their first propane tank. Most of the doorframes had rotted partly and could be pushed open. A few were in good shape, and they needed the pry bar to gain access.

An hour later, they'd only found four tanks; one of them wasn't as heavy as the others.

Oliver drove out of the subdivision, heading back the way they'd come. He hoped that the four tanks would be enough to get the ORV to a propane distributor where they could fill adequately. He considered radioing Chief and let him know they were returning, but with fewer tanks, when Kara ordered him to stop. "Pull in there."

They were passing the remains of an old gas station.

Oliver turned into the lot. "What's there?"

"Go to the other side of the building. I think I saw something."

They maneuvered to the side of the building. Against it was the remains of a large, rotted metal display box, holding about two dozen propane tanks.

They smiled at each other as they got out. The case had two levels, each with twelve tanks. The shelf in between had rusted out and the tanks from the top had dropped onto the ones on the bottom. There was a padlock on the front of the case.

Getting the bolt cutters from the ORV's equipment compartment, Oliver cut off the lock. Carefully, they wrestled the door open part way. They were concerned the tanks would tumble out. The door hadn't moved in over three decades and the hinges took quite a bit of force to move.

They started unloading tanks and found that they could determine, by the weight, which ones were full and which were empty.

They discarded the one light tank they'd previously found and added five more full tanks. Now, they had eight good tanks.

They'd both been disappointed with the idea of returning with only four, but now they'd made up for it.

Chapter Forty-Nine

Tyler and Chief were installing the new tank valve when Kara and Oliver returned.

"How's your leg?" Kara asked her brother.

"It hurts a bit, but I'll be fine. Marsha fixed it up. Cleaned it and then put in two staples."

"Good, but you left a bloody mess on the floor. Be more considerate next time," she said light-heartedly, not sharing how thankful she was that her brother wasn't seriously injured or mentioning that she'd cleaned up the blood.

Several of the others had joined them, and they transferred the tanks to the twelve-person ORV. Two tanks were mounted next to the main tank and hoses tied them into the system. Tyler flipped a bypass valve and opened the tanks. Now, they would run off the contents of the small tanks. There was only room to mount two tanks. When these were empty, they would need to stop and replace them. Fortunately, there was a propane distributor about fifteen miles away. The eight tanks would be more than enough to get them there.

"You still going to be driving this thing?" Chief asked Kara.

"Planning to. Is there a problem?"

"No, just keep your speed to about forty, and we'll take your passengers with us. Slower speed and less weight will get you further on those small tanks."

"No problem," Kara said.

Minutes later, they were loaded up and moving out. They only had to stop once to change out the tanks on 12-6 before they reached the fuel site. It was Sam's turn to get the valves and hoses ready for the propane transfer, and in less than ten minutes, he was pumping fuel.

Surprised how quickly the initial hook-up seemed to go, Chief walked over to see Sam. "Well, you sure got that going quick," he complimented his brother-in-law.

"I wish I could say that I was that good, but somebody had already done most of the work. It was already just the way we needed it. Someone who knew what they were doing pumped from here recently. And the adapter on the hose was the same as we use. I think it was a sheltered ORV."

"That would be nice. I'd like to hear about other shelters. However, there were other propane-powered vehicles used in the days before the comet."

They topped off the fuel in the other two vehicles and were on the road again in forty-five minutes. They made their way back to the highway, having lost two and a half hours because of the attack and damage.

After an hour on the road, Theresa noticed that the drone overhead was showing low power. "We're going to need to swap out the drones again."

They'd kept a drone watching over them since the attack. 4-23 and 12-6 both had drone capability, so they could keep the air cover in place indefinitely. However, it was very hard on the machines that hadn't been intended for constant operations. One positive thing was that the convoy could move faster with the drones watching the road ahead. There was no concern about unexpected obstructions on the road.

"This is 4-23. We need to slow for drone recovery," Sam

said. "This one's battery is low. Our other is recharging and is at eighty-six percent."

"Everyone slows to twenty miles per hour for drone recovery," Chief responded. "Sam, bring yours in from the north. Kara, launch one of yours to the south, so we don't have a collision."

Twenty-five miles per hour was the fastest recommended speed for drone recovery, but there was no reason to push the limits. They all slowed, and the magnets released on the roof on 12-6, and the replacement was in the air and climbing. As soon as the new drone began orbiting and sending data, the other directed itself onto the moving ORV and was locked into place as its batteries began to charge.

In the lead, Sam was about to announce the return to speed when he saw something that momentarily confused him. There was an overturned vehicle to the right side of the highway. That wasn't overly surprising, because they saw lots of disabled cars and trucks. The rear of this one was facing him and he could see a large ripped open pressurized tank on the back.

"4-23 we're stopping. Overturned ORV by me."

"Say that again. What is it?" Chief asked.

Sam ignored him as he came to a stop. The others would be here and able to see it before he could explain it on the radio. They were just far enough past that they could see the designation on the front and struggled to make out the upside-down letters.

"It says 17-4-19. Where is Shelter 17?" Sam asked.

Theresa was already on the computer looking it up. "Shelter 17 was in the White Mountains in New Hampshire."

As they walked to the damaged ORV, Theresa relayed what they'd learned.

Noticing something, Tyler pointed at the ground. "Look here. This wreck has been here a little while." There was considerable damage made when the heavy machine tore up the earth on its way to where it now lay. "See, this ground is all torn up but, there in the middle of it, are shoots of new grass coming up in the disrupted earth. It's been here a week or two."

Kara was the first to get to the front compartment and, fearing what she'd see, peeked inside. She was relieved that there weren't any bodies. There was what might have been some blood on the console, but not much.

After investigating the ruptured tank, Chief said, "I think it was gunfire that breached the tank and caused it to explode."

"Yeah, and it blew outward as designed. There's no blast damage in the passenger compartment," Sam added.

He and Oliver climbed into the overturned vehicle, looking for anything that might be of use. They found nothing. Someone had already stripped everything of value.

Thirty minutes later, they were back on the road. They'd learned much from the wreckage. A lucky shot could destroy an ORV. The design to protect passengers from a tank rupture seemed to work, and there were other Anvil members in the area.

Chapter Fifty

It was four-thirty in the morning. Marsha had just awoken Sam to take his turn standing watch.

They were in the lower level of a parking garage tonight. The team found a clear spot with a half dozen skeletal remains and a few old cars. Two of the ORVs were down here. Sleeping mats and sleeping bags were on the ground around the vehicles. Everyone else was sound asleep, and a few were snoring.

Sam got dressed, found Wilbur's leash, and the two of them slowly worked their way up the ramp to where Marsha was pacing.

"Okay, girl, your turn, go to sleep."

"Not yet. You need to see something up top."

As Sam started following her, there was a single beep sound from her radio. Ignoring it, she kept walking. The beep happened every five minutes and came from the overhead drone. It meant that the flying machine had completed two more laps and not detected any movement.

"When did you last swap out drones?" Sam asked.

"About an hour ago."

They approached the parking structure's top-level and Sam asked, "So, what are you showing me?"

"The sky."

They stepped into the open and saw the expanse of stars. Every night since they'd been on the road, Sam and Chief had looked for this opportunity. Until now, every night had been overcast. Tonight, however, the sky was clear and the stars visible.

"That's so amazing. I swapped out the drone and then spent half an hour looking. I never imagined it would be like this. It's so incredible."

Sam nodded, enjoying the view. "We've been looking forward to a clear night so you guys could see the heavens for the first time."

"I was thinking of waking the others. Should I? I want Jenny to see this," Marsha said.

"Go wake them. They won't complain."

Within five minutes, the others had slowly made their way to the top of the ramp, simultaneously curious and annoyed at being awoken. The annoyance quickly disappeared, though, as they encountered a vast open sky with millions of tiny lights from distant, massive stars.

"This is what I wanted to see the most when we were in the shelter, the open sky, and stars," Tyler stated with awe.

In preparation for the arrival of the comet, everyone had become a little more knowledgeable about the stars and constellations. The surface-born dusted off that long-buried data and pointed out specific celestial features to the younger ones.

Kara went to the ORV and dug out a pair of binoculars, and passed them around. An hour later, when the image began to fade because the sun was preparing to return, no one was sorry for the loss of sleep, and the travelers were on the road several hours ahead of schedule.

By mid-morning, they were north of Atlanta on I75. They'd already had to do some off-road travel because of a collapsed overpass and the burned-out remains of a semi-trailer. They were just completing a drone swap and Chief, driving 4-22, heard the magnets lock the aircraft into the charger.

He keyed his radio. "This is 4-22, coming back up to speed."

Before anyone answered, another voice came across the radio. "Everyone pay attention to your call signs. We don't have a 4-22."

Shocked, Chief thought and then said, "Unit speaking, this is 87-4-22."

There was a moment of silence. "87-4-22, this is 139-4-19, we're northbound on I75 just North of Atlanta."

As he spoke, Lucy had been working on the computer, enlarging the map of the area. She looked over at him. "They're close. Headed this way."

Chief keyed the radio. "We're southbound on 75, about 45 minutes from Atlanta. If you're interested in meeting up, we can find a spot close for both of us."

"Absolutely, you're only the second other team we've encountered on our trip. We started in central Texas almost a week ago and are heading for a settlement in North Carolina. We're planning to stop for a break close to where you are now.

"We've heard that Shelter 189 is in the area, and they've set up a settlement in the Red Top Mountain State Park. Rumour is they're friendly. They have a food supply, and we're hoping to spend the night in their old shelter," the voice informed them.

Lucy found the location on the map. "We just passed the exit for that about 10 minutes ago." She then scanned to see if there were any other drone signals that she could capture. There were none. Typing a message into her computer, she sent instructions directly to the screen in 12-6, which Marsha acknowledged.

12-6 decreased speed. When it was down to 35mph, their crew heard the electric motors spinning. By the time the vehicle's speed was down to 20mph, they were spinning at full speed, and the magnetic clamps released.

Thirty seconds after Lucy sent the instructions, the other screen split in two when the feed from the second drone appeared as it sped south on I75. Twenty seconds later, 12-6 had caught up to the others.

DRONE DATA STREAMED to the three ORVs. The high-speed sprint to find the others had cost the drone one-third of its battery. Now, it orbited slowly, monitoring the progress of the Texas convoy.

The group coming from Texas was much larger than expected. Lucy saw two, two-person ORVs (motorcycles) in the lead. There were also six of the four-person, six of the 12, and three 40-person buses.

"If they scan for a drone feed, they'll see the same thing we do: an overhead view of each group," Lucy stated.

"That's fine. We've got nothing to hide. I just want to make sure that they don't either," Chief said.

The travelers from Shelter 87 turned around and headed toward Red Top Mountain State Park.

"We aren't even exactly sure where this settlement is or if they're friendly," Lucy pointed out. "We could have Kara and Marsha put up their other drone to locate and investigate this place we're going."

Chief considered it. "If we get all three drones committed and run into problems, the only other one we have is on our roof—with a depleted battery. I don't like that. We don't have that far to go. Make a couple more orbits with the one over us to make sure we're clear, and then send it in search of the settlement. Okay?"

Lucy agreed and input the commands. When she finished,

she saw a change on one of the screens. The Texas convoy now had four other vehicles, a few miles behind it and gaining on them.

"Looks to be getting busy out here," she murmured after informing Chief of what she'd viewed.

"139-4-19 from 87-4-22," Chief said into the radio.

"Go ahead," a familiar voice said.

"Strange question, but how many vehicles are with you?"

"17 total. Why?"

"We've had some troubles on our journey and now keep a drone in the air at all times. Four vehicles are approaching you from behind. They're about two-three miles back," Chief explained.

Chapter Fifty-One

Desmond and Shelia secured their boat to the recently installed dock. Others were taking the fish they'd caught for processing. Shelia remembered her grandfather telling her stories about fishing before the comet, and those stories didn't match up with what she'd experienced.

Now, they headed over to assist with the unloading of a trailer-load of lumber and other materials that an ORV had brought. Supplies were coming in several times a day. There were lots of building materials available, too, if you knew where to look.

The repairs on the building, now designated for operations, were complete, and a new project had started.

As they were working, Leo approached them. "As I was returning with the load, I heard radio traffic. It was too far away to understand, but it wasn't any of our people from the bits I caught. I just thought you might want to know."

"Thanks for telling us. We've had visitors before; we'll take precautions. Do we still have teams out?"

"Four teams. I'll head over to the operations building and see if I can get them on the radio," Leo offered. "I doubt there's anyone in there now."

"Good." Desmond looked at Shelia. "Go pass the word that we might be getting guests."

As she turned to leave, she caught motion in the air and saw a drone descending towards them. "Look there!"

The drone hovered at fifteen feet, then shot up and disappeared. The three of them followed it with their eyes.

"Anyone know if that was one of ours?" Desmond asked.

"I don't think so. All our people know not to use them that close to the buildings, after that incident a while back," Shelia replied.

Desmond nodded. "I'll go to operations myself. That drone was intentionally showing itself to us." He walked the seventy-five yards to the operations building, pressed the button for the generator, and waited thirty seconds for it to come up to power.

When the lights in the ceiling stabilized into a constant glow, he pressed the button on the desktop microphone. "Drone operator, this is Community 47-1."

"Community 47-1, this is 87-4-22. Sorry if our drone startled anyone, but we wanted to get your attention and ask if it would be okay to stop in for a visit."

"Certainly, we're always glad to have visitors. How many in your group? We'll prepare lunch."

"We've got nine people in three vehicles, but there's another group coming in behind us that's much larger."

"The more, the better. We're always looking forward to meeting others," Desmond said cheerfully.

He then spoke to the remaining teams outside the area. He learned that they'd made contact with the large group that was on the way and were leading them in. So far, nothing from either of these two groups was concerning.

He peered over at Leo. "Pass the word. We need to get our equipment moved out of the way. We have twenty outside vehicles a few minutes away that includes a couple of 40s. I don't know where we'll park them all."

Leo nodded. "Boss, if they're hostile, we don't have enough manpower here to defend ourselves."

Chapter Fifty-Two

Lucy was apprehensive as their trio of vehicles left the main roads and continued on the route the drone had shown them. The abundance of trees caused the road to be heavily shaded. It was apparent that recent work to remove the overgrowth had made the road passable.

There had been signs which were still readable for a visitor's center, but they were heading away from that and moving toward what the sign had said was the marina.

The group from Texas had made contact with a local team who was leading them here as well, so Lucy had recalled the drone. The two of them now circled, waiting for a break in the tree cover so they could land.

At last, the trees opened and the marina was visible. Chief was surprised to see new construction taking place. There were also several boats on the water.

"This is an interesting place," he commented, impressed.

A woman stepped towards them; she had an assault rifle over her shoulder but looked friendly. Chief stopped next to her.

"Welcome to Red Top Mountain. I'm Shelia. My

husband, Desmond, was the Senate President and is now the Mayor of this community," she informed them.

Chief smiled. "I'm Chief and this is my wife, Lucy. Thanks for letting us visit. You're the first person from another shelter that we've met in person."

"Well, it'll be fun getting to know you," she said with a smile that seemed genuine.

"I see your people are armed; is there danger around here?" Chief asked, glancing around.

"To be honest, we don't know you and are just being careful," Shelia admitted.

"I understand that," Chief agreed, appreciating her honesty. "Where do you want us to park?"

She directed them to park near a building that was under construction. The three vehicles moved ahead and parked as directed. While everyone was exiting, two other men approached.

Before they said anything, Chief called out to his people. "Leave the rifles here. Let's make sure they know we aren't here to cause problems. Also, lockdown each ORV. We don't know about the others that are coming in."

Everyone complied and Chief turned to the two approaching men who had overheard his instructions. "Hello."

The two came up to Chief and the shorter of the two spoke. "Welcome, I'm Desmond. You already met my wife and this is Leo. Glad to meet you."

Chief introduced the members of his team.

"So, there's another group coming in behind you. What can you tell us?" Desmond asked.

"Not much. They claim to be from a shelter in Texas and are heading to the east coast. We discovered each other and decided to meet up. They suggested we come here. They'd encountered someone who knew about you."

"We're trying to make ourselves known. We want to be a

place others can come to, and trade and share information," Leo explained casually.

"You picked a beautiful place, right here on the lake," Theresa motioned.

"It's a great place. You're welcome to join us for lunch under the pavilion. You'll probably get the first fresh fish most of you've ever had, and it's amazing. Our people are still studying it, but we believe that certain plants in the lakes thrived with the extra radiation. These plants are what the fish are eating. The fish have all tested as healthy, but there are tons of them, and they're huge."

Sam spoke up. "Are you smoking the fish too? I smell something familiar."

Leo nodded. "We are. It's the best preservation method we have. There are a bunch of smokers running almost around the clock."

Jenny had worked herself closer to the front; Desmond saw her and Wilbur. Bending down, he pet the puppy. "Sweetie, your dog is cute. There are other kids about your age in the area and a couple of dogs too. I think you'll both like it here."

Jenny was thrilled—imagine, other kids and dogs! This might be a fun stop.

"Now, I need to meet this other group," Desmond advised, "but we'll meet for lunch in about an hour. Have fun and meet some of our people."

"Do you mind if I stay with you?" Chief asked. "I want to get a feel for them too."

"That's fine, follow me. With all their vehicles, we're parking them in a different spot."

Chief nodded to the three other surface-born. "*No one wonders off alone. I'll see you at lunch in an hour.*"

Chapter Fifty-Three

Lucy and Sam led the others away from the parking area. This place had once been a thriving recreational area, and the beauty remained. It was encouraging to see the new construction, happening and knowing that people were putting down roots on the surface again.

"I like it here. It is warmer. More like the temperature we had in the shelter," Oliver commented.

"Feeling the warmth from the sun on my face is nice," Kara added with a smile.

Jenny agreed. "Yeah, but the air is different. Thicker."

"Remember, Jenny, you learned about that in training. That's because there's more moisture in the air than we had inside. Right?" Kara looked to her mother for confirmation.

"That's exactly right. Temperature and humidity constantly change outside," Lucy explained.

As they walked past a four-person ORV that had been modified with a large wagon full of lumber attached, Lucy thought something seemed off.

Theresa was thinking the same thing and spoke first. "With all the work going on here, where is everyone?"

Lucy realized that was what seemed wrong: there was no

one around. It was as if all work stopped when the travelers from 87 had arrived.

Set back off the road were three trailers, similar to the one they'd just passed. Each had a big propane tank on it.

"That's smart," Tyler said. "They can refuel right here."

Agreeing, Sam said, "True, but it must have been a heck of a job to move them here. Each of those tanks holds about 2000 gallons."

Further along, tucked back among trees, there was a small building with a low roof. It was old and had recent modifications.

As they drew closer, Wilbur started barking and pulling on his leash; whatever was over there, he wanted to see it and was fighting Jenny and the leash.

"Wilbur, No. No," Jenny repeatedly said, a little more forcefully each time, frustrated by her fuzzy friend's insistence.

Oliver scooped up the dog, who struggled to get to the building. As they approached, strange sounds and smells were coming from inside. It had been over 32 years, but the three surface-born knew the sound. Before they could explain, two young women with assault rifles stepped out. They were in their mid-teens and appeared deadly serious.

"Are you with the small group or the big Texas group?" the taller one asked.

"We're with the first group, the smaller group," Lucy answered.

The intensity on the teens' faces melted, and they lowered their weapons.

"Sorry about that. We weren't sure. You guys checked out, but we haven't heard about the others," the taller one advised.

"Okay, guys. You can come out," the other called and, from behind the lower building, fourteen children appeared. Two of them were small enough that they needed someone to carry them, and the oldest was almost as old as the two guards.

Theresa was confused. "So, what are you doing? Protecting all these kids?"

"There've been a few problems with visitors that ... weren't nice. A couple of our people died in an attack a few months ago, so we're extra careful. Tracy and I just got weapon-certified last week. They told us to watch the kids until we heard that it was clear. They radioed that you guys were fine," she explained.

"So, where *is* everyone else?" Marsha asked.

"As soon as we learned strangers were coming, they got in position. They're here. You just can't see them." the one called Tracy said.

She noted their puzzled expressions. "Did you see the three boats out on the water but close to shore?"

Lucy's team nodded.

"Well, there's a sniper on each. There are also some in the woods and tucked all around the area where they're bringing in the visitors. You didn't see them because they're very careful. As soon as we get the all-clear and hear that the new group is okay, everyone will return to work."

Satisfied with the explanation, Lucy introduced her people and learned that the other girl was named Daphne. The kids asked for and were granted permission by Tracy to see Wilbur.

As the kids were checking out Jenny and her dog, Lucy asked, "Is that a barn? I thought I heard chickens."

"Yeah, it is ... come see," Daphne gestured.

They entered through a small side door and immediately smelled animals. The first pen held three scrawny chickens and a duck. They walked to the second and saw a single animal.

Kara surveyed it for several seconds. "Is that a baby horse? A ... foal?" She was impressed with herself for coming up with the word.

Lucy chuckled at her twenty-three-year-old daughter, who had never seen animals before Wilbur. "Not exactly."

"No, that's a donkey, and he isn't a baby," Tracy answered.

Daphne caught Kara's embarrassed expression. "Don't feel bad. None of us were sure what it was either. When our teams are out looking for supplies, any animal sightings take first priority. We need to build up their numbers. One of our teams saw a pig but couldn't catch it. But we've got a pair of cows. We keep them in a different place that has more room."

Jenny asked, "So, you get to eat *real* chicken, not from a can or bag?"

"No, we only have three; we can't eat them. We need to do everything we can to help the chickens breed. We won't be eating any for maybe five to ten years. That's if we can find a rooster."

During the explanation, Tracy had held her hand to her ear and was frozen in place. Suddenly, she spoke. "Kids! The other new people are okay too. You can go find your parents."

Chapter Fifty-Four

As Lucy, Sam, and Theresa approached the pavilion, they could smell smoke and cooking fish. The others were chatting with some new shelter-born friends they'd made, discussing their first experiences with the outside world.

They saw Chief sitting at a table with half a dozen others, including Desmond and Shelia. They approached and met the leaders of the convoy from Texas.

"So far, we've learned that shelter life was about as boring in Texas and Georgia as it was in Michigan," Chief summarised with a grin.

"That, and being in a larger shelter was much better," Desmond added with a smile.

Regarding Sam, Lucy, and Theresa, he explained, "Our shelter here was a Level 4. We didn't have a pool, and there were fewer people, only two theaters, so available TV and movie content was much less." He pointed at the Texas contingent. "These guys were in a Level 2 and had a TV production studio and created their own programming, movies, and shows."

Sam nodded, impressed. "We did a lot of that too, but it was by recording on an old cell phone or tablet, and sending it out on the internal network. We were able to maintain a regular release schedule, but a studio with real recording gear would've been much better."

"Without a pool, none of our shelter-born had ever been in water, let alone knew how to swim," Shelia told them.

"That's true. Not only did they have to learn to walk around outside, but then we were trying to get them to function in water," Desmond added. "We still won't let them on the boats until they can swim relatively well, and many refuse to try."

Neil, the group leader from Shelter 139 in Texas, asked, "What are you doing to protect yourself from radiation here? We're limiting exposure by finding an underground place to spend the nights."

"We're doing the same thing," Theresa stated.

"The old visitor's center here had a storm cellar below ground and is somewhat protected but isn't great. We're working to fortify the building and adding sandbags to the floor to improve the protection there. So, we spend some nights there.

"We've got two teams and we do three-day rotations. Each team is out here for three days, working during the day and getting into the visitor center basement at night. Then, we rotate back to the shelter for three days. The shelter is about 10 miles from here, and shuttling back and forth took lots of time, so we went to this rotation. Speaking of that, you're all welcome to spend the night at Shelter 189. The people there would love to meet you. Also, you could see just how small a Level 4 shelter is."

Chief glanced at the others and, despite the desire to get to Florida, saw three heads nodding in agreement.

Sam was curious. "Where are all your work teams? There are less than a hundred people here. Did some decide not to stay with your community when the doors opened for the first time?"

The Anvil

"Our shelter doors opened about six months ago. Of the 940 people, less than a hundred decided to leave the area. The rest are still here. We've got several primary projects.

"This is one of them. The fish are our primary source of protein, and we harvest, process and ship back to the shelter for freezing. There's still limited power there, but it's enough to keep the freezers online. As part of this effort, we've got people working at the visitors center. They're working to make it a better underground area for safe sleeping.

"There's also a bunch of people a few miles from here, working on what had been a reasonably young subdivision. Most of the houses are in okay shape, and they're getting them liveable again. We think that the radiation will be safe enough in ten more years not to need to shelter at night. We'll have a neighborhood ready and in perfect condition by then.

"We also took over two old farms and are working on getting crops planted. There are over a hundred people dedicated to that. We've got a pair of cows at one of them and are trying to find more.

"Our least desirable task is a few miles from here, at the Regional Medical Center. The main hospital building was only a couple of years old when the comet passed by and appears to be mostly in good condition. We want to get it operational again, which is a big undertaking. It means getting power back on. It also means removing the thousands of corpses that remain there. When the comet passed, people flooded the hospitals. There was never time to remove the dead. Thousands of mummified corpses have to be removed, and we've got people working on it."

Upon hearing that, Lucy stood and walked away. Twenty minutes later, when their hosts served the fantastic fish lunch, she hadn't returned.

Chapter Fifty-Five

Sam and Chief walked back from Café B, each with a cup of coffee. It was five in the morning and both were up, early as usual. Since almost a hundred people had left, having rooms for the night in Shelter 189 wasn't a problem.

Sam had only started drinking coffee a couple of years before Shelter 89 had run out of it, and he was glad to taste some again. "This is really terrible," he commented with a dry smile. "I know it's been twenty years or so since I had any, but this wasn't what it tasted like."

Chief chuckled. "They recently found a warehouse with a few pallets of the stuff. It was thirty years expired. They say it's still good, but I don't think they know what it is supposed to taste like."

Nonetheless, they kept drinking it.

As they walked, Jenny, carrying Wilbur, approached. She was visibly frustrated.

"Morning, kiddo. What are you doing up so early?" Sam asked.

"Will one of you go with me to take him outside? He needs to go out. I cleaned up after him twice during the night and don't want to have to again."

Smiling, Sam answered, "Glad to. Let's go. See ya later, Chief."

"You know that dog has legs; he can walk," Chief pointed out.

Jenny knew Chief was kidding but wasn't in the mood, so she ignored him and turned to Sam. "I figured if I were carrying him, he wouldn't make another mess that I'd have to clean up."

Sam was unable to fault her logic. "That makes sense."

They walked a little further, and she said, "This place is weird."

Baffled, Sam asked, "How's it weird? It is just like what we had in 89."

"That's what's weird. The carpet is the same and the furniture is the same. The signs look the same. The rooms have the same names. It even smells the same. But, it's all wrong. The rooms are in the wrong places. Halls are missing." She paused as she glanced around with a frown. "It's like they took our shelter apart and built this one … and left a bunch of parts out and mixed it all up."

Sam thought about it and agreed. There *was* an unnerving familiarity, "I know what you mean; it's weird."

They ascended the ramp and headed out the tunnel—and heard a sound.

"What's that noise?" the pre-teen asked.

"That's rain, and it sounds like it is coming down hard. We might get wet."

"Good, I always wanted to see rain."

They stepped into the open and found a torrential downpour.

"Oh, wow! That's a lot of water!" The child who had never seen rain said.

Before Sam could respond, there was an explosive clap of thunder, followed by a blinding flash of lightning.

Jenny shrieked and dropped Wilbur. She flung herself

against Sam, who held her close. A second later, she composed herself and screamed. "Where's Wilbur? I can't see him!"

It was mostly dark, and purple spots from the lightning bolt obscured their vision.

Sam grabbed her arm. "We'll find him, but the lightning and thunder will happen again, so be ready."

"Wilbur, Wilbur!"

They stumbled into the monsoon-like weather and were instantly soaked to the bone. When the second clap of thunder happened, Jenny was ready; she flinched but didn't scream. After a minute of searching, she heard whimpering and found him. As he ran, his leash caught between the bottom of a small boulder and the ground. She pulled it free and led the dog back to the safety of the shelter.

As they moved inside, Jenny said, "I don't like rain."

Sam smiled. "Did he pee while he was out there?"

"I don't know, but I think *I* did," the girl admitted with a rueful smile.

"Don't worry; no one will be able to tell."

Chapter Fifty-Six

Neil and Desmond entered the storage area in Shelter 189.

Chief saw them and waved them over. "We all want to thank you for your hospitality," Chief said to Desmond.

"We're sorry that you can't stay any longer," Desmond smiled. "Neil here is going to keep his Texas crew around a couple of days before they head back out."

Chief nodded. "We would, but my wife Lucy and Sam were kids when the comet came. They ended up separated from their parents, who ended up in 104 in Florida. They're anxious to get there and see if they're still alive."

"I can understand that," Desmond said. "If in the future, you're looking for a place to settle down, you're always welcome to join us in the Red Top Mountain area. The only requirement is you have to like fish."

They all laughed and Neil asked, "Did you say your wife's parents are in 104?"

Chief nodded. "Yeah, 104."

"Well, the only other group we encountered while heading this way was from 104."

Chief's eyes widened. "What did they have to say about their shelter. And people?"

Neil thought about it before answering. "The ones we talked to were headed west in a convoy even bigger than ours. Remember those videos that were circulated between the shelters years back? Made by that David Cowan and talking about being ready to meet the sleepers when they awaken?"

"Sure, I remember that."

"Well, that David Cowan was at 104. And these people were going to a place he picked out to set up a community and await the awakening of the sleepers."

"Do you know if everyone from the shelter went?" Chief asked.

"No. Like everywhere else, different folks went in different directions, and some stayed at the shelter. I forget how it went, but they were able to extend their reactor life by taking nuclear fuel from an abandoned shelter. I don't recall the details around that."

Chief didn't need an explanation; he had a good idea of what happened. There was good reason to think Sam and Lucy's parents might still be at 104 ... *if* they were still alive.

FIVE HOURS LATER, Lucy was driving as they approached the Florida border. The people at 189 and the Texas caravan were friendly and fun to be with, and the twenty-four hours spent with them were enjoyable. However, it was time to get to 104.

The cooler of smoked fish and full tanks of propane were nice gifts from their new friends in Georgia.

Chief was resting his eyes as they traveled onward. The three vehicles' navigators took turns watching the drone view while the other two rested. Since Lucy was in the lead, she remained focused in case road obstacles were called out.

They had left the highway because of a collapsed bridge and were on a two-lane secondary road. The shoulder had washed away over time, making the roadway more narrow than usual.

"22, there's something stretched across the road about a mile ahead," Oliver transmitted. "Not sure what it is ... working on getting a better view."

Lucy slowed.

"It looks like a log. The road is narrow, partly washed out on the edges. You'll need to slow to go over it. We might just want to stop and move it out of the way."

Moments later, he was back on the air. "All vehicles stop. Don't get close to it. That isn't a log. I think it is an alligator."

Everyone's attention turned to the screens. The gator was enormous and stretched across both lanes.

"So, what do we do? The gullies on both sides are very steep. Not sure if the ORV can handle it," Theresa stated over the radio.

"We could just shoot it." Kara, sitting behind Chief and Lucy, offered.

"No, we aren't shooting it. So little survived the radiation, we don't need to be killing off what did make it," Chief told his impulsive daughter.

Lucy began moving forward again, wanting to get a direct view of the animal. The others followed and found that it was even larger than they imagined. The creature was dark green and tan and looked to be sunning itself. If it weren't for the tail's infrequent movements, it would be impossible to know if it were dead or alive.

"I bet it's twelve feet long," Lucy said, awed.

Oliver's voice came over the radio. "Can we just nudge it out of the way?"

"That beast could tear a tire off one of these vehicles," Chief told him.

"That tail gets real narrow near the end," Lucy pointed out. "I bet we could get over it at fifty miles an hour, before the gator even moves."

Voices of approval radioed back.

Lucy glanced at Chief, who shrugged, not having a better idea. "If he grabs a vehicle, he can do some damage. Maybe even overturn it."

"I can cover them and make sure he doesn't grab them," Kara stated.

Marsha's voice rang over the radio. "I don't mind going first. I'll get this big ORV past him … before he knows what is happening."

"Okay, that's what we do," Chief agreed reluctantly. Kara popped the roof hatch and he said, "Maybe you and I should change places."

"Dad, I can handle this," his daughter replied forcefully.

Lucy moved as close as she could without fearing a reaction from the animal, while Marsha backed away to get a running start. Releasing the locks, Kara brought the weapon around, lining up on the creature, knowing that he would probably move before she needed to shoot.

When Marsha and 12-6 passed Lucy's ORV, they were already going over 50 mph. She kept it as close to the edge of the washed-out road as she dared. Where the tires struck, the tail was about eight inches thick, and the impact shook the vehicle hard at that speed. Marsha, expecting this, managed to keep control and stay on the roadway.

The alligator's response was explosive and it whipped around, folding himself in half to get to whatever it was that had struck his tail. However, he wasn't expecting the assault, and his reaction wasn't fast enough to attack the fleeing vehicle.

Kara was shocked. She'd watched the whole thing through the gun's sights and was in awe that something so big and cumbersome could react so fast.

"We're all fine. We hit him at about 55, and it knocked us around, but no damage. Whoever goes next should take it a bit slower," Marsha advised.

The Anvil

"No one is going next," Chief stated firmly. "He came real close, as in inches, from getting you, and he wasn't expecting it. Now, he's alert. We certainly can't do it again slower."

They could see the animal was agitated. He was in the same spot but his tail was thrashing; his eyes were now open, and he kept turning his head to look in all directions. Even inside, with the engines running, they could hear it snorting loudly.

They jumped in their seats as the loud M240B machine gun fired a single shot.

Chief had been watching and saw as the 7.62mm round blast a baseball-size hole in the old asphalt, three feet from the reptile's head. Seconds later, another round made a similar impact six inches closer.

The reptilian brain in the alligator had no idea what was happening, but he did know that something had happened to his tail, and it hurt. Now, something frightening was happening near his head. With increased agitation, and no ability to reason, he wanted to leave the place where he'd been resting. He started walking to the far side of the road, headed to the gully beyond.

Chief was about to tell his maverick daughter to stop shooting but decided to see what decision she'd make on her own. Seconds later, when he heard the upper hatch close, and her butt drop back into the seat, he knew the answer.

"You just had to shoot the gun," he said.

"It worked, didn't it?" Neither of her parents could see the ear-to-ear grin on her face.

"It sure did," Lucy remarked.

"Nice shooting, gunner," her Uncle Sam's voice said across the radio.

"Your aim sucks, sis," Tyler teased from the other vehicle.

Chapter Fifty-Seven

FOLLOWING THE INCIDENT WITH THE ALLIGATOR, SOMEONE with an assault rifle escorted Jenny every time she walked Wilbur. They'd become quite fond of him, and no one wanted to see him become some gator's lunch.

They were getting back in the vehicles following the latest stop, and the drivers swapped places as necessary. As always, some people changed where they were riding.

Chief scooped up the pup and looked at his owner. "Okay if he rides with me?"

Ever since the thunderstorm, the dog hadn't been his enthusiastic self. He wanted someone to hold him more than usual.

Jenny wasn't surprised by Chief's request. When not driving, Chief often sat with Wilbur on his lap. Before she could answer, he looked at Kara. "Find a new ride. Wilbur and Jenny are with us."

"Dad!" Kara tried to sound offended and they all giggled.

The day before, Jenny had let Wilbur ride in a vehicle without her; neither of them had done well with that.

They headed out and Chief told Jenny, "That should be the last stop before we get to Shelter 104."

"Good, we've been driving a long time."

LUCY'S HANDS were sweating and she felt mildly nauseous. She could tell her heart rate was up. She hadn't felt anxiety like this since her first night in Shelter 87, when she realized she and Sam were all alone. Now, the computer indicated that they were just a couple of miles from where her parents should be.

Chief took the radio. "Shelter 104, this is 87-4-22."

Lucy looked over at him. "Why aren't they answering?" The concern was evident in her voice.

"You watch the road. I'll do this. They might not have anyone near the radio, or their radio might have died years ago. We'll figure it out."

Lucy tried to relax and focus on driving, but she was too concerned.

"Shelter 104, this is 87-4-22," Chief repeated. To Lucy, he said, "Take your next left, and then it looks like you'll be heading into the mine area."

"Go ahead 87-4-22. This is 104," the voice from the radio said.

Everyone sighed in relief.

"We're a convoy of three vehicles approaching. May we come in to visit?"

Several seconds later, a light on a pole came on ahead of them. "The ramp in is by the light. We're opening doors now."

The three ORVs descended the ramp into a parking area that looked a lot like what they'd left in Michigan. Everyone got out, relieved to stretch their legs. A door opened and two men approached. One appeared to be in his mid-thirties, the other in his mid-fifties.

Sam saw them first and raised his hand in greeting. "Is it okay to park where we did?"

"No problem," the taller, older one said.

Sam thought there was something vaguely familiar about the older man. There hadn't been any video communication between the shelters in close to 10 years. Still, Sam immediately knew who the younger man was. "Kevin, right?"

"...Sam?"

The two men who had never met face-to-face but had spoken for many hours in the past warmly embraced. Hearing the commotion, Lucy hurried over.

Kevin Torez hugged his foster parent's daughter, each glad to finally meet the other. He addressed the group. "Guys, this is our Senate President, David Cowan."

Everyone recognized the name, and Sam realized why he looked familiar. He'd seen all the videos that David had circulated.

Chief looked at David. "You're the one whose father was a huge part of the sleeper project. Right?"

"Yup, that's me. Welcome to 104. I started out with Marie and Alex, and Kevin here, in Shelter 16. I was with them on the mad dash when we had to change shelters twenty-three years ago."

Lucy introduced everyone else, and Kevin remembered video conferencing with most of them when they were kids.

David had heard about the grandkids from Alex and Marie many times. "How about Kevin takes Sam and Lucy to their parents? We can let them have some time together, and I'll give the rest of you all a quick tour. We'll end up at the Wilsons' residence."

Everyone agreed, and Lucy and Sam left with Kevin.

This shelter was now the third one the Wilson siblings had been in, so they weren't surprised how much it resembled theirs in Michigan.

"I know I've told you both this before, but your parents are amazing. They helped my mom and me when we first got to 16 and later took me in. They've been great friends."

Doing the math in his head, Sam relished that Kevin had spent much longer with his parents than he had.

"When we opened the doors here, your parents weren't sure what to do. They wanted to leave. They wanted to race to 87 to find you, and they also wanted to go back home. They thought you might look for them at your old house. Some of us convinced them to stay here. They were getting older and taking off on their own was too dangerous. We knew that if it were possible, you'd show up here."

"There was never any doubt," Lucy said. "We knew from the day our shelter doors sealed that we'd be headed here as soon as we could leave 87. Being separated from them all this time has been awful."

They arrived at a door and Kevin said, "Here it is. I'm going to go find the others, and we'll be back in a bit."

"Thanks, Kevin," Sam said with a grateful smile.

Fifty-year-old Lucy raised her fist to knock on the door, about to see her parents for the first time since she was 17. She was excited and terrified.

Chapter Fifty-Eight

ALEX WILSON WAS SITTING IN HIS CHAIR, ENJOYING A NOVEL which he'd never read before. One of the things he liked the most about the shelter opening was the stuff the scavenger teams were bringing back. That included books. He'd read every book in the shelter repeatedly, and something different was a welcome change. Today's treasure was titled *Alternate Purpose*.

Marie was in bed asleep, and he was considering waking her up to get some dinner. The quality of the food had improved since the shelter opened.

There was a knock at the door. Alex didn't move to get up. Almost everyone would knock once and then come in. This time that didn't happen. Mildly irritated, Alex lifted his sore 72-year-old body from the chair and ambled to the door. He turned the knob and found a middle-aged couple standing there. Alex knew everyone who lived in 104 and, for a second, he wasn't sure who these two were. Then it registered, and his mouth wouldn't move ... and his legs crumpled.

His son caught him before he hit the floor and helped him back to his feet. The three of them held one another, crying for over a minute before any of them spoke.

As Lucy held her father, she was horrified at how frail he'd become. She knew his age and that he wouldn't look the same as when they last had a video conference, but she wasn't ready for this.

"I missed you both so much. All we've wanted is to see you again."

"We came as soon as we could, dad," Lucy said, wiping tears from her cheeks.

"We know. This is all our fault. We should never have left you alone to take that cruise."

That statement shocked Sam. "We don't blame you. Deciding to go on vacation wasn't wrong. There's no way anyone could've known."

Seeing that her father's outlook on that subject wouldn't budge, Lucy changed the subject. "Where's Mom?"

"Asleep in the bedroom. You should go in there, but we need to talk first ... unless Kevin told you."

Concern lined Sam's face. "Told us what? Kevin didn't say anything."

"Two years ago, your mother had a stroke. We didn't think she'd survive, but she did."

"How bad is she?" Lucy asked as fresh tears formed in her eyes.

"Fortunately, her memory wasn't affected. Her left arm and leg are very weak. If she's just taking a step or two, I can help her with that, but anything more, and she needs her wheelchair. She's become quite depressed because of it. You being here will be a big help, I hope."

Turning, the kids headed for the bedroom and opened the door—and saw their mother in person for the first time in thirty-three years. Sam's eyes bulged when he saw how small she looked in the bed. Lucy walked up with Sam right behind her. She reached down and took her mother's frail hand.

"Mom, it's us. Lucy and Sam. Wake up; we're here."

Her reaction was almost identical to their father's. At first, she couldn't even speak, but the tears on her face said everything. "I can't believe you're here. I'd all but given up."

"As soon as we could, we headed right here," Sam said.

"Oh, Sammy, you're so grown up. I missed you both terribly."

"We're here now, and we aren't leaving," Lucy promised.

"How long did it take you to get here?"

"We were on the road six days," Sam replied.

"I want to hear all about the trip and what's left outside," Marie said.

"On the way here, we stopped at the house. It's still there. We took pictures and brought you a few things," Sam told her.

"Those will be interesting to look at. I want to see how things held up there," Alex said.

After a few minutes of conversation, Marie insisted on getting out of bed and moving to the living room. She let Sam and Lucy help her walk the few steps. They got her seated in her chair and then took seats across from her on the couch.

"Are the others here? My grandchildren?" she asked with a hopeful smile.

"Of course," Lucy assured her. "Kevin and David are showing them around so we could get a few minutes with you first."

"Kevin and David are wonderful people. David has been a great leader. The people really respect him. The kids sit with him for hours as he tells them stories about how life was before. He has a way of talking that keeps their attention. They affectionately call him 'the old man'. He's going to be headed west to meet the sleepers soon, and Kevin wants to go with him, but he won't leave us behind," Marie explained.

"Kevin and Penny, that's his wife, have been helping with anything we need," Alex told them. "When Mom first had her stroke, one or both were here every night."

Sam was glad that his parents had people to watch out for them. However, he also felt a bit jealous that others were getting time with his parents when he couldn't. Looking at the expression on Lucy's face, he could tell she was feeling that too.

There was a knock at the door, and Chief and Theresa entered.

"Kevin explained the health situation to us, so we decided to come in a few at a time rather than swarm you guys," Theresa explained.

Having stood, Alex embraced his son-in-law and daughter-in-law. As he did, Marie had Lucy help her to her feet so she could too. "We spoke so much on the video calls way back. I missed you both terribly," Marie told her children's spouses.

"When that last satellite failed, and communication was no longer possible, it was difficult for all of us. We had become so attached. I missed the contact we had with you guys," Chief said.

Minutes later, there was another knock, and the rest of the family entered. Kara and her grandmother had been very close and video-chatted regularly. Lucy was concerned about how Kara would react to seeing her in this condition.

Kara went right to her and, with tears in her eyes, took her in her arms. "I missed you so much, Grandma."

"I know, I missed you too. I loved all our talks."

"We'll have many more. I've got so much to tell you about," Kara said enthusiastically. She stepped aside to hug her grandfather and let Tyler have a minute with Marie.

Marie noticed Tyler's limp. "What's wrong with your leg, Tyler—"

"Don't fall for it, Grandma; he just wants attention," Kara interrupted. "He stepped in front of a tiny bullet, just to get everyone to feel sorry for him."

Her grandmother looked at her with a warm smile. "I forgot how much I enjoy you!"

They all laughed.

"Now, Tyler, what *did* you do?" she asked again.

When it was Oliver's chance to talk to his grandparents, he introduced Marsha and Jenny and told them how lucky he was to have them both.

"Can I see your dog?" Alex asked Jenny.

She handed him over.

"What happened to his ear?"

"It was like that when we found him. We think something attacked him," the young girl answered.

"I've always loved dogs. It's nice to see that there are still some around."

Twenty minutes later, they exited the Wilson's residence and headed to Café A for dinner. Kara was pushing her grandmother's chair and Alex was carrying Wilbur.

There wasn't a line to get food, so Kara took a seat with her grandmother and Wilbur, and waited while the others went and got trays. David and Kevin arrived at the Café and joined them.

Much of the food looked like the familiar rehydrated vegetables from ration packs. Surprisingly, there was meat mixed in with it and, on the side, there was a breaded piece of meat that had been deep-fried. It was twice the size of a hockey puck and about as thick.

"This actually smells pretty good," Marsha said.

"Since we opened the shelter up, the food has improved. We can get some fresh meat. Two weeks ago, a team went west and caught fish. That was nice, but it was gone fast," Kevin explained.

"What kind of meat is in this?" Chief asked, eyeing the piece on his plate.

"Well mixed in with the vegetables is python, and the deep-fried piece is alligator tail," Alex explained.

Jenny put down her fork.

"It may not sound appetizing, but they both taste a lot

better than the ration packs. These reptiles are all over the place, and our hunting parties have no problems getting all we need. It seems that the radiation didn't impact them to the same degree," David advised.

"On the way here, my sister tried to shoot us a gator," Tyler told them with a grin. "She was twenty feet away and missed, *twice*."

Chapter Fifty-Nine

Two weeks later, Alex arranged for a family dinner. They gathered and ate, and then Alex brought up something some of them had been thinking about.

"I wanted to get us together to talk about what we're going to do. I asked Kevin and Penny to join us because they're family too. Maybe in a different way but still family. Is that okay?"

Everyone from Shelter 87 nodded.

"We'd very much like to leave here. The new society out west sounds exciting. David is leaving soon to connect with those that have already headed out. Even more, now that we know it is still there, we'd want to go back to our home in Indiana."

Lucy's stomach churned at the thought.

"Unfortunately, Marie isn't up for either of those trips—"

"Dad, if that's what she wants, we can make it happen," Sam interrupted. "Even if that means taking seats out of an ORV and adding a bed."

The others all agreed.

"We can get you back home. That won't be a problem," Chief assured them.

"We do appreciate that, we really do, but there's nothing there. No medical care, no food, no people. It wouldn't make sense. We discussed it and are staying here."

"If that's what you're comfortable with, then that's what you should do," Lucy said. "We support anything you choose to do. We're just glad to be together again."

With great effort, Marie forced herself to her feet. "There's nothing here for any of you. Most of the people have moved on. The future is in communities like the one David will help create and the one you visited in Atlanta. We think that's where you should go too. Build your lives. It's time for you to stop living in the bunkers."

Kara replied, "You guys do need some help. We can't just abandon you. I won't leave you."

Alex nodded. "We just want you to consider it. David is leaving in a couple of days with a group of over fifty people. Almost everyone else who is planning to leave is pretty much already gone. We won't be alone here. Almost a hundred others are staying here with us."

TYLER ENTERED the training room and saw the other shelter-born were already there. "Thanks for coming, guys. I was thinking about what Grandpa said about moving on, and I think maybe we should consider heading west with David."

Confused, Kara said, "They won't leave Grandma and Grandpa again. Not after just getting them back. Are you saying that we should just leave our parents here?"

"There isn't anything for us here in this shelter. If we go west, they can catch up with us when they're able to," Tyler explained.

"You mean after our grandparents are dead! Right?" Kara snapped.

"Kara, I'm just throwing it out as an option. Kevin and

David are going, and I think we should consider joining them."

Oliver and Marsha remained silent, letting the siblings debate.

"I'm not going. Grandma and Grandpa need help, and I'm not leaving them," Kara announced in a tone that said there was no room for debate.

"What about you guys?" Tyler asked as he regarded Oliver.

Oliver glanced at Marsha, who said, "We'll go. I want to get Jenny out of the shelters and into a normal community."

Kara stomped out of the room.

THE NEXT TWENTY-FOUR hours was an emotion-filled ride. There was sorrow, disappointment, and a little anger. In the end, they agreed that Lucy, Sam, Chief, Theresa, and Kara would remain at Shelter 104 until things changed; they would then head west to meet up with the others.

After many tears, the others loaded up the twelve-passenger ORV, joined David Cowan's eight-vehicle convoy, and headed west.

As the convoy departed, Lucy and Sam returned to life in a shelter.

Chapter Sixty

THE LATEST CARAVAN TO TRAVEL WEST HAD BEEN ON THE ROAD for two days and was making good progress. The leader of the convoy was Scotty Reynolds. His goal was simple: get David Cowan and the rest of the group safely to their destination. He was determined to do it.

For young Jenny, this had turned out to be a good group for her to connect with. There were a handful of other kids near her age traveling with them. They'd grown up together under the surface of Florida and knew each other well.

This could've made Jenny feel like an outsider. She was the only kid wearing a tactical vest with a combat knife, but she didn't care. Jenny had something important going for her. She had a puppy, and this made her an instant favorite of everyone.

To keep the travelers from getting too bored, people changed vehicles every time the convoy stopped; most of the other children went wherever Jenny and Wilbur were. For a puppy, Wilbur was getting all the attention he could ever want.

Marsha was driving 87-12-6, with Oliver sitting next to her. Four others were riding with them, and they were becoming steadfast friends.

Jenny and Wilbur were riding in the 40-passenger ORV bus directly in front of them. The kids had taken over the back and were hanging out there. Someone had removed many of the seats to make room for cargo, but there was enough space for them to set up sleeping bags and create a cozy kids-only area.

Looking to the left, Oliver saw movement in the distance. It was a rather barren area, and when he looked, there was a dust cloud a quarter-mile away. It appeared to be coming from a road or trail that was roughly paralleling them. It was visible for a couple of minutes and then gone.

Oliver activated his headset. "4-33 from 12-6."

"Go ahead 12-6," Scotty Reynolds, in the lead ORV, replied.

"We just saw a dust cloud from a vehicle paralleling us off to the left."

"Yeah, we saw it too. We aren't going to chase it down."

Oliver concurred with that decision. "Agreed, but I was wondering if we should get a drone up? Check it out and make sure there isn't anything going on that we'd want to know about?"

"No, we're going to wear out the drones if we keep launching them. Let's just keep going."

Marsha looked at Oliver. "It's easy for him to say that. He's never faced an attack out here before."

"I shouldn't have asked. I should've just launched it," Oliver stated flatly.

"Well, it's too late now. We're the outsiders; we need to play nice."

SCOTTY REYNOLDS WAS DRIVING and alert. They came over a small hill and stretched across the road was a large tree. It was too large to drive over. He slammed the brakes and spoke into his headset. "Emergency Stop. Road blocked." He came to a stop just before hitting the tree.

Thinking of the other four-person ORV directly behind him, he tensed, hoping that the new guy from 87, Tyler, was paying attention. He was relieved when he wasn't hit from behind. Then, he was irritated when he heard Tyler on the radio, giving orders.

"We're way too bunched up ... rear vehicles back away and anyone that can get off the road do it."

Scotty wanted to argue, but Tyler was right; this could possibly be a dangerous spot.

JENNY WAS RIDING in the back of a forty-person ORV with a handful of other kids when the emergency braking happened. All the kids slid and laughed, shouting because sliding around was fun. She looked for Wilbur and he was among all the kids.

Suddenly, he stood up and released a vicious growl. He'd never sounded or looked like he did at that moment, and Jenny's blood went cold. She was the first person to sense there was real danger.

SLAMMING ON HER BRAKES, Marsha came to a stop, almost striking the forty-person ORV that Jenny was riding in. Oliver looked at her and the momentary terror on her face, "That was close. Back away/ We shouldn't be right on top of them."

"I can't. The guys behind us are almost touching."

They heard Tyler's concerned orders coming across the radio.

"I guess they can be mad at me," Oliver said as he took the controls and started spinning up a drone.

The drone was only six feet in the air when the first explosion occurred. The raiders were targeting the propane tanks on large buses that often had usable cargo. The shots came from high-powered rifles, not small handguns like those that failed to cause serious damage in the previous attack.

As designed, the tanks blew outward, protecting the inhabitants and cargo.

That design didn't anticipate another ORV to be only a few feet behind the exploding tank—but that design saved Jenny and the other kids. But not 87-12-6, only feet away. The explosion and fireball easily blasted through the front of the passenger compartment, enveloping everyone within.

The bus directly in front of Jenny's was also a target. However, there was more separation between the vehicles, and while the explosion penetrated her bus, the damage wasn't as extreme. The handful of kids and a dog were all but flat on the floor, and the diminished fireball passed overhead, causing minor burns and scalded hair.

The kids were in shock from what had happened and then panicked and started crying. Jenny was aware of other explosions and the sounds of gunfire outside.

The kids wanted to head for the door of the ORV, but Jenny blocked their path. They would be running directly into the battle. She watched the front of the vehicle. Her eyes kept bouncing between the melted plastic, which had once been computer screens, and the crumpled forms of the two adults who had been at the controls. Fortunately, the seatbacks hid most of their bodies from the girl's view. She could feel the flash burns on her face and left arm and smell the damage to her hair.

After a minute, two people with mismatched assault rifles entered the bus. They moved down the aisle, checking some of the cargo that was on board. The one in the lead noticed Jenny and the other kids behind her.

"Look here. A bunch of kids." He approached to see how many there were. "Looks like there are nine of them."

The one behind him responded, "We don't need a bunch of kids to deal with; shoot them!"

The Anvil

As the man brought up his assault rifle, his attention was distracted by the movement of a young dog, approaching and growling.

Jenny's right hand flew to her vest; she drew the knife and pounced.

EVERY INSTINCT in Tyler told him they were in great danger. They were stopped and bunched up. Parked like this was a perilous position to be in.

Almost bumping the vehicles in front and behind, he managed to maneuver the four-person ORV off the road while calling out a warning on the radio. Penny and Kevin Torez were riding with him and seemed confused by his reaction to the obstruction in the road.

No sooner had he made it off the roadway than the first explosion occurred. The device was buried by the tree stretched across the road. It was directly in front of the lead ORV, which tumbled back to where Tyler had been stopped less than a minute ago. Flames engulfed Scottie's vehicle.

Thinking about the propane tank in the fire, he sped to a safe distance, relieved that the driver behind him followed. By then, there had been several more blasts, and he now heard gunfire.

He released the assault rifle from its mounting bracket and sprinted back to the roadway. On the way, he saw several people approaching the rest of his convoy. They were armed and not part of his group. He shot them and continued, aware that Kevin was following.

His first concerns were Oliver, Marsha, and Jenny, and he knew how far back in the eight-vehicle procession they were. As he advanced, he came across several people from their group who were on the ground, including David Cowan, who was bleeding from a gunshot wound to the thigh.

Tyler signaled Kevin to watch David and he continued

looking for the others. He passed a forty-person ORV. There was smoke in the rear, but the rest was intact. The occupants were barricaded inside and armed. He figured that was the best place for them to be and moved on to the next bus.

The exploding tank at the rear of the first bus had incinerated the front of the second, which was where Jenny had been riding. He heard a scream from inside and climbed aboard, careful not to touch the frame that was still hot from the fireball. In the aisle, there seemed to be two battles going on. An intruder was fighting with Wilbur. The man was bringing his gun around toward the dog, who was ripping into his leg. Before he got the gun in position, Tyler fired a single shot.

The second battle was on the floor and already ending. Jenny was straddling the other intruder. She held her knife in two hands and had it buried in the man's chest. She glanced up at Tyler, and for a moment, he thought she'd attack him next. He saw her relax as she recognized him.

"My mom and dad, are they okay?"

Tyler noticed that this was the first time he'd heard her use that term for Oliver. "Not sure. I'm going to check on them next."

"I'm coming with you," she stated firmly.

"No, you aren't." Tyler drew the 9mm semi-automatic handgun from the holster on his vest and handed it to her. "You remember how to use this?"

"Of course."

"You're responsible for these kids. If anyone else comes aboard, and they aren't one of us, *shoot*."

Her expression made it clear that she didn't like being left behind. Still, she took the weapon, worked the slide advancing a round into the chamber, and nodded, indicating that she was ready.

Stepping off the bus, Tyler proceeded toward the back of the convoy. It was clear that the attackers had targeted the tanks on the buses. Probably to disable them, to steal their cargo.

He reached the back of the bus and saw ORV 87-12-6. It was almost touching the bus he'd just left. The flames were roaring as they consumed the vehicle. All the doors were shut. No one had gotten out.

Chapter Sixty-One

8 YEARS LATER

Lucy and Chief stood outside Shelter 104, enjoying the sunset. In the morning, there would be five of them finally departing for the west.

They painfully missed the others that had preceded them on this trip and were anxious to see them again. They'd never expected their stay at 104 to be this long. The assumption was that Marie only had a couple of years, at best. The unspoken plan was that after Marie'd passed, they would pack up Alex and take him with them to meet up with the kids.

Marie had a different plan and lived just short of six years. By that time, Alex's health had deteriorated to the point where he would never be able to make the trip.

Sam and Lucy were thankful for the time they had with them, but the extended nature of their stay had been difficult for all of them. Years of frustration at feeling stuck had ground on Theresa and Chief. Relationships were stressed, almost to the breaking point.

Twenty-four hours earlier, they'd gently transported Alex's body fifteen miles to a local cemetery. It was the same place they'd been two years prior, when they'd buried Marie.

Now, it was time to leave.

They turned and went back inside and headed to Café A. They found Kara and Sam in the kitchen. Kara was dropping fish in the fryer and Sam was removing gator tail from a pressure cooker.

"Thanks for making dinner," Lucy said.

"It's our last one here. We might as well make it good. Maybe someday we'll miss having gator, fish, or python with every meal," Kara replied with a wry smile.

"I don't see that happening," Chief stated.

"Is Theresa coming to dinner?" Lucy asked.

"She was finishing up packing. Said she'd be here soon," Sam replied.

As Kara served the meal, Theresa walked in. "Smells like gator."

"All packed and ready to go?" Kara asked, then realized that wasn't the right thing to ask.

Fortunately, Theresa held her comments to a minimum. "More than." She'd been the most frustrated by the extended stay at 104 and made sure everyone knew it. She loved her husband's parents and never suggested abandoning them. Nevertheless, everyone knew her feelings about the situation.

When they sat and started to eat, Chief spoke up. "We hit the road tomorrow. There are a couple of logistical things we need to discuss. This trip will be different from last time. There are fewer of us, and more people have come out of the shelters. So, we're more likely to encounter others. Also, the radiation levels are in the safe zone again. There's no need to go underground at night.

"Then, we've got the big issue. We're no longer in the best of condition for a trip like this. I'm 60 years old, and Lucy, Sam, and Theresa aren't too far behind. This means that a lot of the physical work will fall on Kara. We need to plan this so she can handle it."

"Does that mean that I'm in charge?" Kara asked with a smile.

"No," was the loud reply from four people.

When the laughter and side comments ended, Chief said, "There are five of us, so do we take a twelve-person ORV or two fours? I spoke to those remaining here, and we can do either." He had an opinion on this but wanted to hear what Kara would think.

"One will be easier," Sam stated.

Kara shook her head. "If there's a vehicle problem, having two keeps us from being stranded."

"That means fewer drivers for rotating and more work for you with fuelling. We'll help as we can, but we have limits," Lucy pointed out.

Kara ignored the concern. "Two. With two of the fours, we can have firepower and drones. Sam and Theresa aren't quite as old and can still do most things. We'll make it work."

"With just two drones, we won't be able to keep the batteries charging fast enough to keep one in the air all the time," Sam pointed out.

Chief started to open his mouth with a suggestion but closed it, leaving the pressure on his daughter.

She looked at him, knowing the game he was playing. "We can mount one of the portable chargers inside and have extra batteries available."

"That would work. We can get that done quickly tonight. Let's get our stuff loaded so we can leave first thing in the morning."

Chapter Sixty-Two

For the second time, the five of them were driving away from a shelter that had been their home. The last time, they headed out to find their parents, and this time it was their kids.

Radiation levels had been on the edge of healthy for the last few years, so they expected that most everyone would've cleared out of the shelters by now. They were making good progress and were halfway through the second day on the road, but Chief was frustrated.

"Honey, it isn't your fault," Lucy told him.

"I don't want to be the reason for our having to keep stopping."

At 60 years old, his body was showing its age, and he found that he needed to stop for bathroom breaks more often than before.

"Dad, this isn't a problem. It's really just like it was before. Back then, we had to stop a lot so that Jenny could walk Wilbur."

Two of the three occupants of the vehicle burst out laughing; one didn't.

A couple of hours later, Lucy looked up from the drone

view on her screen. "There are several vehicles partly blocking the road ahead. You'll need to slow down."

They slowed as they approached. There were four destroyed ORVs. In the back was a 12 followed by two 40s and then a 4.

Sam's voice came across the radio. "These look like they've been here a long time."

"We're stopping to check it out," Chief radioed back and he looked at his wife. "All clear from above?"

"The screen is clear."

They pulled to a stop and got out. Glad to stretch their legs.

Chief headed directly to the twelve-passenger vehicle. It was clear that there had been an explosion and devastating fire. He examined the front quarter panel from several directions. He was hoping to make out a designation on the fender; unfortunately, the fire and passage of time made that impossible.

"There's no trace of the designation," he reported.

"Not on the others either," Teresa said.

All the vehicles were empty of anything useful. Even some engine components were gone.

"It looks like these have been stripped repeatedly over the years. Everyone who finds them takes something else."

"I found two bodies in one of the 40s. They've been there a long time."

After a little more exploration, they drove off, fearing that this might have been the convoy their family was in.

Chapter Sixty-Three

ADAM AND DAWN SAT IN THE LIVING ROOM OF THE HOUSE they'd occupied for the last week. The sun was going down, and the kids were in bed, hungry again. Adam had removed his shirt and Dawn was replacing the dressing on his shoulder. Three days before, a bullet had found his upper arm as he'd tried to get his family to safety.

"What's that noise?" his wife asked, glancing around in alarm.

Adam was confused at first, but then he heard it too. Something was approaching.

She blew out the candle so that they wouldn't be visible, and they took up positions on either side of the large bay window that overlooked the street. Seconds later, two vehicles came down the road. They looked similar, with big wheels and high suspension and the tank on the back.

They'd seen things like this once before. Three days earlier, he and fifteen others had spotted five similar vehicles and had attacked them, hoping to confiscate their supplies. That hadn't worked as planned. He still didn't know for sure who these people were, but he had a good idea.

The two ORVs proceeded past their house and stopped up

the street. A couple of people got out and approached a house. After several minutes, they drove up the driveway and disappeared into the backyard, out of sight.

"I think this is our opportunity. We go up there when they're asleep and take one of those strange cars," Adam suggested.

"Or, maybe we ask them for help?" Dawn suggested.

"We don't know how they would react to that. They might be hostile or refuse to help us."

"The last time we attacked one of those, someone shot you, several of our people died, and we got separated from the rest."

"I'm not going to attack them. We'll simply wait until they're asleep and take one of the vehicles."

"I don't think that's a good idea."

"I don't care. That's what we're doing. Get some rest. In a few hours, we'll wake the kids and get ourselves transportation."

FOUR HOURS LATER, the kids, ages eight and ten, were awakened and told to get their stuff together. They all dressed, and the children put on the backpacks they'd found in a house. They contained water bottles, toys, spare clothes, and a blanket. Using the moonlight, they made their way down the street and to the backyard of the neighboring house.

There were two vehicles parked there. They were nearly identical, other than the big gun on the roof of one of them. Adam liked the idea of having the gun, even if he'd no idea how to use it. He assumed it wouldn't be hard to figure it out, and he would teach himself.

There were four doors on each, and they each went to one and lifted the handle. The doors wouldn't open. After attempting several times, Adam noticed a red light on the dashboard blink once. He mentally kicked himself for not considering this possibility.

Examining the door, he noticed that there was no keyhole, but there was a digital keypad. He started randomly entering numbers. When he entered the sixth digit, the keypad flashed red once. The light on the dash blinked twice.

Cursing, he whispered to his wife, "See if the other one is unlocked."

She walked to the other ORV to comply, and he entered another random string of numbers into the keypad. When he entered the sixth number, the keypad blinked red again, and now the light on the dash blinked three times, and an ear-splitting alarm started blaring.

His ten-year-old daughter screamed and dropped to the ground in a fetal position. Their eight-year-old ran for the comfort of his mother.

Adam turned to run away. The same way he'd done three days ago when his team attacked similar vehicles and the owners had fired back. "Come on, let's go. Run," he yelled to his family.

Dawn gripped her terrified youngest in her arms and started after her husband, then noticed her daughter on the ground, with her hands covering her ears. She turned toward her,

With the noise of the alarm, they never heard the door to the house open. Suddenly, people were pouring out, with a middle-aged woman in the lead. She had a handgun and was immediately on the cowering child. She grabbed her by the backpack, lifted her, and kept a controlling hand on her shirt collar.

Refusing to leave without her daughter, Dawn screamed and approached, still carrying the other child.

Other people were all around them now with a mix of handguns and assault rifles raised. Several of them appeared nearly elderly. The one with her daughter looked to be the youngest. The oldest of the group was a tall male; he went to the first vehicle and was inside right away, and the horrible alarm stopped.

The silence from the alarm was a huge relief; she looked at the woman holding her daughter. "Give me my daughter. *Please!*"

"No. Get over here," the middle-aged woman said. Her face was dead serious, and Dawn complied.

Another man took her son from her and then removed her backpack. She didn't resist. They then removed the backpacks from the kids.

Another older woman asked, "Do you have any weapons?"

"There's a knife in my pocket."

They searched her and took the knife. As this was happening, all three backpacks were opened and dumped out, and the contents searched.

"Who else is with you?" one of them asked.

"Just my husband. He set off the alarm."

"Where did he go?"

"He called for us to run when the alarm started. I guess he thought we were with him."

"And, he *hasn't* come back for you?" the tall man asked with disgust.

ADAM STOPPED RUNNING when he heard the alarm stop. He turned around, looking for his family. They weren't there.

This situation reminded him of a few days ago, when his family became separated from others in their group. They never did find them. With his gun in his hand, he started back to see what had happened.

As he approached the house, he saw that the two vehicles were running, and their lights illuminated the area. A man was sticking up through the roof of the one he'd tried to access. He was ready with the big gun if needed.

Dawn was talking to some strangers and the kids were sitting on the ground. It looked like these people were preventing her from getting to the kids.

An older woman was knelt, talking to the children.

He continued to move forward, not sure what to do. Part of him wanted to turn and run rather than have them capture him. As he approached the property line, the man atop the vehicle yelled, "Gun! Drop the Gun!"

Two women quickly moved in with guns leveled at him. One was middle-aged and the other quite a bit older. "He said, drop it!" one of them yelled.

They both looked alert and focused. Slowly, he tucked the gun back into the back of his pants.

The younger of the two went from looking concerned to enraged. "I said, *drop it!*"

By now, they were just a couple of feet from him, and she moved behind him and ripped the gun from his waistband. The front sight tore into the flesh of his lower back, and he yelped in pain.

They marched him over to where Dawn was and searched him.

Chapter Sixty-Four

As Theresa and Kara escorted the man over, Lucy asked the kids, "Is there anyone else with you guys?"

They both shook their heads.

She could see that Kara's adrenaline was spiked, and she needed to take a step back before she went too far. Lucy suggested, "Okay. There are no more weapons, and everyone's accounted for. How about we go inside and talk?"

"I think we're just going to leave," the man said.

"No, you aren't!" Kara growled.

Lucy gave her daughter a look that she'd used many times over the years. "We're going to talk first. Head inside."

The short woman with stringy hair and a noticeable speech impediment said, "Please don't hurt us."

"We don't plan to hurt you, but we're going to talk," Theresa advised.

Sam escorted everyone to the spacious living room, and the four would-be thieves sat together on the couch. The adults looked to be in their mid-twenties. The kids were snuggled against their mother, clearly preferring her over the father.

Chief stood in front of them. "Explain. Who are you, and what were you doing?"

Dawn answered, wanting to keep Adam from saying something that would make things worse. "I'm Dawn and this is my husband, Adam. We were part of a large group. We're heading for a settlement we heard about near San Diego. Three days ago, we became separated from our people and have been on our own since. We don't have any food, and the kids are hungry."

"So, what were you going do with our vehicle?" Chief demanded.

"We were hoping there might be food inside. We didn't want any trouble."

"And you didn't think to just ask for help instead of stealing?" Kara asked, the edge still in her voice.

Before his wife could answer, Adam said, "Dawn wanted to. I choose not to. We couldn't know if you were hostile."

"We aren't hostile when people aren't trying to steal from us," Kara declared.

Seeing that Lucy was getting frustrated with her daughter, Theresa said, "Kara, come help me get some food for the kids."

Reluctantly, the youngest in the group followed her from the room.

"Excuse our daughter. Being the youngest, there's lots of responsibility on her, and she takes that seriously. She tends to be a bit intense at times," Lucy said with a brief smile.

Ignoring the comment, Adam asked, "I take it you were in one of the underground shelters?"

"We were. What do you know about the shelters?" Chief inquired.

"We were born in one of them, sort of."

"What do you mean by 'sort of'?" Sam asked.

Dawn took over. "I don't know how accurate all of this is,

but from what we heard, the US government was building a few hundred shelters around the country, and no one knew what they were for. Our grandfathers did construction in Arkansas, and they worked on one of these shelters. No one would say what it was, just that there were deadlines, and if the project didn't meet them, the job site would close down. They worked around the clock for two years and were ahead of schedule.

"One day, they had to get things ready for an important delivery. It was a giant box, the size of a train car. It was coming in on a massive truck. Before it ever reached them, the truck was in an accident and rolled over.

"Later, they learned that the delivery was a nuclear reactor. Fortunately, it didn't have any nuclear fuel in it. When the truck rolled, the reactor toppled off the truck, and the external casing became damaged.

"For two days, the leadership was in a panic. There was talk of trying to repair it, but that wasn't possible. They wanted to replace it, but that would take too long. They wanted to bring one in from another site, but that also got shot down.

"One morning, the leadership told the workers to go home, that the project was canceled. Things were too far behind schedule. But the workers knew that wasn't true. They'd been ahead of schedule. The truth was that they didn't have a way to replace the reactor in time.

"A couple of days later, our grandfathers returned to the job site, and the place had been abandoned. All the construction equipment was gone, but everything else was exactly as they'd left it.

"They didn't know why the shelters were needed, but they knew the situation was imminent. They gathered some friends who had worked the site, and they pooled all their money and started finishing as much as possible. They took out loans and mortgages and started buying everything they could think of to stock the shelter.

"Some supplies had already been coming in before the project was canceled, including furnishings and emergency rations. But no vehicles.

"They had already installed the emergency generator, and it was operational, as was the water supply. The lights in the hydroponics area ran off banks of low-voltage batteries. They could keep them charged by running the generator for an hour a week. So, they were able to grow food.

"Six weeks later, the comet passed by, and the crisis was apparent. They all fled to the unfinished shelter and remained there until seven years ago. There were thirty people in a shelter designed for over a thousand. Our parents were kids when this happened. We were born there and our kids too—"

"What's that smell. It smells real good," Adam interrupted.

"We aren't going to let the kids go hungry," Lucy explained.

"What is it? How are you cooking it?" Dawn asked.

"We've got a small propane generator and an old electric skillet. And you don't want to know what it is."

Adam gave her a curious look.

"Python and wild grapes; it's what we had for dinner. We had some in a cooler from where we were last staying," Sam explained.

"Is there any for my wife and me? We're hungry too," Adam asked with a bit of sarcasm.

"You should ask Kara. She's the one preparing it," Lucy answered flatly.

She smiled as Adam deflated a little more.

"Either way, thank you," Dawn said. "Food for the kids is what matters most."

Lucy, Sam, and Chief noted the condescending glare Adam gave his wife when she said that.

As all four were eating, Sam went outside and retrieved their backpacks and belongings.

"Where's my gun? I want it back," Adam said.

"Not tonight," Chief said. "If you go off on your own in the morning, you can have it then."

Chapter Sixty-Five

The following day, Chief and Sam were up first and spoke quietly, hoping not to awaken the others.

"So, what do you think we should do with them?" Chief asked.

"I'm hoping they sleep in, and we can just leave before they get up."

Chief nodded. "Dawn's okay, but I don't care for Adam. He seems slimy."

As they spoke, they started getting breakfast together.

"Lucy wanted to offer to let them ride along with us. Safety in numbers and Adam's youth would take some of the workload of Kara," Chief stated.

"That would be a tight fit. We've got seats for eight, and that would be nine," Sam pointed out.

"She said if they want to go, they'll have to squeeze in. We aren't going to."

Kara, Theresa, and Lucy joined them, and they started eating.

"So, do we save them some or not?" Kara asked bluntly.

"We made enough to include them. But, if those guys

aren't up by the time we're ready to leave, I'm not waking them. We'll leave them here," Chief said flatly.

As they were finishing up the meal, the four guests got up.

"Good morning," Sam greeted solemnly.

No one but Dawn said anything. "Hi guys."

"So, you were eating without us? Did you even save us any?" Adam asked, frowning.

"We didn't have to, but we did," Chief replied.

Sam slid plates their way.

"Thanks for the food," Dawn said with a humble smile.

"There isn't much here. Is this the same amount your people got?" Adam asked sarcastically.

Seething with rage, Kara's hand slid toward the hilt of the knife in her tactical vest.

"Don't even think it, Kara," Lucy advised.

Kara returned her hand to her side. Her mother hadn't even been looking at her. If she weren't so angry, she'd be amused. Instead, she decided to leave the room. "I'm going to get the ORVs loaded and ready to go."

"So, what are you four planning to do next?" Lucy asked casually.

"We need to find a community where we can settle down. Either San Diego or somewhere closer," Dawn explained.

"We're headed for a settlement on the Arizona, Utah line. We hope to be there in a couple of days. If you're willing to help with the work, you can join us," Chief said.

"So, we can go with you, and we'll have to do all the work? That's what that sounds like to me. Not such a great deal," Adam snapped.

"Well, so far, we've fed you twice, and you've been nothing but trouble and constant complaining," Chief pointed out.

Lucy was ready to take back the offer but said, "We're going to go load up and leave. If you want to join us, be at the vehicles with your stuff before we depart."

"If we go with you, do I get my gun back?"

Chief glared at the younger man. "No. As long as you're with us, we'll hold onto the gun."

"Fine, but I want to learn to drive."

"No." Chief turned and headed outside to help get the stuff loaded.

As they were all filing out, Theresa took Dawn by the arm and led her to the living room. "Do you guys want to ride with us?" She asked quietly.

"Yes, we do. I appreciate your offering," Dawn answered in a sincere voice.

Theresa wanted to be kind to this woman but needed to get her point across. "Well, we're all ready to leave you behind. If Adam doesn't keep his rude opinions to himself and learn to shut up, you're all walking and not riding. Got it?"

Dejected, she nodded once. "Yeah, I know. He's caused problems for all of us before. Many times."

"If you want, you and the kids can come with us, and we'll leave him here," Theresa offered. "My people would gladly do it."

Dawn thought before answering. "No. He's the children's father and my husband. I can't do that."

"Okay. Get your kids and your stuff and get in an ORV. Chief will tell you which one."

"Thanks for the offer. I do appreciate it." She left the room, gathered her children, and headed outside. Finding her husband, she took him by the arm and led him off to the side to talk.

When they rejoined the group, Chief and Sam were discussing seating options with the others. Hearing this, Adam said, "We'd like to ride together."

"Well, that's a problem. We don't have enough seats, and our people are in the front seats of each vehicle. So, unless you all want to squeeze in the back together, you'll need to split up," Chief explained.

Adam looked at the cramped seating in the rear of the ORV and then at his wife.

"No," she said adamantly.

"Fine. Where do you want me?" Adam asked.

Kara opened her mouth to answer but caught the glare from her father and kept the comment to herself.

"You'll be riding with Lucy, Kara, and me."

Before a comment could come out, Chief glared at his daughter again.

Chapter Sixty-Six

Two days later, it was mid-afternoon, and the mood in the ORV Lucy was driving was unpleasant. Within an hour of starting the journey, everyone was ignoring Adam. He would comment on anything someone said, so everyone stayed silent. Now, they were into their second day of the journey, and it was tense and uncomfortable.

When they stopped for fuel, Chief told him to help, and he agreed but did nothing without being explicitly told and was more in the way than helpful. It didn't help matters to learn that Sam and Theresa were having an enjoyable time with Dawn and the kids. So, now, they rode in silence.

It was late in the afternoon, and the overhead drone had recently had the batteries replaced. Chief sent it ahead, knowing that they should be getting close to the location David Cowan had spoken of. Ten minutes later, with Sam driving the other vehicle, Chief triggered the radio. "Theresa, check out the drone view."

It was several seconds before she answered, but on his screen, he could see that she'd taken control and was maneuvering the aircraft for views with different angles.

"Looks like an active community. I see a handful of ORVs in the area. Think this is it?" she asked.

"I hope so. See anything concerning?"

"Not yet."

He talked to Lucy. "The next exit looks to have an active community. We're going to check it out."

"What are you seeing? I want a vote in if we're stopping here," Adam said.

They ignored him. As they took the exit, the road led directly into a downtown area. There were storefronts on both sides of the road. Most were in use, with indications of recent rebuilding. There were many bicycles, some parked in front of stores, others going up and down the street. They saw a large parking lot with a hand-painted sign: "All New Arrivals Stop Here."

There was an adjoining lot with dozens of parked ORVs. Lucy backed into a spot at the edge of the lot and Sam, parked next to her. As they exited the vehicle, Adam reached for one of the mounted assault rifles and started to pull it from the bracket. Chief swatted his hand away. "Leave that alone."

"We don't know if we might want it."

"No."

"You always have to be the boss, don't you, old man?" Adam stomped away.

Seeing the fury in her father's eyes, Kara approached him. "You know, this is all your and Mom's fault."

"How is this our fault?" Chief asked, puzzled.

"I wanted to shoot him when we first met him," Kara said.

"Yeah, well, your mom and I were wrong."

As the group walked away, a small laser beam shot down from above and found the sensor. The drone followed its laser and descended perfectly into position, locking into place and starting the charging cycle.

Chapter Sixty-Seven

It was a warm, pleasant late afternoon as they exited the parking lot, with Sam and Theresa in the lead. There was a small visitor's building that had kept its intended purpose. A hand-painted banner that said, "New Arrivals Check-in Here."

There were two women with assault rifles roaming up and down the street. They each had a blue armband. When they noticed the arriving party, they slowly headed toward the Visitors Building.

As they entered, Chief and Lucy made sure to be in front of Adam. They didn't want his mouth to cause problems.

A couple, who seemed to be a little older than Chief and Lucy, was working at the desk.

"Welcome to Tri-Town," the tall thin woman said in a friendly voice.

"Thank you," Lucy responded.

"Are you here to visit or relocate?"

"We're looking for family members in the area; if they're here, we'll stay."

"Great. I hope you enjoy the town. Just a few things you

should be aware of. I see that most of you are armed. Firearms are permitted, but responsible behavior is required.

"This community works on a barter system. I'll give you each one meal voucher. After that, you'll need to trade goods or work for more. The same goes for lodging. There's free camping in the fields east of town, but there are available motel rooms. You'll need to go to the Barter Office if you want one."

As they spoke, one of the women with the armband entered and looked around before leaving.

"There's the old community building up the road. That's the communal dining area where the meal vouchers are good. Any questions?" As she said that, she handed over nine laminated cards.

"I don't think so," Lucy answered.

"Okay, one of the security officers with the blue armbands outside will speak to you as you go. This is a nice community. If you decide to relocate, stop back, and we can get that process started."

"Thanks," they said and turned to leave.

Outside, the security officers were waiting. "Hello and welcome. We need a minute of your time."

"What can we do for you?" Sam asked with a smile.

"I assume you have a vehicle?"

"We've got two ORVs in that lot over there," he pointed.

She held out a pencil and paper. "Give us the complete designations. We'll try to keep an eye on them tonight."

"Is there reason to be concerned?" Chief asked.

"There are those that don't live in the Tri-Town area. They often sneak into town and cause problems. They steal and sometimes kill. They can be quite dangerous. We refer to them as raiders."

Chief nodded. "Thanks. We appreciate the info and for you watching the vehicles."

"It sounds to me like you need better security," Adam smirked.

"We do the best with what we have. Only a few hundred people are living right in town. We have many teams scattered about at different project sites. There's farming, the hydroelectric dam, the propane drilling, and refining facility, and the hospital are just some of them. These projects cover a huge area. We have the same security concerns at all of them."

The other security officer said, "You need to know that we're a law and order community. We don't tolerate violations of the rules. There aren't many, but we do react harshly to violations. If you're respectful and don't cause problems, there won't be any concerns.

"That sounds like you're threatening us," Adam said angrily. "We haven't done anything, and you think you can just threaten us?"

"This is the same thing we tell everyone," the shorter of the two advised him.

Seeing the scowl on both officer's faces, Dawn took Adam by the arm and led him away from the conversation.

"Thank you for the information," Lucy said to them. "They aren't with us. We just found them on the road yesterday."

With the officers watching, Sam took four of the meal vouchers and handed them to Dawn. "These are yours. Take him and go. We'll talk to you later, maybe."

They turned and walked away, leaving Dawn and her family standing on the road.

"What do you mean, *maybe*? You have our stuff and my gun," Adam called after them.

They kept walking and didn't look back.

"I'm hungry. Is anyone else?" Chief asked.

The other four agreed, and they started towards the community building. On the way, they saw the Barter Office and went inside.

"Good afternoon," a short pleasant African American woman said.

"Hello, we just got into town, and the welcome center suggested that we stop in," Lucy explained.

"Great, come over here and have a seat. I'm Lydia, one of the barters. You're free to barter with individuals, but the idea of this office is to bring all of that here under one roof. If any of our citizens are looking for something, they can list it with us, and anyone who might have it will see that it is wanted. That's the listing here on the wall." She pointed to a massive list of items printed on paper on the wall.

Lucy glanced at some of the items: a 24-inch bicycle tire, insulated cooler, boy's swimsuit size small, and cooking oil, among many other things.

When she returned her attention to Lydia, she continued, "Also, if you want goods or services, we'll make trades."

"Like hotel rooms?" Chief asked.

"Exactly. Hotel rooms, meal passes, propane, medical care. It is all available."

"What would two hotel rooms cost?"

"Depends on how long you're staying. One of your handguns would get you four to six weeks."

"Probably just one night. We think we've got family here. We're looking to connect with them."

"I could do two rooms for one night for six rounds of 9mm ammo. Maybe for a blanket or a half dozen ration packs. We're flexible if you have suggestions."

Speaking up, Kara suggested, "How about for a couple of pounds of fresh alligator steaks?"

The woman's eyes lit up. "You have *fresh* meat?"

"It's in a cooler on ice. Well, most of the ice is gone, but it is still plenty cold enough," Lucy stated.

"That would be a fair trade," the barterer agreed.

"Okay, we'll let you know. We're going to try to locate our people first," Chief advised.

"What are your people's names? I know many of our residents."

"Oliver Wilson," Theresa offered.

"Sorry, I don't recognize that one."

"What about Tyler Brown?"

"Tyler! I know Tyler. He and his wife are always helping with things around here."

Giggling, Kara said, "Tyler went and got married. I want to meet this woman."

Thinking about their son getting married without them, Lucy and Chief became quiet.

"What about Kevin Torez?" Sam asked.

"Councilman Torez? His wife is Penny?"

"Yeah, that's her name," Sam verified.

"They're real popular. He's big in local politics. They say he's a big part of why Tyler gets away with ignoring the housing regulations."

"What do you mean?" Lucy asked.

"From what I hear, Tyler grabbed up a street with a bunch of nice houses and won't let anyone move there," Lydia replied. "He says he's saving it for his family. Hey, is that you?"

"I don't know. Maybe," Lucy answered.

"People like him well enough, but there are rules against that, and he ignores them, and the council refuses to make him stop. He's had the houses for years."

"Well, that sure sounds like my brother," Kara observed casually

"Where does Tyler live?"

Taking out a pencil and paper, Lydia drew a crude map. "You can drive, but it's an easy walk."

"We're stopping at the community building for dinner first," Chief said.

"Well, then you'll want to walk for sure. You'll be more than halfway there already."

"Thanks for your time," Lucy said.

"Even if you don't need rooms, I'd be glad to take the gator off your hands. I could get you a good trade for it."

Chapter Sixty-Eight

A CREAKING FLOORBOARD AWOKE HIM FROM HIS NAP. HE KNEW precisely which board it was and could tell who was walking in the house. He didn't want to get up; his inner ear hurt again. It had been raining this morning, and water had got inside. That always happened and that's why he hated the rain. His head would hurt for a day or two, and there was nothing he could do. He wished that Mom understood what the water did to him.

He'd been extremely young but still vaguely remembered when the ear was damaged. He'd been attacked and shaken by the ear until it had ripped away. The pain had been terrible for a long time after that.

Slowly, he got his aging body off the bed and went looking for Mom. He could tell that she was getting ready to go out and that he should go with her. There was nothing he liked more than spending time with her. She'd been with him since almost the beginning.

For a long while after getting here, she'd leave him in the house and go away during the day and come home and snuggle with him in the evening. Now, she was here all the time, now that she was changing. He instinctively knew why but didn't care. All that mattered was spending time with Mom.

He had a dad now, too, and he was great, but he wasn't Mom. She was the best. He slowly walked down the stairs and met her at the bottom. She smiled, "Are you ready to go?"

She opened the door and the two of them went outside. The rain was gone, and his apprehension disappeared. He knew where they were going. The same place as they always did in the evening when Dad wasn't around.

He was glad that mom was changing; she walked slower and his aching legs didn't have to move as fast to keep up. They worked their way down the street, and people occasionally called greetings out to both of them. They often used Mom's new name.

Walking with Mom was always one of his favorite things to do. He became aware of some people on the road coming toward them. Good, more people to make friends with! Wait, there was something familiar, he knew them! He remembered them! They were his friends! He called out once and sped towards them.

"Where are you going?" his mother called.

The people stopped as he approached. At first, they looked a little concerned. He kept going, even though it was painful to run.

Do you remember me? I missed you. Do you remember me? He thought over and over.

As he approached, one of them said, "Look at the ear and feet! It's Wilbur!"

Yes! They remember me!

He wanted to jump up on them, but his legs couldn't do that anymore.

They all crouched and greeted him.

Backing away, he thought, *Come see Mom, Come see Mom, she's changing.*

They stood back up, and one of them called out, "Oh my gosh! Jenny, you're pregnant!"

Yup, she is.

They hurried to each other and embraced. Then, he felt a change. Mom pulled back, full of pain, fear, and sorrow.

They seemed confused by her actions, and then she burst into tears. *I hate it when Mom cries. It makes me hurt inside.*

Chapter Sixty-Nine

Jenny composed herself and asked, "Have you seen anyone else yet?"

"No, you're the first one we've run into. What's wrong?" Theresa asked anxiously.

There was a bench nearby, and she directed them toward it.

"Did something happen to Oliver?" Sam asked quickly. "Or Marsha."

Kara helped the very pregnant Jenny to sit. Then, she started the story, "On the way here, our convoy was ambushed. We lost most of our vehicles and a quarter of our people. Mom and Oliver died in an explosion. The propane tank on the bus in front of them blew, and they were very close. It consumed their ORV."

Theresa screamed and collapsed, her worst fears confirmed. Sam tried to hold her, but he was in shock. Their son had been gone for eight years, and they hadn't known it.

After several minutes of tears and silence, Kara asked, "What about the others? Are they okay?"

"They all made it here, though David took a bullet to the leg. After the massacre, Tyler took over. Using the remaining

ORVs, he shuttled everyone to a close-by neighborhood. He then loaded up as many people as the vehicles would hold and then raced here to get more transportation. Five days later, he was back with three 40s, and we all made it here about a week late."

"On the way here, we passed the remains of a group of a destroyed convoy," Kara informed her. "They'd been there a while. There were a couple of 40s, a 12, and a 4 off the side of the road. That was into our second day on the road."

"Yeah, that would be it. We had no way to get them off the road."

With a trembling voice, Theresa asked, "You were okay, not hurt?"

Tears returned to Jenny's eyes. "I was in the back of a 40 with the other kids when the attack happened. The attackers boarded the bus and said they were going to kill all the kids. Wilbur and I fought them. I killed one, and Wilbur slowed the other enough for Tyler to get there and finish it. I was a mess for a long time. I still sometimes wake up and see the blood on my hands and knife. Just like it was yesterday."

Sam slid next to her and held her, just as he'd done when she was a child. She was the closest he would ever get to having a grandchild.

Theresa's voice was hushed. "Did they get buried?"

Jenny nodded. "All of the dead were moved with us to that neighborhood. While Tyler was gone getting transportation, those of us that were waiting took care of that."

As they were talking, a group of older kids walked by. They waved and called out, "Hey Wilbur, hi Doc."

Wilbur wagged his tail in response, and Jenny waved back.

"What's with them calling you 'Doc'?" Kara asked.

"Shortly after I got here, I located the clinic and found two old physicians on staff. They had some younger people they were training, and I convinced them to take me on as one of their students.

"I started unofficial medical school when I was fourteen years old. For four years now, I have been one of the doctors at the clinic. We hope to be able to move back into the hospital soon. Repair work there's moving along. But we need reliable electricity first. We can run the clinic on propane generators, but not the hospital. Tyler is one of the team leaders working at the old hydroelectric dam, trying to get power back on. They're hoping David's sleepers will arrive soon; they need some expertise."

"Has there been any news on the sleepers?" Lucy questioned.

"No, and radiation levels are mostly in the safe range. We expected them by now, but there has been nothing. The council is concerned that they planned to sleep for twenty years, and we more than doubled that before the radiation dropped. They wonder if they all died in there."

Through the conversation, Sam and Theresa sat in silence, absorbing the information as they smothered in grief.

"So, where can we find Tyler?" Chief asked quietly.

"He's working. He usually gets back home in a few hours. We can go to his house, and I can introduce you to Becca, his wife. It would be funny for you all to be waiting there when he returns."

"Well, where were you headed when we met you?" Lucy asked.

"To get dinner. But we can do that later. I doubt Sam and Theresa have much interest in food. Going to the house might be a better option."

Theresa objected. "No, we can go eat. Everyone's hungry, and I need to stay active. Once I sit and relax, I'll lose it, so I'm better off being busy for now."

They got up and headed back to the road, and Jenny led them back in the direction they'd come.

"They told us that dining was in the community center," Kara said.

"That's communal dining. It's quick and easy and similar to what we had in the shelters. Cafeteria-style. There're a few smaller restaurants in town. I'm taking you to one of my favorites."

"Will our meal vouchers work there?" Lucy asked.

"You won't need them. Hold onto them for another time."

They entered one of the shops they'd seen near the Welcome Center. It was small and clean, with a few tables that were all occupied.

"Hey, Doc!"

"Hi, Wilbur."

"Hi, Doc."

Everyone greeted them as if they were celebrities.

"Everyone sure likes Wilbur," Kara noted.

"When we first arrived, he was the only dog, and everyone loved him. There are more now, but he's still very popular."

As they spoke, a woman called Wilbur over and handed him something from her plate.

Jenny approached the counter and the girl standing behind it greeted her. "No husband tonight?"

"No, he's still at the clinic. But my family finally made it. They arrived a couple of hours ago."

"Oh good! Hopefully, that will help Tyler."

After Jenny introduced everyone, she asked, "Any chicken tonight?"

"We've got a little left. How many do you need?"

"Chicken? *Real* chicken?" Kara asked. Hope reflected in her eyes.

"Yeah, we got some in this morning. It's either that or fish," the woman explained.

Everyone agreed they wanted the chicken and, soon, breaded chicken strips and French fries appeared. They took their food to a large outside table and sat.

Confused, Chief asked, "How do you have chicken and potatoes?"

"We've been here almost nine years. Farming was one of the first priorities. Several parties that have come in had live chickens that they found on the way here. Also, we've had teams scouring the countryside for years, rounding up every usable animal. Eggs are readily available now, and when a chicken stops producing eggs, they're available for food.

"Some settlers who arrived from the north came across an old potato farm on the way. Everything was overgrown and in bad shape from decades of neglect. Still, they realized the treasure it was and dug it up and brought several hundred potatoes here. We planted them out at one of the farms. For the first two years, a hundred percent of the crop went to increasing the number of plants. By the third year, ten percent was available to eat, and that percentage increases each year. Now, they're always available on the menu.

"We've done that with all crops, and vegetables are now plentiful. Many settlers brought plants from their shelters' hydroponics, so we've got a good variety. The first couple of years were hard. David insisted on letting it hurt for the first few years, so we would be in a good place going forward, and he was right."

"David Cowan?" Sam asked.

"Yeah, he's the head on the council. He has been all along, and everyone reveres and respects him. Nothing much happens without his approval. ...He took a bullet to the leg in the attack on our convoy and walks with a cane now. That further enhanced the 'Old Man' nickname," Jenny explained.

"We didn't pay for our food or use a meal pass. How does that work?" Chief asked.

"There's no payment. You're supposed to have to show an employment card, but they know me." Seeing the confusion, Jenny continued. "David instituted a Work-to-Eat program. Needed jobs get posted and, when you work, your card is updated. If the card doesn't show that you've worked, you don't eat. Since there's plenty of work, everyone should be eating."

"What if someone refuses to work?" Lucy asked.

"Everything is free to those that contribute and nothing to those that don't. No work means no housing, no food, no medical care. Those that are difficult about the rule don't last here, and it can be dangerous outside of the towns."

"I wonder how long Adam will last," Kara chuckled.

Shaking his head, Chief said, "The problem is that his wife and kids will end up leaving too."

"The girl inside said something about Tyler. Is there a problem with him?" Lucy asked.

"The more time that has passed without you guys arriving, the more he has wondered if you ever would. He's become a bit depressed and difficult to deal with over the years. I think seeing you'll be great for him. For years, he has been working on the homes he picked for you. It's become a bit of an obsession."

They were all quiet, concerned about Tyler's mental state.

Kara broke the silence first. "Tell us about this husband of yours."

Jenny smiled. "His name is Conner. He came in with a group about five years ago and works in the clinic. He recently finished our version of medical school and is now a doctor too. We got married a little over a year ago, and this will be our first child."

"That's great. We're all looking forward to meeting him," Chief assured her.

They finished the meal and got up to leave.

"Our overnight stuff is in the ORVs. We should probably get it," Kara said.

"There's parking at each house. We could just bring them up there," Jenny suggested.

Everyone agreed and they walked to the parking lot and

found an anxious Adam pacing the lot. His kids were playing in the grass while Dawn sat on a log.

Seeing them, Adam called out, "There you are! We've been waiting. We need to get our stuff. We've got nothing to trade, so we're going to spend the night in the camping area, but we need the blankets we have in our bags. Who's the pregnant babe?"

Chief's first thought went back to Kara's earlier comment; they should've shot him when they had the chance. He smiled and shook his head to chase the dark image away.

Chief waved Dawn over. "First, she's none of your business. Second, as much as I want to leave you in the field for the night, we're going to help you one last time. Dawn, do you and the kids want beds for the night and food in the morning?"

"That'd be great. What do we need to do?" she answered with a grateful smile.

"Come with us and keep your husband's mouth shut," Chief answered. "It's going to be a bit more cramped, but we need to ride up to the Barter Office."

Lucy, with an arm around Theresa, said, "Theresa and I will walk. We'll meet you there."

As the two women left, Dawn approached Chief. "What's wrong with Theresa? She doesn't look right?"

"We just learned that Theresa's and Sam's son and daughter-in-law died on their way here."

Dawn's eyes went wide and she climbed into the back of the ORV, trying to think of something to say.

As Chief was getting in, he noticed Adam approach Sam.

"I know you don't like me, but I really am sorry about that."

Sam merely nodded in response.

They boarded the vehicles and headed to the Barter Office. Upon arriving, Chief took Dawn and Adam inside while Kara and Sam stayed outside with the kids.

"Welcome back. Did you bring me the gator meat?" Lydia asked.

"No, we're still thinking about that one. I did bring these guys. They're new here and, if they stay, will need to get settled. It's the two of them and two young kids. So, they need a place to stay and meal passes while they get processed."

"We can work something out. What do they have to barter with?"

Pulling out the 9mm automatic that he had tucked into his belt, Chief ejected the magazine and worked the slide to show that there wasn't a round chambered and handed it to Lydia.

"Hey, that's my gun!" Adam said.

"No, it's your price for admission," Chief corrected him flatly.

Adam started to object, but Dawn drove an elbow into his ribs.

"How many days lodging with meal passes for two adults and two kids can they get for this?" Chief asked.

Inspecting the gun, Lydia worked the slide and even sniffed it. "Someone didn't maintain this very well, but it's in okay condition. Any spare magazines or extra ammo?"

With a depressed and resigned voice, Adam answered, "No."

"I can offer three weeks with food. That should be long enough for you to secure employment and be assigned permanent lodging."

"Employment? What are you talking about?" Adam sniffed.

"Everyone fifteen years old and above must work to stay here. You work, you eat," Lydia explained.

"What kind of work?" Adam asked suspiciously.

"I'll finish this transaction, and then you can go to your rooms. It is too late now, so in the morning, go back to the Welcome Center, and they'll walk you through the relocation process. That'll include discussing available employment positions, as well as housing and school registration for your children."

Setting the magazine for the gun on the table, Chief walked out of the room, leaving Adam and Dawn to deal with the rest of it.

Chapter Seventy

The ORV pulled up to the curb, and the three passengers got out. Tyler drove away after saying goodbye to the co-workers he usually dropped off on his way home. He dreaded their departure. Now, he was alone with his thoughts —the same thoughts whose torment was steadily growing stronger.

He tried to stay busy to keep his mind on something else. However, that strategy was proving less and less effective, and his mood and attitudes were slipping into unpleasant places. The people around him were feeling the side effects.

His wife, Becca, had been understanding at first, but her tolerance for his negativity and explosive reactions was running out. He loved her dearly and knew that he would soon lose her because he couldn't change. He had been trying for years.

Everyone thought his problems were because he missed his family, but it was much more than that. He wanted to see them and, as time went on, he was terrified as to what had happened to them. But the part that was unknown to everyone was how horrified he was at the thought that they might show up. He wanted them to be safe but hoped he would never see them again.

Seeing his parents would mean seeing his Aunt Theresa and Uncle Sam. If that happened, he would have to face them, knowing that he was responsible for their son's death. That thought had haunted him for the last eight years, and he had cried himself to sleep many nights as he dwelt on his guilt.

As he turned onto his street, he made himself the same promise that he did every night; he wouldn't let Becca see his inner turmoil. She was terrific and didn't deserve to see the ugliness that lived within him.

As he approached his house, he saw an ORV parked at the home next to his. The house was one of the ones he had prepared for his family, should they ever arrive. He knew many people were angry that he held a tight grip on three extra houses, but he didn't care.

Tyler knew that someday he would have to give them up and let someone else have access to them, but not today. Whoever was there would be leaving immediately, he thought, as he felt his rage building.

He parked in his driveway, hurried from the vehicle, and headed next door to deal with the intruders. As Tyler approached the house, he heard the door of his home open behind him and cringed, knowing that Becca would again see his fury.

"Where ya going, big brother?"

The mental shock at hearing Kara's voice stunned him. He didn't know what to do. He was thrilled and horrified at the same time. He wanted to run and see the family ... and also wanted to run and hide.

Ignoring the fear, he ran to his sister and took her in his arms and held her as he wept. Within seconds, he was aware of his parents surrounding them and joining in. With his parents and Kara in his arms, the longing for them and fear for their safety melted away, diminishing much of the pain he had held onto for years.

"I missed you guys so much. I was starting to think I would never see you again," Tyler said softly.

"Things took longer than expected. But we're here now," his father said with a grin.

As they spoke, Tyler became aware of two others approaching and knew who it was before looking up. His blood went cold. Pushing away from his parents and Kara, he walked to his Aunt Theresa and Uncle Sam and, looking at the ground with renewed tears, said, "I'm sorry. I'm so, so sorry. It was all my fault."

Even as a child, Sam and Theresa had never seen their nephew so emotional. Confused, Theresa spoke for the first time since learning the news of Oliver's and Marsha's deaths. "Tyler. What's your fault? Why do you think you're responsible? Jenny told us what happened. You were nowhere near them when the explosion happened."

"Coming here was my idea. I asked them to come too. If I hadn't done that, they would never have been killed!" The anxiety in his voice increased.

Shaking his head, Sam said, "That isn't true. I remember when you asked them. And I remember that they had already told us they were planning to go with the convoy. They were planning to ask you to go, but you asked them first. Either way, they would have been there. This isn't your fault." As Sam spoke the lie, he hoped Theresa would back it up. The trip might have been Tyler's idea, but they didn't blame him. He'd done nothing wrong.

Theresa nodded. "That's right. This isn't your fault." As she said this, she grabbed her precious nephew and held him as they both wept.

Chapter Seventy-One

6 MONTHS LATER

Sam stood, waiting inside the door of the home he and Theresa had moved into. Tyler had scooped up seven upscale homes that were in good condition. He had been working on fixing them up for the last eight years.

It was a lovely house, if not a bit larger than Sam and Theresa needed for themselves. Tyler had even made sure that the furnishings were in good condition. Sam was curious how each of the homes managed to have a small propane generator. Those were in short supply but, somehow, Tyler managed to have one waiting at each house.

Since he was alone and the houses were large, David Cowan had moved in with Kevin Torez and his wife, Penny, which left one of the houses available. David had instructed Tyler to find someone needing a home and offer it to them. Sam and Chief talked to Tyler to ensure that he understood the one specific family *not* to mention it to.

David has suggested that one of the new arrivals serve on the leadership council. The family discussed it and decided that Sam would be the one. Usually, the council met every Saturday, but David had called for an emergency meeting this Thursday evening for some reason.

The ORV pulled into his driveway, and Sam sprinted into the pouring rain and climbed inside, greeting Kevin and David.

The council met on the outskirts of town, inside an old Civil Defence building, which had become the local government administration building.

They choose this site because there was a significant amount of radio gear that was all still functional. Every Saturday, the Council would meet in the morning to power up the generator and the radios. Then, the scanners would seek out radio transmissions, hoping for word from the sleepers. During that time, the Council would conduct business for an hour or two. It was then an open session, where anyone could come and discuss any topic they wanted. Each Saturday, when they shut down the generator for the week, there was renewed disappointment that the sleepers still weren't heard from.

They arrived at the council building and parked among the other ORVs. Sam and Kevin assisted David to the building and out of the rain. When they entered, ten voices called out to David in greeting. He smiled and waved his hand.

The room had dim lighting from kerosene lamps and candles.

"Is anyone working on the generator?" David asked.

"The boys are out there now. It should be up soon," a member answered.

"Very good. In the meantime, let me tell you the reason for the special meeting. Something exciting happened. The team out at Farm 6 saw and heard a helicopter today."

"Are they sure?" an excited voice asked.

"Two people saw it, and four others heard it," David verified.

"Do you think it's them?" Kevin asked eagerly.

"One way to find out," someone answered.

At that time, the lights came on as the ancient generator came to life.

They heard a voice from the intercom by the radio console. "Generator on."

David was standing by the radio console, hit the intercom, and answered, "Thanks, boys."

Owen brought up the radios and was getting the scanners started on their search.

After a couple of minutes, the silence in the room was broken by the thing they'd spent close to a decade looking for: a radio transmission.

A female voice spoke. "Greetings, this is the commanding officer of a team of specialists who were prepared before the comet devastated our civilization. We have a team of over ten thousand men and women specifically trained for rebuilding our once-great nation. We have the technology, tools, and knowledge of the past with us and will be helping to rebuild. Please contact us on this frequency, and we'll send a team to meet with you to start the long project which lies ahead of us all. Thank you."

The room erupted in cheer. Some were crying, some shouting in joy, and others clapping. In the middle of the celebration, the back door slammed open, and two soaking wet teenage boys raced in. One of them was covered in mud and the other held an ancient revolver.

The room became silent.

"We were in the generator shed and heard screaming. We thought something must be wrong," one of the boys said.

The sight of the muddy, wet confused boys made the whole room burst into laughter.

The other boy, confused, asked, "What's going on?"

"Quiet," Owen at the radio console ordered. "It's starting again."

The message they'd heard, repeated every three minutes.

"What do we do now?" a woman asked.

"I'll answer them," David said.

He stepped up to the radio console and faced his people. "For years, I've been telling you the stories about the past. Many of you as children heard me speak of how one day we'd rebuild. I said that people would be there to help us as we fought to turn things back to where they were. These are the people I spoke of."

Chapter Seventy-Two

THE NEXT DAY

Lucy stood with her husband and grown kids and watched the proceedings. Most of the town had come out for this historic mid-morning meeting. The summit signaled hope for the future. Not just for Tri-Town but the whole human race.

Just a few minutes later, a UH60 Blackhawk helicopter appeared in the distance. It rapidly grew in size and circled the downtown area before landing in the center of town, in an area previously roped off.

Ever since word had gotten out that the sleepers had finally awakened and were coming, everyone was out doing what they could to make the town more presentable. The first impression would set the sleepers' opinion about how capable the community was to work with.

They had done an excellent job; there was no trash on the ground. All clutter was removed. Someone had found an old push mower and the grass was trimmed.

Many of those gathered had never seen an aircraft in flight, let alone been present to watch a helicopter land. They stood, transfixed, as they watched the technology from the past arrive.

The Anvil

After a full minute on the ground, the deafening engine noise decreased, and the rotors began slowing. No one exited the aircraft until the rotors stopped moving. The first to exit was half a dozen armed troops, who took up positions around the helicopter. Lastly, two men emerged and the female pilot.

The man who had been in the front with the pilot took the lead and shook hands with David Cowan. They spoke briefly and then David talked to the pilot. After a brief discussion, the pilot embraced David, and it appeared she was crying.

"What was that about?" Chief asked, puzzled.

"I don't know, but I plan to ask. It was almost like they knew each other," Lucy answered.

Almost as an afterthought, David shook hands with the other man. Then the Council, including Sam and Kevin, were introduced to the new arrivals. After a brief discussion, the man David spoke to first, the pilot, and the council boarded a twelve-seat ORV and left for the Admin building.

Several people, including Jenny and her husband, approached the third new arrival. Lucy recognized many of them from the medical clinic. They also spoke briefly and then boarded separate vehicles and left, heading in the clinic's direction.

"That helicopter is amazing," Kara said, awed. "I hope these guys live up to all the expectations."

"I agree," Tyler said. "We need some assistance at the dam. We're close to getting power back on, but there's a lot we still need to figure out."

"That would be good. Reliable power would make a huge difference," Chief agreed.

LATE THAT AFTERNOON, word spread through the community that a town meeting would occur at 7:00 PM in the town center.

The crowd that formed was larger than the one that was

there in the morning. On a hastily constructed platform, David Cowan waited, seated next to the man he first met in the morning.

At precisely 7:00 PM, he stood and the crowd became silent.

"We have worked very hard to build this community over the years. We have fought and sacrificed to get to where we are today. I think every last one of you should be proud of what we have accomplished. Today begins the next phase of this work, the part we have all been waiting for. We'll work hand-in-hand with the sleepers to continue to rebuild. Up here with me is Brad Warren. He is the second-in-command of the sleeper team and has a few things to say."

Brad walked to David. Instead of shaking his hand, the two men embraced, showing the sincerity of the connection between the two groups. The audience applauded as Brad prepared to speak.

"Thank you for the warm welcome. David told me that you were afraid that we might not be waking up after so long. We had the same concern. When we awoke, and so much time had passed, and radiation was much worse than expected, we feared there would be no one out here. Finding this community and learning that there are others is a huge relief. Our mission isn't to do the rebuilding but to come alongside you to assist in doing that work together.

"That means that we will be assisting and guiding, not taking over. Our security people will support and train yours. Our medical personal will teach and guide yours. You have done a great job rebuilding, and the tools and equipment we have will make your jobs easier. Starting in the next few days, you will be aware of more vehicle traffic as we begin assessing the situation and developing a detailed list of priorities.

"So far, we have determined that the power plant at the dam is priority one. I have looked at the progress reports. Because of all you've already done, I believe we can have limited power available within the next month. Priority two is to increase security to stop the attacks from outside. Farming will be next. We'll be having experts visit all the farms that you have established and determine what we can offer at each. In case you weren't aware, we have a wide assortment of livestock asleep in our facility. Once we are sure the farms can produce enough feed for them, we'll be getting those animals out and breeding. ...We have a lot of work to do, and so far, what we see here is *very* encouraging."

Epilogue

20 YEARS LATER

The 42-year-old woman walked to the podium. Her hands were sweating and she was queasy. More than anything, she wanted to sit back down, or better yet, go home and go to bed. However, the two women who meant more to her than anyone had asked her if she would be willing to say a few words, and she wouldn't deny them.

Those gathered in the hall fell silent as she prepared to speak.

"My adopted grandfather was a wonderful man. I was about eight years old when I first met him, and I remember how kind he was to me from the first day. When I was struggling, I would seek him out and sit with him and just talk, and things would be better.

"When he arrived here, he was selected to serve on the leadership council. That launched his incredible twenty-year career. During that time, he was instrumental in negotiating trade agreements with fifteen of the seventeen existing US colonies. He established relations with the East Canadian Survivors Coalition. He met and repeatedly negotiated with both the leadership of the Nation of Europe and the London Community.

Relations within Europe were proving impossible. It quickly became apparent to those communities that the US government had early warning about the comet, which wasn't shared. This had prevented other governments from developing their own shelters. Their understandable resentment proved to be unyielding.

She scanned the audience before continuing. "Following the retirement of David Cowan, the Council, who had chosen my grandfather to lead this community, he was later elected as the first Regional Governor. His leadership has allowed us to continue to thrive and grow and live in peace with our neighbors.

"Project Anvil was intended to take the scraps leftover from the disaster and rebuild them into a new society. My grandfather was one of the blacksmiths that helped forged all we now have on that anvil. I consider it an honor to be able to share the story of his amazing life."

As she said that, Jenny turned and looked at the framed photo of Sam Wilson sitting on the casket with a ragged, long-loved, and well-worn eighteen-inch stuffed bear next to it.

CHRISTOPHER COATES

This book is a parallel story to another of my books, *The Ark*. You can read the two books in the order you prefer. *The Ark* can be obtained through the link provided in the next page.
Thank you

About the Author

Christopher Coates writes action / adventure / sci-fi novels. Having spent 30 years in Fire / EMS and an overlapping 20 years in Information Systems, his books tend to have the occasional integration of medicine and technology.

Christopher grew up in Cape Cod Massachusetts and moved to Michigan to attend Davenport University. He currently lives in Kent City, Michigan with his wife, 2 grown kids, and their 2 dogs.

To learn more about Christopher Coates and discover more Next Chapter authors, visit our website at www.nextchapter.pub.

Made in the USA
Columbia, SC
18 January 2024